FALLING OUT

OF

Grief

FALLING SERIES BOOK ONE

NICOLE THOMPSON

Falling Out of Grief is a work of fiction. Names, characters, places, and incidents are the product of the author's imagination or are used fictitiously. Any resemblance to actual events, locales, or persons, living or dead, is entirely coincidental.

Copyright © 2025 by Nicole Thompson

ISBN 979-8-9938386-1-8 (trade paperback)

TRIGGER WARNING

If you have any triggers, brace yourself for spicy moments, family drama, witty jokes, second-hand embarrassment, belly laughs, and ugly cries. On a more serious note, the following detailed depictions are present in the story: sexually explicit content, death due to terminal illnesses, infant loss, sexual abuse, grief, panic disorder, depression, post-traumatic stress disorder, and religious trauma.

While these topics are heavy, the intent is to provide emotional processing, enlightenment, and healing, woven in a beautiful love story.

TLDR: There's tough shit in here, but it's a damn good romance!

CHAPTER ONE

BILLIE

S ign here, Ms. Carlisle."

I'm transfixed. I can't move. I can't speak. The tears are welling, but I am fighting it. There's a high-pitched ring in my right ear. My surroundings are a blur.

"Ms. Carlisle?"

The hollow sound of my name jolts me from numbness to reality. I clear my throat and blink rapidly several times. It's no use. The tears splash onto the admission papers. I sign my name and pass them over. "Yes, sorry. Here you go." I grab a tissue from the desk to blot my eyes.

"I know this is difficult, but we're here for you," empathizes Roberta, one of the hospice nurses. "Claire will take you to your father now."

I sniffle and nod my head quickly several times. "Thank you. I appreciate that," I croak.

The nurse leads me down a long corridor—at least it seems long. Everything feels surreal, from the floral decor on the beige walls to the sparkling white floors. It smells like lemon cleaner and death—whatever that smells like. I peer into my father's room, where he's resting comfortably. He's wearing his favorite Pittsburgh Steelers sweatshirt, which consumes his frail frame. His salt-and-pepper hair lies neatly, just like his hands placed over the white comforter. His dark stubble is peeking through his smooth olive skin. His eyes are closed. He doesn't seem to be in any pain.

"If you need anything, even a cup of coffee, just use this call button here," offers the nurse. She hands me a call pad, and I place it on the end table beside the bed.

"Thank you again. For all your kindness." I look up at her with a pained smile.

What's her name again?

Claire.

Her badge says Claire. She looks familiar. I think we may have attended high school together, but I can't be sure. It's been nearly two decades. Her long golden-brown hair is pulled tight into a low ponytail, her beach waves flowing halfway down her back. She has that natural beauty women would kill for. Clear skin. Cerulean blue eyes. Not a wrinkle in sight. She's naturally thin, but I can tell she works out. Her complementary blue scrubs really make her eyes pop.

"We will take great care of him. Of both of you," Claire soothes. She places a comforting hand on my shoulder as she leaves the room. I walk over to my dad to kiss him on the cheek. Resting my hand on his, I sit down beside his hospital-style bed.

"Dad?" I whisper. "It's Billie. I'm going to be right here." Dad scrunches his brows ever so slightly.

I scan the room and see a large dark-brown couch against the left wall and a flat screen television mounted to the wall across from my dad's bed. There's a door in the far right corner open just enough for me to see it's a bathroom. There's a silk flower arrangement of yellow roses sitting in a glass vase that decorates the cherry coffee table placed in front of the couch. On the table lies a stack of magazines, and the television remote sits next to the flowers. The warm-beige walls hold landscape paintings by someone named Cecil. They're mesmerizing and should definitely be adorning the walls of an art museum.

The room feels homey. Well, it's as homey as it can feel, considering death is imminent.

My dad is dying.

Since my dad won't be dying at home, this is the second-best place. I really wanted to keep him at home until the end, but his care is beyond my abilities at this point. He needs around-the-clock care, and I simply can't afford full-time private staff.

This evening, I checked him into Bellevue Community Hospice Center, where he will pass away soon. He's in the end stages of ALS, which stands for Amyotrophic Lateral Sclerosis, commonly known as Lou Gehrig's disease. It is by far one of the worst diseases I can imagine a person enduring. The neuro-degenerative disease paralyzes the person until the body stops working. Medically speaking, the person typically dies from respiratory failure. In layman's terms, the person can't fucking breathe anymore.

My father was dealt the shittiest hand. He is the best person I've ever met. There's no one on this planet who doesn't love my dad. He's lived a modest and faithful life, and this is the hand he gets dealt? Bullshit. Complete and utter bullshit, yet there's nothing I can do but watch him deteriorate.

I thought I was going to lose him today.

I woke up this morning, like I do every Sunday, to make breakfast and stream Mass on YouTube. I used to make us both breakfast: pancakes, bacon—the works. My dad has a feeding tube now, since he can no longer chew and can barely swallow his own saliva.

ALS...such *bullshit*!

I still like to go to Mass in person, so I typically go Saturday evenings, when the home health nurse bathes and readies my dad for bed. This morning, though, my father wouldn't wake up, so I dialed 911. My dad is a DNR—do not resuscitate.

That's when I knew I couldn't do this alone anymore with only part-time help. I've been my dad's primary caretaker since his diagnosis two years ago. When my parents divorced, my mom basically left and never really looked back. I don't think she ever really wanted kids, but I showed up and, from what I gathered, she felt trapped and smothered by motherhood.

Don't worry, I'm in therapy to work through all that.

We talk occasionally when she calls, but I really stopped making an effort after the big blowup the day I graduated from college. My special day ended up being all about her, and I had enough. I was a grown woman, after all, and she was not a fan of me setting boundaries with her. Three weeks later, she met Tony, then Troy, then another Tony, Nick, and now Chuck.

I give my dad credit. He's never uttered one negative word about her. But as a young teenager, I picked up pretty quickly that her behavior as a wife and mother was not typical in a family. My mom knows Dad's sick and expresses her sympathy, but she hasn't come around once. I doubt she will even show up for the funeral.

Now that's typical.

A person with ALS could live two years or twenty, and each person's experience is different. My father is on the short side of survival, but, given what I've seen, I'm honestly relieved it's happening quickly. I would hate to watch someone struggle with this for decades.

My dad stayed in the hospital for only several hours before we got placed at Bellevue. The ambulance transported him here this evening, and we're finally settled in.

At promptly 7 p.m., I put *Wheel of Fortune* on the TV because we watch it every night when he's awake. Not tonight, though, since he's already asleep. And not for many more nights. I take this as an opportunity to go outside and breathe.

Decompress.

Process.

A cool blast of air startles my face as soon as the automated doors slide open. I smell a freshly lit cigarette and follow the smoke trail to a man sitting on a bench, about twenty feet from the entrance, taking the first drag. He meets my eyes, blows out the smoke, and offers the pack my way.

"Would you like one?" he asks.

"Oh, no thank you," I reply. "I don't smoke."

"Neither do I. But it's been a shitty day. I needed a menthol."

"You're right about it being a shitty day," I huff. "Since you said menthol, I will take one."

I grab a cigarette from his pack of Pall Malls. Talk about a core memory. I haven't had one of those since college, when I actually smoked. Of course, that was back in the early 2000s when practically everyone lit up on campus between classes and at parties.

The man takes a purple lighter out of his pocket to light my cigarette. I take a long drag and hold the smoke in my lungs for several seconds before exhaling. I'm not sure if I should sit down or not, so I stand awkwardly beside the bench.

"Ah," I blow out. "I forgot how great menthols are."

"That instant calm is quite relaxing," he agrees.

"Right? I hate everything about smoking other than the immediate stress release and the coolness in my lungs. I hate the smell, though. It reminds me of college, and that wasn't exactly my idea of a good time."

"I can relate," he chuckles. After some breathy silence he asks, "Do you remember flavored cigarettes?"

"Do I? Oh, I used to love the mango ones until they were banned for appealing to teenagers to start smoking. Ha, that was back when a pack was like two bucks. I cannot fathom they're more than ten dollars a pack now."

"Yes, that is crazy."

We stand silent for several more minutes, puffing, inhaling, and exhaling. I take that time to look him over inconspicuously. He's tall and lean, with brown hair that grazes the nape of his neck. He's wearing a black hat backwards, a dark-gray hoodie, and black joggers. He has stubble that defines his sculpted jaw. His piercing eyes are peridot green, and his lips—well, they're quite full.

I wonder what it would be like to kiss them.

I snap myself out of my reverie and take the last hit. "Thanks for the cigarette. I hope your evening gets better." I place the butt in the large outdoor ashtray. He looks at me inquisitively but offers only a "You're welcome."

I turn to go back inside when my brain compels me to spin around and say, "I'm Billie, by the way. My dad's here in hospice."

The man offers a warm smile and says, "I'm Scott. It's nice to meet you. I'm sorry about your dad." He extends his hand, and I shake it firmly. I was always taught that a solid handshake is the most respected type. The coolness of his skin sends tingles up my arm.

"Thank you," I say sincerely as I regretfully release my hand. "Well, I should get back there. Have a nice evening."

"You too, Billie."

When I return to Room 218, I set my backpack on the coffee table and pull out my laptop. I'm not sure how I'll be able to work right now, but I don't have a choice. Shortly after Dad's diagnosis, I took a remote position creating interactive digital training content for the manufacturing company from which my dad worked. The company has been so supportive of us. In fact, he's still technically an employee on medical leave, and the company covers medical insurance costs. The plant is a family-owned company unlike any I've ever encountered.

My dad gave Steele Manufacturing forty great years. It was the only adult job he ever had. He went on medical leave at sixty-two, a few years earlier than he wanted to retire. But he had already been having some mobility issues prior to being diagnosed with ALS. Doctors thought it was arthritis or Lyme. But, nope. A death sentence. A slow and miserable fucking death sentence.

When I needed to leave my full-time corporate job in professional development, I humbly reached out to Rick, my dad's best friend and CEO, to see if he had any work I could do remotely while I cared for my dad. He ended up creating an entire department so I could have a job. Instead of outsourcing training, Rick created an in-house team. I get to create videos, visuals, and documentation to help train and inform employees on the equipment, processes, and procedures. It's not glamorous or imaginative, but overall I enjoy it, and it works for my current lifestyle.

I write for several hours. At some point, I drift off to sleep, my hands resting on the keys.

CHAPTER TWO

BILLIE

I wake up to a nurse humming a tune as she props up my dad with fresh pillows and adjusts him. I check the time. It's 8:18 a.m. Okay, well, I got some decent sleep at least. My neck is a little stiff but, other than that, I feel semi-rested. I stand up, let out a long yawn, and stretch.

"Good morning," says the nurse. "I hope you slept okay. I brought you a blanket and pillows in case you decide to stay this evening. Stanley will be in shortly to clean and tidy the room. Is there anything I can get you?"

"Uhhh, I don't think so. Wait, a toothbrush and toothpaste?"

"Absolutely. I will be right back."

The nurse walks briskly out of the room. She's in such a good mood. I don't know how hospice nurses can remain positive or remotely cheery when everyone around them is dying. However, it's a welcomed emotion right now.

I hear a dog bark in the hallway.

"Easy, Bruno. It's too early to be so excited," a male voice says gently.

I'm curious, so I head to the door and peek down the hall. Menthol man is standing outside a resident's room with a gorgeous Great Dane. The gray dog speckled in black spots wears a vest that says "therapy dog" on each side. He has giant floppy black ears and stands at least three feet tall when on all fours. He's a beast. My heart skips a beat. Seeing menthol man during daylight is even better than last night.

What is his name? *Gah.* I can never remember when people tell me their names in general conversation.

I didn't think I'd see him again, so I didn't bother to emblazon his name into my core memory.

Just as he's about to enter the room next door, he glances in my direction. My hair is in a messy bun that's falling out all over the place, and I am definitely not enjoying this morning's post-cigarette breath.

Yuck.

He nods in my direction and smiles. He's not wearing a hat today. I discover his luscious curly hair. Perfect loose brown coils that fall to his cheeks in the front and to the nape of his neck in the back. He's sporting a navy hoodie and fitted white joggers.

I return a smile and turn back into the room. Then it hits me.

What if he's coming here next?!

I rush into the bathroom to get a shower. Practically everything I need is already in there. Shampoo, conditioner, even a razor and shaving cream. There are white towels hanging outside of the step-in shower, and a brand-new loofah waits for me on a hook next to the seashell-patterned shower curtain. I turn on the water and wait for it to heat. I love hot showers, the kind that practically melt your skin off. I breathe in some steam and step in.

Finishing quickly, I throw on a pair of black leggings, a sports bra, and a loose maroon sweatshirt that hangs off one of my shoulders. I comb out my wet hair, snagging the toothpaste and toothbrush from the coffee table. I brush my teeth vigorously and moisturize my face.

I feel rejuvenated. It's amazing how refreshing a shower can be. I bid my dad good morning, kissing him on the cheek, as I normally do, and giving his hand a squeeze. His eyes are open. He appears to be watching *Good Morning America*.

"Morning, Dad. I hope you're feeling better today."

He blinks twice—that's our signal for *yes*. One long blink means *no*. Even blinking is becoming difficult for him as his flutters are slower and more spaced out.

I cannot imagine what he's enduring, especially since his mind is still sharp. He's a prisoner in his body, just waiting for it to give out so his misery can be over. The father I once knew is gone, a soul fading from the shell of his body.

This disease is fucking bullshit.

I hear a knock at the door, and my heart skips a beat. Menthol man and his dog are waiting in the doorway.

"Good morning, Billie. May we come in?"

He remembers my name.

Swoon.

"Sure. Please, come on in." The Great Dane walks right over to me, ready for his pets.

"This is Bruno," the man gestures.

"Hi, Bruno. Aren't you gorgeous?" I look up at menthol man. "He is majestic." Those gorgeous spearmint-green eyes pierce my emotional armor.

"Thank you. We visit several days a week in the mornings before my shift starts at the hospital."

"Oh, what do you do, Mr.—"

"Call me Scott. It's actually Dr. Scott Bennington."

Of course he's a doctor.

"I'm sorry." I squeeze my eyes shut and put my hand to my forehead. "You told me last night, but everything was a bit hazy."

"As to be expected. This situation isn't ideal. But that's why Bruno is here. He brought joy and peace to me in a dark time, so now I share his light with the residents here."

This guy is a walking green flag.

I don't see a ring. How is he not married already? Or maybe he just doesn't wear a ring. My dad never really wore one because of the type of work he did at the plant.

"That's beautiful." I cup Bruno's massive head in my hands. "You sure are a sweetie pie."

I turn my attention to Scott. "You're more than welcome to let him visit my dad. He can't move anymore to pet Bruno, but I'm sure the positive energy alone will brighten his day." I glance toward my dad. He blinks twice.

"He says *yes*. Well, with his eyes. He can't speak anymore either. It's too difficult with his weak muscles and the ventilator." I close my eyes and sigh reluctantly. The ventilator breathes for my dad because he can't breathe on his own anymore, like at all. If my dad didn't have the ventilator, he would die. When we first arrived at the hospice center, Dad was going to be given comfort measures only, which doesn't typically include monitoring or machines of any kind in inpatient hospice. However, I bargained (well, pleaded) so that he could stay monitored for a while because he would die quickly without the ventilator. I'm just not ready to lose him yet.

Scott nods at me sympathetically.

"Come on, Bruno. Over here, boy." Scott leads Bruno to the hospital bed. Bruno rests his head on my dad's lap. My dad blinks twice again. I see a tear form in the corner of his eye and trickle down the right side of his temple.

"Aw, Dad. Don't cry. It's okay." I lean over him and hug him. "It's okay," I repeat. "We're here."

"I hope I'm not upsetting him. I can go," Scott offers.

"No!" I say a little too enthusiastically. "I mean, that's not necessary. Having visitors is much needed too. That's what therapy dogs do, isn't it? Evoke emotion and joy?"

"I suppose you're right," Scott smirks. "That's typically the goal."

The three of us sit quietly for a while, surrounding my dad with love. When his eyes remain closed for more than a few minutes, I know my dad is sleeping. He is on some pretty heavy sedatives most of the time to keep him calm. I suppose not being able to breathe and move independently would feel like being buried alive in a casket. Except when he's in a casket, he'll be gone.

Scott slowly stands. That's Bruno's cue that it's time to leave.

"I wish I could stay longer, but we need to head out for the day."

"Thank you for coming, Scott, really."

"My pleasure. We visit Mondays, Wednesdays, and Fridays. I work later those days, so I like to come here for a bit in the mornings before I go in."

"That's really nice. Do you work over at St. Teresa's?"

"Oh, no. Actually, I work at the children's hospital. Pediatric Oncology."

This guy is surrounded by death, too. I wonder what he's been through.

CHAPTER THREE

SCOTT

Billie, Billie, Billie. I like that her name is rather androgynous. It's mysterious, and I am eager to find out more about her. Billie Holiday. Billie Jean King. Billie Eilish. Billie Rogers.

Billie is a good name.

Mysterious Billie is gorgeous. She probably doesn't even realize it either. Even in those tight leggings and oversized sweatshirt, I could barely keep my composure with those curves. Ah, those curves. I'm intensely attracted to her.

I want to believe there are no coincidences, but I rarely come to Bellevue in the evenings. Out back, there's a gazebo where my wife and I would sit and watch the sunrise and sunset when she was a resident here. I'm not sure why, but lately I've been struggling with her death, so I've been coming out to the gazebo to watch the sunset when I have the evenings off. Christine loved watching the sunsets. I think coming out here every evening kept her going longer, just as it's kept me sane.

Breast cancer.

Christine was diagnosed shortly after we found out we were expecting Maggie. Given her circumstances and the risks, she wanted to forego treatment until after Maggie was born. She insisted she would battle the cancer head-on as soon as our daughter arrived. At twenty-six weeks, however, Christine went into labor, and there was no stopping it. It was quick, fierce, and the most traumatic event I've ever experienced—even as a doctor who specializes in oncology.

The cancer and the pregnancy were stealing so much energy that Christine's body just couldn't handle both.

When Maggie was born, everything was quiet. The baby never took a breath, never cried. Nurses whisked Maggie away and began working on her in the NICU. After thirty minutes and multiple doctor attempts, Dr. Angelo called her time of death at 5:45 p.m. August 11. We were devastated. We learned later that several of Maggie's organs weren't developing properly, so her chances of surviving after birth were not in our favor. The twenty-week ultrasound hadn't shown anything of concern, and I had studied those images myself.

Neither of us could grasp how so much pain and sorrow could plague us. That is, until Christine stopped responding to treatment and decided palliative care was the best way we could spend what little time we had left together, enjoying each other's company rather than running to endless appointments and treatments.

We spent a beautiful summer together. As the leaves started to change and die, so did Christine.

Christine was at Bellevue exactly one month when she passed, precisely fourteen months after Maggie died. It was October 11, and the nurses let me know the end was near. I asked if we could take her out to the gazebo so that we could watch the sunrise one last time. They, of course, agreed. The weather was crisp but not cold; it was the perfect fall morning. I laid in bed with Christine, and we watched the most magnificent sunrise. I held her. I kissed her. I told her it was okay to go and how much I loved her. She wasn't too coherent at this point, but before she passed, she whispered, "I will always love you." She took several more labored breaths, and her soul left with her final exhalation. It was a beautiful and devastating experience. I laid with her until I was ready to let go. Then the grieving process began.

I haven't been the same since. I mean, who could be?

The other night, I was just leaving the gazebo when I saw Billie come out of the front doors. I don't normally smoke. I'd be a hypocrite. Smoking causes cancer, and I even treat cancer from the effects of secondhand smoke in children. But, for whatever reason, I've needed something to help me cope with this wave of relentless sorrow, or I don't know if I'll make it. I'm not much of a drinker anymore, after my month-long bender in the Bahamas post-funeral, and weed has never really appealed to me. I already work out regularly, so an occasional cigarette it is.

I want to see Billie again, but I don't want to make my advances too obvious. I know what's coming her way soon, and I don't want to be a distraction.

She's a welcome one for me, though.

CHAPTER FOUR

BILLIE

The next morning, I arrive at the hospice center right at 9 a.m. I went home last night to try to get a full night's sleep, which I really haven't had in I couldn't tell you how long, but I still tossed and turned all night.

It's Tuesday, so Scott won't be here today.

Bummer. I'd love another gaze at that eye candy.

The center is much louder and busier this morning: nurses talking and checking in with their residents, custodial staff cleaning and maintaining the common areas, and a gentleman working his way into each room with a tray of food. The center smells of pancakes and sausage, with a hint of that lemon cleaner. No death smell today, thankfully. The man won't be walking into my dad's room, though.

When I walk into Room 218, my dad is wide awake, and I swear his mouth curves into a smile.

"Good morning, Dad." He looks at me and blinks twice. "Wow, Claire. He seems much more alert today."

"He sure does! Isn't that right, Mr. Carlisle?" He blinks twice. "Billie, I was hoping we could chat a moment privately about your father's accommodations," Claire says as she finishes administering my dad's medicine via IV.

We meet outside where there are picnic tables under a covered concrete patio. After some surface-level small talk, Claire again explains that, generally at this stage of hospice, there are no measures taken to prolong life, such as monitors, a feeding tube, and the tracheostomy tube attached to a ventilator. I tell her I'm not ready to stop all of that, for he could die today. I ask for just a little more time with my dad, to make him as comfortable as possible: only monitors that alert in case of a huge spike or dip in heart rate, the ventilation to help him breathe for now, and the feeding tube slowly easing off his nourishment.

I understand he won't be here much longer, that death is very close, but I don't feel right cutting everything at once, especially since he is aware of his surroundings. That's what kills me about this disease. How can I let him die when he knows what's going to happen? Claire sympathizes and says that we can try those accommodations for now and just take one day at a time. I'm not sure the reality of the situation has set in yet.

A while later, there's a knock at the door. It's Rick Steele. Rick co-owns Steele Manufacturing with his brother, Roger. Rick used to go by *Dick* as a kid but quickly changed that in middle school when kids called him *Steel Dick*. He's dressed in a plain mahogany polo, Levi jeans, and Adidas tennis shoes. His salt-and-pepper hair is perfectly barbered, his beard to match. His cologne smells of cedar and musk.

"Mr. Steele, good morning." I rise from my chair and extend my hand. He shakes my hand briefly. I used to call him Rick, but since I became an employee, it seems awkward since he's *the big boss*.

"Billie, I've known you since you were born. Just because you work for me doesn't mean you have to change your demeanor. Please, call me Rick."

"Yes, sir—I mean *Rick*."

Rick turns his attention to my father. He holds a vase filled with yellow roses, sprinkled with baby's breath and orange tulips. It nicely complements the silk ones on the coffee table.

"How ya doin' today, Ted? I figured these flowers would perk up your room a little bit." My father blinks twice. The corner of the right side of his mouth curls again just slightly. Rick hands me a paper. "I brought this sign-up sheet of people who plan to visit each day so that you can go home and rest or grab something to eat. Is that okay with you, Billie?"

"Oh, yes, of course. I actually have some work I need to catch up on, so that'll be really helpful."

"Now don't you worry about work anymore. Neil is going to cover everything assigned to you for now. Shut down that computer. Just be with your dad. Your job will be here whenever you're ready to come back, if you decide that's what you want to do. No obligation whatsoever."

My eyes grow wide in surprise. "Wow, Rick, that's so very generous of you. I just..." I lower my voice to a whisper and lean in toward him. "I can't...I can't afford to take time off."

"Paid leave, Billie. Everything will be paid. Insurance too. Any costs here at Bellevue. You just focus on your dad and yourself."

"I don't know what to say other than thank you. That's very kind of you." My expression softens in appreciation.

"You're family to me, kiddo. You will always be taken care of."

Rick is one of the most generous souls I've ever met. There's no doubt he will be writing those checks to me from his personal bank account, along with the payments to this facility. We haven't gotten a single bill since my dad's treatment started and haven't paid a dime for anything. Any time I tried to tell him "no," he'd smirk and shake his head in amusement. That's just the kind of man Rick is. You don't see people like him running multimillion-dollar companies anymore. But Rick and my father have been best friends since they were kids, so he is like an uncle to me.

Rick even tried to pay for full-time private nurses to keep my dad home, but I wouldn't accept it and put my foot down. Realistically, the house isn't set up for everything he needs right now. And I think we both feel happier here. There are other people around and a full staff that takes care of everything. It's less isolating at the hospice center, and there's a lot more emotional support too.

Plus, I'm not sure I could live in our house if he died there. It would be too much for me to handle emotionally.

Rick's late grandfather, Albert—the founder of Steele Manufacturing—made an obscene amount of money prior to the stock market crash in 1929. That's how he managed to found Steele Manufacturing in 1935.

When Albert passed away from a massive heart attack right after World War II started in 1941, his son Beau took over the company. Steel and manufacturing industries skyrocketed during the war, bringing in millions of dollars, which, at that time, was an unspeakable amount of money for most people recovering from the Great Depression, particularly in the outskirts of Pittsburgh.

Beau was always humble, though. When he retired in the early 1980s, his son Rick took over the company, fresh out of college, along with his other son, Roger, several years later. Roger is a nice man too, but Rick has a heart of gold. I can see that Rick inherited his father's gentle nature and modesty regarding wealth.

Everyone knows Rick is filthy rich, but he doesn't really act like it. Sure, he drives a classic 1954 Rolls Royce Phantom, but his clothes are simple, not designer, and he always donates to charities. The community college even has a scholarship named after him, and he sponsors $25,000 in scholarships each year.

I really admire Rick, and I will be forever grateful and appreciative of how generous and caring he's been through this journey. Torture Road as I see it.

Rick is chatting away to my dad, talking about all the happenings at the plant, so I take this as an opportunity to run some much-needed errands and grab something to eat. I order a coffee and breakfast sandwich at a local bakery, then stop by Reader's Cove, a vintage-inspired bookstore. I'm in desperate need of more novels to read. Since I'm not going to be working anymore right now, I have a lot more time to fill to keep my brain alert.

As much as I want to spend all my time with my dad, I do get bored because he sleeps most of the time. It's very quiet if the TV isn't on. It creeps me out a little. When he is awake, we can't carry on a conversation, so there's not much I can do to keep myself occupied.

I arrive back at the hospice center later in the afternoon and figure I'll stay until he's asleep for the night, which is usually no later than nine.

Tonight, however, my dad is asleep by seven-thirty, but I'm not quite ready to leave. I haven't really been anywhere other than his room, so I want to scope out the place a bit. I check out the common area that's set up for visitors to play games, watch movies, and eat. There's also a kitchen area where you can make yourself something simple to eat. On the counter is a tray of cookies and some bakery buns, with a handwritten sign that says, "Leftovers from the community dinner. Please help yourselves. Food is in the fridge."

There are white chocolate macadamia cookies on the tray, so I snag one and make a cup of hot chocolate. It's chilly this evening but not frosty. I throw on a thick hoodie and grab a blanket, one of my new romance novels, and hot cocoa, and head outside to see if there are any swings or areas where I can read. I see a gazebo about thirty yards past the back patio. There are white string lights outlining the structure and several autumn-themed hanging baskets at the entry. I walk in and notice several wooden benches and a plastic lounge chair with a puffy seafoam-green cushion. I snuggle up on the lounge chair and begin reading. I feel at peace right now, so relaxed that I doze off with the book in my hands.

CHAPTER FIVE

SCOTT

After work today, I went to the gym and made a nice dinner for myself. Anything I do at home anymore just reminds me that my wife and child are gone and I'm all alone. I think that's why I've been going to the hospice center so much. I've gotten to know the nurses, especially Claire, since she's near my age. She hasn't worked at the hospice center that long, but she's really nice and someone I'd consider a friend.

Plus, Bruno loves Roberta. John usually works night shifts, but I am never there that late, not since Christine passed. Then there are a few other nurses I've seen in passing. Even though I'm constantly reminded of the pain I endured there, the hospice center somehow brings me comfort, particularly the gazebo.

I'm trying to keep myself busy around the house, but I think I'm going to go back to the gazebo tonight. Most of the time, I sit on the lounge chair and listen to music or read. If I'm feeling creative, I'll draw. I'm not really good at it, but I can doodle. Tonight feels like a music night.

It's dark when I arrive, so I use the illuminated gazebo to guide me. I'm startled to see Billie asleep with a book in her hands as I enter. She looks angelic. I am stunned by her beauty. Not just physically, but mentally and emotionally too. She's been caring for her dad relentlessly, and knowing exactly what that's like makes her so much more attractive.

But physically, wow! Long, flowy chocolate-brown hair grazes her waist. Caramel eyes. Sunkissed skin. She's a little shorter than average height, which I like because shorter women tend to be a bit feisty. And her curves—they're in all the places I love on a woman. I'm not sure which I like more, her boobs or her ass. Either way, she was generously gifted in those areas. I need to stop thinking about her, but she's been popping up quite frequently since we met, and something of mine is starting to pop up when I see her.

Billie is the opposite of Christine, who had shoulder-length blonde hair and blue eyes. She was tall and slender, with some sculpted curves and the warmest smile. Her personality was gentle and timid.

I don't want to wake Billie, so I put in my earbuds, sit on the bench, and close my eyes. I zen out and relax for a good hour, and then I'm ready to go home for the night. Billie is still lying in the lounge chair. I'm not going to leave her outside on this cold November night.

I walk over to the chair and crouch down.

"Billie," I whisper.

Nothing happens.

She must be in a deep sleep because she hasn't moved since I got here. "Billie," I say with a little more volume. "Hey, it's getting cold. You should go inside."

She yawns and stretches. When she opens her eyes, they meet mine. She shoots up off the chair like I scared her to death. "It's me, Scott. I'm sorry. I didn't mean to scare you."

She registers that she recognizes me and relaxes her defensive stance. "It's okay. I must have dozed off. I definitely wasn't expecting you, or anyone really, here this late at night. What are you doing here, by the way?" She eyes me curiously.

"Well, a few years ago my wife was a resident here, and she passed away. When I'm struggling with grief, I come out here. She died in my arms in this very gazebo. It probably sounds a little morbid, but coming here brings me comfort."

"Wow, I am...I am so sorry for your loss. Do you mind me asking what happened?"

My jaw hardens. I stare at the ground, then look out at the blackened landscape. "Metastatic inflammatory breast cancer."

"That is so unfortunate. You have my sympathy. How long ago did she pass?"

"It was two years this past October. Some days, it feels like yesterday." I continue to stare into the black abyss of night.

"My dad was diagnosed two years ago this past October as well. October 11. I will never forget it." Her voice trails off.

"Wait, did you say October 11?" My heartbeat quickens and my mouth becomes dry.

"Yeah, why?"

"That's the day my wife passed away, two years ago. What are the odds?"

"I would say extraordinarily slim," she says, bewildered.

How uncanny we both felt such extraordinary pain on the same day. I'm not sure what to say next, so we end up just staring at each other. Her long eyelashes dance along her high cheekbones when she blinks, and even though the light in the gazebo is dim, I see her chest rise and fall quicker than normal.

"Well, I should probably get you inside. You're shivering." I would stay out here with her longer, but I'm starting to shiver too. And the silence is awkward.

"Yes, I'm feeling the frost," Billie chatters.

"Here, let me help you," I offer.

"Thank you. I would like that."

She gathers up the mug, half full of now-cold cocoa, and her book. I pick up the blanket and place it around her shoulders.

"Thank you, kind sir," she says emphatically.

"You're most welcome, my fair lady," I reply with mirrored emphasis.

Once we get back to her dad's room, I wait outside the door. I'm not really sure what I should do at this point. Going in seems inappropriate, but part of me wants to. At the doorway, Billie quietly announces, "Well, we're here." She grits a smile. I can't help but to do the same.

"Yes, we are. I guess I'll see you tomorrow?" I ask hopefully. She nods at me, her eyes heavy from exhaustion.

"I look forward to it." Billie walks into the room and shuts the door.

I'm looking forward to it too.

CHAPTER SIX

BILLIE

I probably haven't slept that well in months, even though it was on the plush brown couch in my dad's hospice room. That lounge chair really did me in. I will most certainly be spending more afternoons out at the gazebo while my dad is resting.

I'm anxiously awaiting Scott's arrival this morning. It's a new feeling for me because I haven't so much as had a crush on a guy since Benji Myers. He was in my corporate ethics course in college. The class curriculum, including the title, was an oxymoron.

When I finally got the nerve to approach him, we were promptly interrupted by his boyfriend, David. So, that's how that went.

The end.

This is different, though, with Scott. He and I have both gone through a lot, so we have that in common. That part sucks, but he's not gay and not seeing anyone to my knowledge, based on what he said last night, so that's fairly reassuring.

I am insanely attracted to him. I hope it's not obvious, but I'm drawn to him. I get butterflies in my stomach when I see him, even after just these few encounters. Plus, he has been a kind and respectful gentleman.

Another green flag for him.

When I hear familiar nails clacking and tags jingling down the corridor, I know Scott and Bruno will be here soon. I go into the bathroom to brush my teeth again and spray some perfume. I even throw a few loose curls in my hair. But I don't go overboard because I don't want him to get weirded out by full glam on an early Wednesday morning.

I sit with my dad, who's watching an old western, and shortly after, I see Scott and Bruno approach the door.

"Good morning, Scott," I offer first.

"Good morning, Billie. Fancy meeting you here."

He is witty. I like that.

"Yes, such a surprise to bump into you here, of all places, again," I say slyly.

"May we come in?"

"Absolutely. Hi Bruno!" I welcome the pup with open arms. "Ya know, this therapy dog stuff really works. I've been looking forward to your visit all morning."

It's not a lie, Bruno is a great dog, but I'm more interested in seeing Scott again.

"I was looking forward to seeing you too." Scott smiles coyly. I immediately feel heat flush in my cheeks.

He caught me. Okay, so maybe he feels something between us. I feel like we're both walking on eggshells because we're going through so much painful shit. Neither wants to intrude, but we are steadily testing the waters.

Scott and Bruno visit for at least thirty minutes before heading out for the day. They usually spend about ten minutes in each room, so Scott's clearly more interested in visiting with us.

Even if I'm right, though, I've never pursued a guy before. I have no idea what I'm doing, and I don't want to mess up what's happening right now. I should probably give him some kind of hint that I'm interested, but I'm also worried he will clam up and ghost me. I'm thirty-six years old, and I feel like I'm eighteen—worried about rejection and abandonment.

Thanks, Mom.

Besides, as much as I don't want to lean on anyone for, well, for anything, I know I will need some kind of emotional support when my dad passes. I'm secretly wishing that'll be from Scott. A girl can dream, I guess.

After lunch, I pop out to the back patio again, book in hand. The weather is rather warm for a November afternoon, but the air is crisp. Perfect for reading and relaxing. Claire is eating her lunch at the picnic table, so I take a seat beside her.

"Did you see the sandwiches in the common area?" Claire asks, sinking her mouth into a turkey sub. "They were donated this morning from the deli."

"Yes, I did. The spicy Italian was excellent. I'm in a food coma, so I figured I'd get some air and clear my head while my dad is resting."

"It can get pretty stuffy in there. Have a seat," Claire offers. "Let's chit chat."

I take a seat and stare out toward the landscape. "I will say, the view here is breathtaking." I look wistfully at the rolling hills and faint tree line in the distance, my mind wandering.

"It's half the reason I work here," Claire admits. "I love my job, and I'd like to think I'm making a difference for people who are dying—and their families too—but it's emotionally draining. I always seem to find peace here. Coming outside even for just a few minutes every day helps rejuvenate me enough to get through each shift, no matter the time of day or year. Although—" She ponders a moment. "Fall is my favorite. The leaves are gorgeous. All the leaves have pretty much fallen now, obviously, but when the snow comes, it's majestic."

"I'm sure it is," I reply softly, staring absent-mindedly into oblivion.

"Well, it was nice chatting with you," Claire says as she crumples her empty sandwich wrapper.

"Sorry, I'm just...not really with it today," I say resignedly, finally making eye contact with her. Claire looks back at me sympathetically.

"No sweat, really." She pauses and then carefully offers, "I know it's not my business, but maybe it'll do you some good to get your girlfriends together for dinner or something. Relax, let loose a little." She gives me a light squeeze on the shoulder.

"I would love that. Except I don't actually have any," I admit, rather embarrassed.

"What? Come on. Everyone has girlfriends," Claire says in disbelief.

"Sorry to disappoint, but I do not. Not since my dad got sick, anyway. And I just don't care enough to rekindle those relationships, honestly." I shrug.

"Well then, I am taking you out this evening. Nothing crazy, just some margs, chips, and salsa. Trust me. I've never seen anyone sad while they're indulging in authentic Mexican cuisine." She is persuasive. I let out a chuckle.

"That is true. I do enjoy a good margarita."

"It's settled then. Here's my number." Claire taps her phone against mine, which creates new contacts on our phones. "I get done here at four, so I just need to go home and shower. Want to meet at Caliente's at six?" Her bubbliness is contagious. I feel a small flip in my stomach and smile.

"Perfect. Seeya there."

This afternoon, my dad has a few more visitors from the plant, so I go home, shower, and get ready to have dinner with Claire. I slip on a form-fitting, long-sleeved teal top. The cut is square and low across my chest. I have a generous amount of cleavage showing. The pushup bra also squeezes and perks up my boobs so that they're the perfect roundness and fullness.

Va-va-voom.

I select dark denim jeggings that make my butt look bangin'. I curl my hair into beach waves and pin the top half back. I leave out some curled pieces to frame my face, more of a messy than sleek look. I finish off with a dark, smoky eye and a pop of red lipstick. I even break out my heeled sparkly-black ankle boots and complementary crimson leather jacket.

I look hot. I don't tell that to myself often, but I feel it tonight. Claire made me feel good about myself today, and I'm looking forward to doing something fun with another woman. When I pull into the restaurant, my phone dings.

CLAIRE
I'm in the back booth in the bar area.

ME
Be right in.

I scan the restaurant and spot the bronze bombshell in the back corner. Her hair is pulled in a high ponytail, and she's wearing a bright-red turtleneck. Claire is a stunning woman. Now that I'm thinking about it, we did go to high school together. She did some of the musicals while I was a techie running the soundboard and curtains.

"Hold on a second, girl," Claire says, extending her palm out toward me. "We have to go out tonight. You're turning me on, and I'm not even gay."

I blush. "You're funny," I comment as I proceed to sit down and grab a chip.

"No, seriously, Billie. Your boobs are like, 'hello, here we are!'" Claire shimmies, and I put my hand over my cleavage. Maybe this shirt is too low-cut. I don't own a lot of scandalous items, but I wouldn't mind having a man notice and desire me.

"Stop it right now and take your hand away. Do not be ashamed of that bod. See? Look around." She opens her arm like she's presenting the entire bar area to me. I observe several men sneak a peek over at me, but none of them remotely spark my interest. I smile and give Claire a desperate, wide-eyed look to stop.

"Do you have a boyfriend or something?" Claire takes a sip of her margarita.

"Absolutely not. Never even had one." I'm not sure why I'm admitting that so openly. I haven't even ordered my drink yet. Claire rolls her eyes and flags over a server.

"Get this woman a strong margarita, an extra shot in it too, please." I abruptly stop Claire. "No way. Not unless you want to carry me out of here." I look up at the server. "I will have a house margarita on the rocks, please."

"Would you like salt on the rim?" she asks pleasantly.

"Yes, please."

"I'll get this in and be back shortly to get your dinner order."

"Can you bring us a side of guacamole too, please?" I love guacamole. I'm what people would call a guac connoisseur. Give me all the guac.

"Sure thing. I'll be right back." The server turns to greet people in another booth behind us. Claire picks right back up where she left off.

"Never a boyfriend, ever? I find that hard to believe." She shakes her head and bats her lashes.

"Mary Palmer," I respond. I grab another chip and wait for it to register.

"Mary who? Hang on, do you have a *girlfriend*? Oh, my gosh! Are *you* gay?" Claire gets this excited look on her face like she half-expected me to be.

"No, not gay, but I love the gays. And yes, Mary Palmer. Remember? You played her in the senior high school musical. I was the weird techie running the soundboard."

"Get outta here! Yes, now I remember. You look a bit... different, though."

"I was in my emo phase," I scoff playfully. Now, I wasn't full goth, because my parents would have scheduled me for an exorcism, but I did wear a lot of black and heavier eye makeup in school. I purchased the Linkin Park and Panic! At The Disco CDs with my birthday money and hid them in my underwear drawer. I wouldn't dare listen to them without headphones either. That, too, would have warranted a visit from an exorcist. Maybe I'm exaggerating just a tad, but that music would have been in the trash if my parents had found it.

"Well, it's good to reconnect," she chimes. The server brings my margarita the moment Claire raises her glass. "To surviving high school and being successful, functioning adults." I clank my glass with hers and take a nice big gulp. She's right. I'm not sad at all right now. In fact, I'm feeling pretty damn good. And the guac is A-plus. I don't think I've had any this good since my spring break trip to Mexico my senior year of college.

With dinner and two more margaritas under our belts, Claire and I reminisce about high school, laughing maniacally when she reminds me of the time Liz Sousman doused Carter Christiansen with a full bottle of Fruitopia because she found out he was cheating on her. The entire cafeteria was in hysterics. Then I bring up the time members of the marching band pranked the band director on senior night by gathering their instruments and playing the half-time show outside his house at 1 a.m. I wasn't in the band, but I tagged along for fun. It was awesome, and he was a good sport about it. We didn't stay long because I'm sure the band woke up the entire neighborhood. Afterward, a group of us went to a taco joint because it was the only place open that late, and I promptly got food poisoning.

We go on and on until we admit we are drunk. There's no way either of us is driving.

"Let's do one more, please?" Claire begs. I should probably stop, but I'm enjoying myself for once, occasionally munching on chips and salsa, even though I'm stuffed from dinner. It's not like I have to be anywhere tomorrow other than the hospice center.

Fine. What the hell.

We get one more round. I'm borderline smashed. "How the hell are we going to get home?" I slur a bit.

"No worries. I'll book us an Uber. We can get our cars in the morning." She grabs her phone and pulls up the app.

"Too bad you can't call that Scott guy. Now that...is a hot piece of man right there. He is *yummy* to look at. I'd take him home in a heartbeat." Claire flashes me a quick, mischievous smile, but I'm too far gone to process why. Fifteen minutes later, Claire waves toward the door, and two men start walking toward us.

Since when does Uber send two drivers? Or maybe she booked two, one for each of us. Who knows. Wait, do drivers enter restaurants to pick up people? I'm not paying too much attention, though, because—margaritas.

Then I smell him.

The invigorating scent of sweet, musky cologne violates my senses. I meet that gorgeous man's eyes staring widely back at me. I don't move. I don't speak. I just gawk at him. He's dressed in butt-hugging dark-wash blue jeans and a fitted pale-blue t-shirt. His muscular arms fill out the sleeves, and I swear I can see the ripples of a six-pack. I always heard tequila makes the clothes come off, and I really don't want to find that out drunk. Right now, though, it's pretty tempting because I want to see what's under his clothes.

"Scott. Glad you could make it. Have a seat," Claire gestures. Scott breaks his gaze from mine, and Claire scoots over to make room for the other man, who has the same face as Scott but straight dirty-blond hair and periwinkle eyes. He has a piercing on the left side of his bottom lip and is dressed in a black polo, black jeans, and a black denim jacket. I shoot Claire a *what the fuck are you doing?* look, and she just smiles innocently and bats her eyelashes again. I move in too because, well, I don't want to be rude, but if I keep smelling his masculine scent, I might be in trouble tonight.

"I thought you said it was an emergency." Scott squints his eyes at Claire, realizing he has been lured here.

"I lied. Sue me. We still need rides home, so it's not for nothing. Have a beer. It's on me." Scott naturally takes a seat beside me, and the other guy sits beside Claire. The men indulge and order a draft beer.

"Ladies, this is my brother, Ryan," Scott says, gesturing in introduction. "This is Claire and Billie."

"Scott, you didn't tell me your brother was smokin' hot," Claire says, not giving a fuck. Now that I'm getting to know her more, I actually think she never gives any fucks. Ryan's cheeks flush and Scott snickers. I can tell Ryan is shy because he's rubbing his hands back and forth on his pants and looks completely embarrassed. He has to be younger than Scott because his features look more youthful.

"And how many of these margaritas have you ladies had?" Scott probes.

"Four!" I say way too loudly. I hold up my hand and show him four fingers. Scott looks at me amusedly and just nods his head, smirking. "Here, high five, man," I say, grabbing his hand and giving us a high five.

Yikes, I have had way too much to drink, and I'm making a complete fool of myself. I stop sipping the margarita and switch to water.

The four of us talk and laugh for a solid hour. We promise to generously tip our server for camping at her table for so long. She doesn't seem to mind. She has most of the bar area to herself, and there's no wait at the door.

Ryan has started to loosen up a bit, and Claire has had no problems warming up to him. Her flirting is obvious, stroking his hair and resting her head on his broad shoulder. Meanwhile, he's squirming like a nervous teenager about to make out for the first time. Scott and I sit rigidly, but I can feel the heat radiating from him. We're sitting close enough that our legs are touching, and I don't dare move to break the warmth between us. I intentionally brush my hand against his when I move my hand from my lap to take another drink of water. He glances at me, and I flash him a genuine smile. He moves his hand onto my thigh, gives me a light squeeze, and rests it there. My breathing becomes more shallow because the surge of energy at his touch is making me feel a little lightheaded. I stay close to him until I absolutely have to excuse myself to go to the restroom.

"I'll come too!" Claire chimes in, and we all get up from the table. Claire puts her arm around me, and we walk like we've been best friends forever. Once the restroom door shuts, I shoot Claire a snide look.

"Hey, you said he was hot," she says defensively. "I have his number, so I figured, hey, why not get laid tonight? You probably need it right now."

"How do you know he's even into me? Gah! I am so embarrassed. I'm beyond buzzed. I made such an idiot out of myself he'll never like me now!"

"How...old are you?" Claire rolls her eyes. "Billie, we are not sixteen years old. We're grown women interested in grown men. Besides, I saw Scott look at you. I bet a Benjamin that he would take you home tonight. I mean, he *is* taking you home tonight, but home as in the big O." She clicks her tongue. I slam the door to the stall and do my business. She does the same.

"Claire?" I say when it's quiet.

"All day every day," she replies.

"Thank you...for inviting me out tonight. You were right. I needed it."

"I like you, Bills. You're a cool cat. A Billie-cat."

Scott is driving Claire home first since she lives closest to the restaurant. I am exhausted and dreading tomorrow's hangover because I never drink. I'm already feeling achy. I'm starting to doze off when I feel Scott's hand slide onto my thigh again. I don't even look over. I just hold onto his arm and lean against him. He's so warm, so comfy.

The only sound in the car is rock music. We're all in our mid- to late-thirties. Anything past 9 p.m. is considered late, and it's 10:15. Tonight was such a fun, relaxing night. When we get to Claire's condo, Scott unlocks the car doors, turns down the music, and presses on the overhead light.

"Dude, what are you doing?" Scott admonishes. My eyes fly open and I turn around. Claire and Ryan are making out. His hands are all over her. She's practically sucking his face off. The poor sap is taking it like a champ. Maybe he's only shy in public places because he has no shame right now.

"What?" Ryan asks, brushing off Scott's alarmed tone.

"We're here, Claire." Scott says with a little more control in his voice.

"He can stay with me tonight, Scott. Don'tcha wanna come in, baby?" She bats her eyelashes (which must be a signature expression of hers) at Ryan. He nods his head yes, accompanied by a devilish grin.

"Nope. No drunken sex on my watch." Scott interrupts. "You guys can reconnect later. Good night, Claire," he says in a singsong voice.

"Call me," Claire whispers to Ryan, then gives him a throaty kiss and exits the car.

"Thanks for cockblocking, man." Ryan groans. "She's hot as fuck."

"Listen, I am not letting either of you wake up with morning regret. I'm sober and driving, so I'm in charge." I haven't said a word this entire ride home. I don't intend to, so I press my lips together and turn back around.

"Fine, but you're giving me her number," Ryan orders.

"Fine."

About ten minutes later, Scott pulls up to my house and, of course, being the gentleman that he is, gets out of the car and opens my door. He walks me onto my porch and to the front door.

"Well, this is me," I declare.

"Yes, it is. Nice house." Scott rolls his head, admiring the porch and wooden craftsmanship outlining the door. It becomes quiet and super awkward.

"I guess I'll see you Friday?" I ask.

"Yes. No. Actually, no." Scott pinches the bridge of his nose. "I have a flight tomorrow afternoon. I'll be gone until next Tuesday for a conference." He looks at me apologetically.

"All right. I will see you when you get back." I offer a warm smile before I turn to unlock the door.

"Do you want to grab breakfast tomorrow? My flight isn't until later in the afternoon, and, well, you need to get your car somehow. I could pick you up in the morning for breakfast and take you to your car after."

Is he asking me out on a date?! No, it can't be a date. It's breakfast.

Breakfast. Isn't. A. Date.

Scott sways and bites his lip like he's a teenage boy asking a girl to a dance. He stuffs his hands into his front pockets and gives me the puppy dog eyes. My heart flutters, but I'm trying to act cool. Damn it, he's so cute. I wouldn't mind asking him for a sleepover tonight, but I know he won't be a hypocrite.

"That would be nice." Scott huffs in relief at my acceptance.

"Okay, then. Is nine good for you?"

"It's perfect."

"Goodnight, Billie."

"Goodnight, Scott."

We anxiously gaze at each other. I'm not sure if he wants to kiss me—or should I kiss him? I mean, I want to kiss him, but if he wanted to, he would, right?

"Okay, well, I'm gonna...." He hitches his thumb behind his shoulder and heads down the porch steps. I open the door and turn in for the night.

CHAPTER SEVEN

BILLIE

T hankfully, I do not have a hangover this morning. The two ibuprofen and bottle of water before bed must have done the trick. I hop in the shower and quickly wash off because I overslept and now have only thirty minutes to get ready. Makeup is simply mascara, some bronzer, and lip gloss. The look is just as relaxed—jeans, white t-shirt, and my favorite crimson leather jacket. My doorbell rings right on time. I am greeted with a bright smile on Scott's face. I'm glad he's relaxed, too, in his jeans, t-shirt, and casual jacket. He has his hat on backwards, and his luscious brown curls touch his neck. He smells just as good as he did last night. I'm intoxicated again, but by him this time.

"Good morning, Billie. How's the hangover?" he muses.

"Actually, I have no hangover," I brag.

"Impressive! Shall we?" He offers his arm and I accept.

"We shall."

He takes me to Bess's Homecookin', the best mom-and-pop breakfast joint in town. The decor is original, straight out of the '60s. I'm sure things have been replaced or restored along the way, but it's retro. Not like a diner, more like my grandma's house. I order a Belgian waffle with strawberries and whipped cream, and he gets the biscuits and sausage gravy.

"So, what conference are you going to?"

"It's for oncology doctors. I'm presenting research on my study on the success of stem cells treating leukemia in children."

"That's incredible. How long have you been conducting research?"

"Five years. I still see patients daily, but more often than not I'm researching and studying my patients and their cases. I spend a lot of time in our lab, particularly on Mondays, Wednesdays, and Fridays. That's why I go in later. I prefer to be at the lab when the daylight shift is gone." He talks about it nonchalantly, but I am intrigued.

"So this is like a really big deal, isn't it?"

"I mean, I guess you could say that." He's being modest, but I guarantee if I look up this conference there will be some flashy acknowledgment of his presentation.

"Good for you," I encourage. "Truly impressive."

"Thank you. So, tell me. What do you do for a living? I feel like you know a lot about me, but I don't know much about you," Scott says in between bites of his breakfast. I sink back into the booth, sip my coffee, and run my index finger around the rim of the coffee cup.

"Well, I have been working for the manufacturing company my dad worked at doing professional development, like training modules and documentation. I started there shortly after my dad got sick because I decided to move out of the city and back to Bellevue to be with him. The commute and traffic wasn't worth it, so I quit my fancy corporate professional development job about a month after I moved back. Right now, though, I'm on leave. The CEO is my dad's best friend, so Rick's been looking out for me, which I appreciate."

"I'll say. You don't often see CEOs taking care of their employees like that these days."

"Not at all. He's been very kind and generous. But it's not just because he's best friends with my dad. He's this kind and generous to everyone. This guy Jonald suffered an aneurysm last year over Christmas break, when the plant completely shuts down annually for two weeks. Rick made sure his leave was fully paid. The guy was out for like five months, too."

"That's a terrible and frightening situation, but it sounds like a really nice place to work."

"It is. I'll have to decide what I'm going to do after my dad... well...you know...but I'm not thinking that far ahead yet." I coax a smile, but my lip quivers. Scott puts his hand over mine. My urge to cry dissipates, and I find his sympathetic expression.

"As you shouldn't. Right now is all about you and your time with your dad, making sure he's as comfortable as possible. It's a really delicate season." Scott squeezes my hand and pulls back to continue eating.

Talking any more about my dad is going to make me emotional, so I quickly change the subject. "So, what's the name of this conference?"

"The American Leukemia Research Initiative Conference," he spills out. "Most of us just call it ALRIC."

"That's quite a mouthful. Where's Bruno staying while you're gone?"

"With Claire," he snickers. "She owes me for tricking me into thinking she was stranded with a dead car battery."

"She is quite a firecracker, that one."

"A live wire even. I'm glad she did, though." He gazes at me, grinning from ear to ear, and my heart leaps. I return a smile.

"Me too."

We make small talk for the rest of the meal, and when the check comes, he snatches it, refusing to let me pay for my portion.

"My treat," he asserts.

"You do not have to do that," I protest.

"I know, but I want to, and because I'm the keynote speaker at ALRIC, I can afford it."

"Show-off!" I jest. "Must be nice."

"Eh, I'm comfortable. But it is true what they say."

"What who says?"

"I don't know—the proverbial philosophers of society. That whole adage that money can't buy happiness, yada yada."

"Are you...not happy?" I question with furrowed brows and concern in my voice.

He flashes another smile, and his eyes appear to shimmer at me when he says, "I am today."

A while later, Scott drives us back to my car in the naked parking lot of Caliente's, reminiscent of the kids who used to do the "walk of shame" in college. You know, the ones who stayed out all night partying, walking home when everyone else was on their way to class. Being the prude that I am, I was always the one on my way to class or the library to study.

I unlock my car and he blurts, "Give me your phone." My heart pitter-patters. She's been quite acrobatic since I've met Scott. I hand my phone over without protest.

"Please text or call me anytime. I am texting myself from your phone, so I have yours too." He doesn't look at me, but he's smiling as he's programming and texting.

"I will keep that in mind, thank you," I reply, trying to remain cool and not burst into a childish giggle. He hands the phone back to me, and my hand touches his when I take it. My breath hitches just slightly because I am ready for something to happen if it's going to. I feel like a kid on Christmas Eve waiting for Santa's arrival.

We're in the staring contest again, like we were last night. I will not kiss him first. I can't. I don't have the confidence either. I'm too afraid of rejection.

Thanks again, Mom.

He leans in and...hugs me. He hugs me! Okay, fine.

I eagerly accept the embrace, wrapping my arms around his strong, solid body. We hold each other for a few moments before he gives me a gentle squeeze and releases.

"Have a safe trip, Scott. Please keep me posted. I want to hear all about it when you get back. Thank you for breakfast."

"The pleasure is all mine, Billie. And I will." He nods and turns to get back into his car. My heart flips again and seems to each time he crosses my mind, which is quite frequently if I'm being honest. I jet over to the hospice center, since I haven't been there since yesterday afternoon. I've only called five times to check on him. Claire is undeniably hung over. She groans and mopes over to me when I walk through the automated doors.

"Rough night?" I smirk.

"Maybe a little. See, my mind thinks I'm still twenty-one. My body is screaming at me, clearly reminding me I'm thirty-six."

"Ha, I can relate. So what's this with you and Ryan? Do you know him?" I query.

"Nope. Met him last night. He's a phenomenal kisser. I wish I coulda taken him into my condo. Scott killed the kitty vibe."

"The kitty vibe?" I raise an eyebrow at her.

"You know...the coochie meow-meow kitty cat. The vageen supreme vibe." I shrug like I have no idea what she's talking about, but I think it's hysterical. "He lady cockblocked me."

"Ohhhhh. I see what you mean now," I simper.

"You're such a prude, Billie. Anyway, you and Scott need to get together, and Ryan and I need to get together. Just think—we could be sisters someday!" I guffaw so loudly the people in the reception area look over at us. I lower my volume.

"Scott won't even kiss me. I'm not even sure he's interested in me like that. He seems like he is, but then he just...stops."

"Girl, just kiss him!" Claire coaxes and nudges me with her elbow. "That's what I did with Ryan. He was all about it."

"Maybe you're right," I say resignedly. "He doesn't get back till Sunday, so I won't be seeing him until Monday anyway. It gives me a few days to stress out about it. Anyway, how's my dad?"

"He's stable. I had to sedate him earlier this morning because he was getting quite agitated. He's resting comfortably now."

"Thank you, Claire. I appreciate you."

"No worries. I've got you, Bills."

CHAPTER EIGHT

SCOTT

I won't reveal how many times I have stared at my phone since I gave Billie my number, waiting to see if she has texted me. Nothing yet. I'm waiting to board my flight, and I'll be sans service for several hours. Maybe I'll text her after my flight lands. But is that weird? I mean, I won't have much to say other than I made it safely. I hear the announcement that my flight is ready for boarding, so I make my way onto the plane and get comfortable. My mind buzzes restlessly, processing all of last night.

When my phone dings, I fumble wildly to see if it's Billie.

Sadly, no. It's Claire.

CLAIRE

U haven't kissed her yet?! What r u doing?!

ME

How do you know she even wants me to kiss her?

Did she say?

CLAIRE

Give me a break. U know she wants u. U 2 need to pull up ur big kid pants and stop stalling. Just let it happen.

ME

Are you sure she likes me?...

CLAIRE

I just talked to her. KISS HER!

The flight attendant begins his announcement over the intercom, so I turn my phone into airplane mode and try to relax. Claire's texts were reassuring. Maybe I should just go for it like she said. I don't know why I'm so scared.

It is a big deal, though. Christine and I were together since we were kids. She's the only one I've kissed, the only one I've slept with. The idea of being with someone else makes me feel torn between the life I had with her and a new one with someone else.

I guess a kiss wouldn't hurt. If there's nothing there, then we know, and the tension will be over, one way or another.

But what if I like it? What if I want more? Then what? I guess I'll cross that bridge if I come to it.

Fortunately, I fall asleep shortly after the flight takes off and don't wake up until we land. Within an hour, I'm set up in my hotel room and order room service. While I wait, I settle into bed and text Billie.

ME

I made it safely to Chicago.

She replies immediately.

BILLIE

That's good! I was wondering when you'd get in.

How was the flight?

ME

I think it was good. I slept the entire time. Lol.

BILLIE

Haha. That's nice. What are you up to now?

ME

I just ordered room service. Chillin' for the rest of the night. You?

BILLIE

Just grabbed dinner too. Someone donated the leftovers from their funeral luncheon. The guy in room 204 passed a few days ago.

I suck in my breath. I've been trying to put it out of my head, but my daughter Maggie was due in November. She would have been three next week, and I am just not handling it well. Anytime I hear anything about someone dying, I become really anxious and angry.

ME

Sorry to hear. He was a really nice man. Such a shame.

Way too young.

That man had stage four pancreatic cancer at forty-five years old. His kids haven't even graduated high school yet. Time is a thief.

Billie doesn't respond. Thankfully, my room service arrives just in time, because I'm famished. Even though I slept the whole flight, I'm probably going to crash after I finish eating. Besides, I have an early day tomorrow, so the more rest, the better. I shoot her one last text for the night.

ME

Turning in early. I have to be up at 4 a.m. Good night. :)

BILLIE

Sleep well. I'll be thinking about you tomorrow. Good luck! :)

The fact that she will be thinking about me tomorrow is reassuring that the signals I'm sending are being well-received and reciprocated.

Finally.

In the morning, I get ready for my presentation, feeling confident yet nervous. It's 6 a.m. in Pittsburgh, but I really want to take a selfie and send it to her. Is that too juvenile for a man who's approaching forty? I need to know if she's into me or not. She said she would be thinking about me today, but I could be reading that message the wrong way.

Fuck it. I'm doing it. I send the picture with the caption, "Ready to tackle the day and kick ass during my presentation." I don't expect a response because it's early, but sure enough my phone buzzes.

BILLIE

Wow, looking good there, Doc.

ME

I'm surprised you're awake.

BILLIE

I couldn't sleep.

ME

Is everything okay?

BILLIE

I guess as good as it can be…just lots on my mind.

ME

I'll try to call you later. We can talk about it if you want.

BILLIE

Okay.

Ugh. This is dumb. She said I looked good, but a friend could say that. And now she has a lot on her mind—of course her dad and not me. He's dying, for Pete's sake.

So what am I even doing?

CHAPTER NINE

BILLIE

That selfie this morning was hot... no...HAWT! Yeesh, I can't jump him through the phone, but I wish I could. He's the reason I couldn't sleep last night. I keep thinking about the heat and stares between us during our drinks at Caliente's. I can cut the sexual tension with a knife. And now, physically, my lady parts are burning so badly for the company of a man I can barely stand up. No, really, I am hurting down there.

When he returns, it's happening. I'm going to throw myself out there and see what happens. If I get rejected, then fine. Nevertheless, he's the freakin' keynote speaker at ALRIC and needs to focus on that this weekend.

To add to the misery, my dad had a rough night last night. He's becoming increasingly more agitated. Other than his lungs, his other organs are functioning.

How disgusting for a disease.

When do I know it's time? I know he's at the end of his life, and it won't be much longer now. How can I be sure when he is ready to go? I imagine turning off the machines, and he feels terrified as he dies this gruesome death, unable to breathe. I'll be the one responsible for his suffering. How can I do that to him?

I wonder what's going through his mind, knowing that part of him is still intact. I would feel bitter, so very bitter. Despite it all, the man relentlessly clings to his faith, because his vitals show he is calm and more relaxed when I'm praying.

I've been reading novels out loud to him too because the weather is starting to get pretty chilly. If I go out to the gazebo, it's for about thirty minutes max, right after lunch when it's the warmest.

After breakfast, I run home to shower, change, and check on the house. I'm so tired by the time I'm done, I curl up on my dad's old bed upstairs in his bedroom to take a nap. It still faintly smells like him, and I quietly cry myself to sleep. I dream about the time we boated at Magnolia State Park all afternoon. We had some beers, listened to music, and chowed down on sandwiches. We talked about my childhood and laughed for hours at all the memories. Then I caught a bass so big I almost capsized us. We grilled that sucker up for dinner, and it was delicious. I will never, ever forget that day. That was only three summers ago.

When I wake up, I feel rested but forlorn. If I feel this way, I can only imagine how my dad feels right now. I pack up some fresh clothes and start a load of laundry before I head out. I haven't tended to the house at all, but no one's been here, so it really doesn't need anything. And worst case, I'll call a cleaner. I have zero desire to scrub a toilet right now.

When I arrive back at Bellevue, Father Pete is sitting with my dad. He's been our parish pastor for seven years. He's a younger man, mid-forties, I'd say, with brown eyes and a short brown quiff. I'm guessing he's about six feet tall, with an athletic build. In his spare time, he runs marathons and coaches the St. Leonard School's boys' varsity basketball team.

Everyone loves him...especially Betty Ann Barber. She's in her late-fifties, with a white pixie hairdo and a petite build. She wears more makeup and perfume than a busted drag queen. I call her the church hypocrite: she acts like she's devout but is the most judgmental person I've ever met. One time I watched her squeeze her breasts in and up as she lifted her hands to receive Holy Communion. Father Pete didn't look, but I'm pretty sure I saw a sweat bead trickle from his forehead. Not because he was attracted to her, but because she makes him feel uncomfortable. And being a priest, in the Catholic Church, no less, is a pretty big burden to carry. Everyone's watching you, waiting for you to fuck up.

If he weren't a priest, I'd probably shoot my shot, but I would never, ever do it because he's a priest. He could leave the priesthood, claiming he's hopelessly in love with me, and I still don't think I could do it. I wouldn't be able to live with the guilt of tempting a man out of the most blessed role of the Church.

I involuntarily shiver at the thought.

"Good morning, Father," I greet him.

"Hello there, Billie. Good to see you. How are you?"

"About as good as I can be, given the circumstances, so pretty terrible." The one thing I like about him is that I feel safe to tell him exactly how I feel about anything, and I don't fear judgment.

"It's a devastating process to go through for all parties. You both are in my daily prayers. I was just about to anoint your father. Would you like to participate?" Father Pete starts getting out his oil and booklet.

"Of course. I'm glad I didn't miss it. I know you're a man in high demand. I really appreciate you coming here today. It means a lot." I affectionately but platonically pat him on the back in appreciation. He doesn't tense or drop a bead of sweat, so we're good.

I've never watched a priest anoint the sick before. It's a beautiful sacrament. Usually, people pray for healing over a person, but we're praying for a peaceful passing—more of a healing of the soul rather than the body. Father Pete also gives me a blessing for courage and strength. Right now, I'm emotionally exhausted.

Once my dad is asleep, we go to the common area and make some coffee. Father Pete pulls out a binder with information about the funeral Mass. My dad has everything he wants pretty much set in place, so I relay the music selections and readings to Father Pete. I still need to select pallbearers, though. I won't be participating in any Mass parts because I don't think I'll be in any kind of condition to do so. My goal is to be there and reverently bid farewell to my father. That's enough for me.

"All right, Billie. I think we're about as ready as we can be for now. Please don't hesitate to text me if you need anything. And please call me when you need me to give him last rites. Again, I'll be thinking about you both." He gives me a reassuring squeeze on the shoulder, and I simply nod my head.

Before bed, I shoot Scott a text to see how the presentation went.

ME

Hey, fancy pants. How'd the presentation go?

Flawless, I'm sure.

He doesn't answer. That's odd, considering he said he would try to call me this evening. Oh, well. Maybe he's just busy with conference stuff.

The next morning, still nothing. I go about my day as usual, which is becoming long and awfully repetitive. However, since the anointing yesterday, my dad is showing more signs of decline. Maybe an anointing is what he needed to finally start letting go.

The next day passes. No response. I could text him again, but why? Maybe he's ghosting me. He's supposed to be back today and bring Bruno tomorrow, so I'll just see him then.

Monday arrives and Scott never shows at Bellevue. I ask Claire if she knows what's going on, since he never came to visit. She says he was acting weird yesterday when he picked up Bruno. He was quick and abrupt and left. She texted him later to see if he was okay, but he didn't answer her either.

Something's going on. I just wish I knew what.

CHAPTER TEN

BILLIE

Thanksgiving is nine days away. My dad is fading more rapidly now. Claire discussed with me this morning that I need to consider when to stop the machines and prepare for the end. I still need to speak to my dad about this, because ultimately it's his decision. Regardless of how long we prolong the inevitable, he's going to die. After Thanksgiving we will begin, unless he miraculously goes on his own beforehand or chooses to wait. We always talked about having this Thanksgiving together and, selfishly, I need it as part of my closure.

This mother-fucking disease!

My father made his burial arrangements a while back, so everything he wants is pretty much set in place.

I'm not sure exactly where he's supposed to be buried in the cemetery, so when Rick visits my dad this morning, I decide to hunt for his plot.

When I arrive at the cemetery, I don't even know where to start. I scan the grounds, observing rows and rows and sections upon sections of headstones. I have a burial plot number and a roundabout location where I think he's supposed to be buried, but it's going to take some searching. I'm not one to go to cemeteries often. It creeps me out. My grandparents are buried here, so I assume his spot is near them. It's been so long since I've been here that I don't remember where they're laid to rest. I figure I'll start from the middle and work my way back. I know they're not buried near the entrance.

I peruse the rows and notice several people visiting this morning—an older couple, what looks like a widow who is praying in front of a headstone, and a man who is kneeling beside a headstone, placing two yellow roses in front of it.

The man's back shakes to the rhythm of crying. His hands are covering his face. I try to mind myself, but I feel so bad for him, and soon that's going to be me kneeling there, crying over my father's grave. I can't brace myself for the impact of it all.

The sky has turned ominous oddly fast, and clearly there's going to be a downpour any moment. The other visitors scurry to their cars. Thunder rumbles in the distance. It's time to go before I get soaked. I can find the burial plot another day.

This man doesn't move though. His crying becomes louder until I hear his sobs. I feel so terrible that I walk quietly toward him.

I can't just leave him there like that.

As I get closer, I recognize the sea of brown curls.

It's Scott.

Oh my gosh, it's Scott. Is this why he's been ghosting me?

Before I get to him, the clouds unleash a fury of raindrops.

"Scott!" I call.

He doesn't answer, so I walk closer until I am only a few steps away. It has been mere seconds, and I'm already drenched.

"Scott?" I ask, with more comfort in my tone.

Without even seeing my face, he stands up, paces back and forth from one end of the burial plot to the other, flailing his arms, and lets everything out—screaming. "What kind of God steals my beautiful, perfect wife and my newborn daughter, who never even got to take a breath before she died? She never even took a breath!" he moans.

"Why did he give Christine cancer? Why couldn't she survive it? How is God all-loving? I watched them both die, and…and I'm supposed to—what, move on? Act like I'm healed and happy? That everything is going to be okay? Because it's not. Fuck that. Fuck. That. This world is cruel and unfair!"

Scott's tears pour as fast as the sky releases raindrops. He looks up into the sky, droplets pricking his open eyes, and surrenders with a guttural cry.

"Why did you take them from me?" he cries out to God. "Why? WHY?! I hate you. I fucking hate you!" He falls to his knees and continues to sob, pounding his fists into the grass and growling in frustration.

I'm too stunned to move at first. My breath is quick and shallow, and my hands are shaking. I'm not afraid of him, but I think I'm in shock. I take a deep gulp of air, make the last few deliberate steps toward Scott, and sit down on the puddling wet grass, placing my hand on his back. I quietly cry with him, tears colliding with the raindrops on my cheeks. After a few minutes, Scott inhales deeply and exhales, beginning to regulate himself. He peers up at me with the most pained, agonizing look on a man I've ever seen and groans, "Why?"

I instinctively pull him toward me and wrap my arms around him. He reaches his arms around me and tightly embraces me, resting his head on my shoulder, holding onto me as he continues to calm down. I take several deep breaths to regulate myself because my senses are heightened and extremely alert.

Soon his breath rises and falls with mine, and we hold each other for a while longer, breathing in unison. At some point, the rain slows to a sprinkle.

I don't know what possesses me to do it, but I give him a soft kiss on the head.

Ugh, maybe that was inappropriate. I don't know.

We're practically strangers, but I feel like I've known him for years. There's something that attracts me to him like I've never been to any other human in my life. But he's actively grieving his wife and child, which is probably why he doesn't want to kiss me and why he stopped texting me altogether. Everything is starting to make more sense. And here I am, practically throwing myself at him.

He looks up at me, a bit surprised by the kiss, I'm sure, and murmurs, "I'm sorry, Billie." He clears his throat. "I don't know what came over me. In the two years since they've passed, I've never cried like that. I don't know what happened to me. I'm so sorry you had to see that."

He huffs heavily. "Today was supposed to be Maggie's birthday, her due date actually. Between this and Christine's death anniversary, the last few weeks have been hitting me hard with grief."

Good grief, that's horrendous!

He's a pediatric oncologist and his wife died from cancer. Damn, that has to feel like an excruciating spiritual slap to the face. He mentioned her passing before, but the gravity of the situation just hit me. It makes perfect sense as to why he's angry. I feel a similar rage about my dad's gruesome disease.

"Don't apologize for your grief, Scott. It's a complicated feeling, process...everything. I'm here for you. And I'm not leaving until you're ready to leave," I assure him.

I pull him into another embrace. He returns the hug.

"I think I'm okay now, really. We're soaking wet. It's cold out. Come on." He gently presses off me and stands up, reaching for my hand. "I'll take you to my place and make some coffee. Get you some dry clothes. Cook us something to eat."

He can see my hesitancy.

"It's the least I can do. I hope I didn't scare you. And I'm sorry I never reached out over the weekend. I've always been alone in my grief, so that's why I pulled away."

"I wasn't afraid at all. This is going to be me soon, and I didn't want you to go through the moment by yourself. I won't want to be alone either when I'm visiting my dad's grave."

As much as I feel I shouldn't go, I can't stop myself from taking his hand. It feels so...inappropriate? I mean, that was his wife. I know our spending time together isn't cheating, but I feel like I'm intruding. I release my hand and stop walking while my head battles its decision. Scott looks at me quizzically.

"Are you sure this is okay? I mean, is this...am I?" I throw up my hands in frustration. "I don't even know what I'm trying to say."

"I don't know anymore, Billie. But I know I don't want to be alone right now, and I feel safe with you. You can leave your car here so the inside doesn't get wet, and I'll bring you back right after breakfast."

He feels *safe* with me? That's incredibly impressive for a man to admit, at least in my experience.

Yet another green flag for him.

My dating history is the epitome of pathetic since that toolbag Brad Sylvan took me out on a date as a bet when I was a senior in high school.

What a humiliating disaster!

After that, I swore off men and haven't met anyone I felt connected to since. But Scott? I think I feel safe with him too. He makes me feel things in my heart and all through my body.

Besides, I do need to come back later and find this burial plot so I can finalize the order for Dad's headstone.

And I'm starving.

I place my hand back in his and say, "Okay. Let's go."

CHAPTER ELEVEN

BILLIE

W e arrive at his surprisingly modest house. It's a ranch-style red brick home. He has a small wooden porch with a swing and a private fenced-in backyard. Lily plants adorn the front of the house but, other than that, the landscape is minimal. I'm not sure what I was expecting, but the neighborhood feels nostalgic. It reminds me of my grandparents' neighborhood.

"This is quaint." I say pleasantly.

"Were you expecting a huge mansion with maids and butlers?" he asks sarcastically.

"Oh, no. I wasn't sure what I was expecting. I like it. It's simple. It's not unnecessarily massive with maids and butlers." I match his sarcasm.

"When you come out of med school and residency completely broke, with $300,000 in student loan debt, it's impossible to afford anything more than *simple*. Christine and I were very frugal for the first few years after I landed my job at the hospital, so I'm now debt-free, including the house. After she died, I never felt ready to move out of here. I mean, why? It's only Bruno and me. Anything bigger than this would be wasteful."

Scott cuts the engine and we make our way to the house. He punches the passcode into the padlock and opens the door. We're excitedly greeted by Bruno. His paws clack on the hardwood floor, and his tail whacks my legs. He wriggles with excitement and waits for me to pet him.

"Wait here. I'll be right back." Scott disappears down the hall.

"Hey, Bruno. Hey, buddy. How's it going? Happy to see me?" I kneel down and give him the attention he's been waiting for, and he licks my hand in appreciation.

"For such a big dog, you are quite a sap," I say, massaging his ears. Bruno lets out a relaxing groan and doggie-smiles at me.

Scott reenters with a towel, a t-shirt, and some gym shorts. He has changed into a plain black t-shirt and gray sweatpants. Why did he have to put on the gray sweatpants? If I didn't know any better, I would say this is a thirst trap. But pictures of him with his wife are hanging on every wall I can see so far, so I truly believe he's not thirsty for anything other than a cup of hot coffee, especially after what I witnessed this morning.

"The bathroom is the first door on your left. Feel free to shower and freshen up. I'll toss your clothes in the wash."

I stand up, wiping my dog-slobbered hands on my cold, wet jeans.

"Thank you, but you don't have to do that. I can wash these when I get home."

"Nonsense. I have to toss mine in too. Everything will be done by the time we're finished with breakfast."

As soon as I shut the bathroom door, I suck in a deep breath.

What is happening to me? Why am I crushing on this guy so badly?

This whole thing seems incredibly fucked up. I should just shower, eat, and leave. But I don't want to leave. I want to kiss those sultry lips because I need to know what he tastes like.

What am I doing?

What am I thinking?

Damn it, I am thirsty, and water isn't going to quench it.

After a much-needed hot shower, I put on the Green Day t-shirt and black gym shorts. I wipe the steam off the mirror to take a look at myself. My boobs fill out the shirt, and the gym shorts hug me right around my hips. My ass fills out the shorts. I feel completely awkward but kind of sexy. I don't have a bra on, so it's only a matter of time before my headlights become abundantly clear.

Maybe that isn't such a bad thing.

My long, dark-brown hair has that messy fresh-out-of-the-shower look, and my caramel eyes have flickers of gold that appear to be dancing in my reflection.

Get it together, Billie. It's just another breakfast. You're in the friend zone.

I take one last reassuring look at myself before heading into the kitchen.

"I hope you're hungry because I have pancakes, bacon, and...."

That's when we lock eyes. A surge of energy courses up my arms and down my legs, landing smack in my lady bits. My heart starts pounding, but I'm trying to play it cool. Thank goodness I'm not a dude or I'd have a raging boner right now. Shit, I am hopelessly attracted to this man.

He scans me up and down.

"Cheesy scrambled eggs," he says.

"Mmm, it looks and smells amazing. I'll pour us some coffee."

"Sounds good. This will all be ready in a few minutes." He motions over the sizzling bacon and skillet of eggs. "I like a splash of cream and two sugars."

"Got it!" I salute and walk over to the coffee pot.

Oh my gosh, Billie, you saluted? Get a damn grip. Seriously. You're embarrassing yourself.

I pour us each a cup, loaded with our cream and sugar preferences, and grab hold of both of them. I turn to walk to the table and—

"Coming in hot!" Scott turns around just as I step forward and—*bam*—we slam into each other, the scalding coffee spilling down the front of me.

"Ow, ow, ow! Hot! It's *hot*!" I yelp.

"Oh, Billie!" Scott quickly sets the hot skillet back on the stove and takes the coffees from me. Instinctively, I peel off my shirt that's melting my skin and toss it on the floor.

Boobs. My boobs are out.

"Oh, my God!" I shriek and place my hands over my breasts in an attempt to shield myself from further embarrassment. But it's too late. Scott gets a full view once the coffees are secured on the counter.

"Towel!" Scott panics, tossing me a kitchen towel to cover myself. "I am so sorry. Are you hurt?" he asks, concerned.

I close my eyes and press my lips together. "My ego is a little bruised but, other than that, I think I'm fine."

"Please, don't feel embarrassed on my account. You have nothing to be ashamed of. You're...you're beautiful."

That moment I look up at him, and his eyes smolder at me. My heart responds by beating double time. He can probably hear it pounding in my chest. I would love to pound him right here and now, but I stand still, unable to speak. I want to kiss him, yet I cannot bring myself to initiate it. He denies the opportunity by saying, "I'll get you some fresh clothes. I'll be right back."

Scott heads down the hall and, after snapping back to reality by watching his ass disappear from view, I follow, thinking I would meet him outside of his bedroom. I knock lightly on the door and open it.

"Scott?" I peer in and freeze midstep. It's not his bedroom but, rather, a nursery. The room is staged perfectly, just waiting for a little baby girl to arrive home. Before I can close the door, however, Scott emerges from his bedroom.

He stops dead in his tracks.

His jaw hardens.

I gasp.

"I'm sorry. I opened the wrong door." I swiftly shut it, take the clothes, and haul ass to the bathroom.

How humiliating!

Here I am with a tea towel barely covering my boobs, and now I've unlocked a whole new shitstorm by accident. I need to get out of here. But first, another shower because I reek of coffee and feel sticky from the creamer. I wash off quickly and get dressed. When I walk into the kitchen, I am fully prepared to excuse myself and leave. But he has two plates set on the table, filled with what looks like paradise on a plate, with fresh fruit and new coffees set directly behind the plates. I hear Scott come up the steps and close the basement door behind him.

"I switched over the laundry and threw the other clothes in the washer. Your stuff will be dry in a little while. Sit, let's eat. I'm famished."

"Are you sure? Maybe I should go. I just feel—"

"No, please don't leave. I'm sure you're feeling embarrassed, and I hope I didn't make you feel uncomfortable. It's just...I haven't had a woman here since Christine died, and, well, I guess I'm nervous."

"As long as you're sure," I say hesitantly, easing myself to the booth side of the table and bench.

"You're fine. Trust me, I've already forgotten what your boobs look like." He grins at me, trying to make light of the situation.

"Ha, well, I'm not surprised you bumped into me. They're definitely hard to miss. I *am* surprised you didn't bounce across the room when we collided." Scott chokes on his coffee and laughs.

"Is that an invitation?" He coughs and chuckles at the same time. His cheeks flush as he smiles before taking another gulp of coffee.

Is he flirting with me now?! What the heck is going on?

I manage a giggle and cut into my pancakes. I can't even answer, but the smile on my face says *yes*. I take a bite and feel more at ease with sitting through a meal.

"Wow," I say, as I go for a second bite. "Where did you learn to cook like this? They're so fluffy and perfectly round, and I love that you added extra vanilla."

"You noticed! I love a prominent essence of vanilla in my pancakes. My mom and I used to cook together when I was younger. When you have four other siblings, everyone has to do their part."

Without even thinking, I blurt out, "Your mom had five kids? Her poor vagina."

Scott guffaws and I redden with embarrassment.

"I don't know much about my mother's vagina, but I'm pretty sure she's okay." He winks at me, probably because he thinks I'm a complete idiot.

Why do I say stuff like that without thinking first?

"Five kids," I repeat. "Kudos to her." I attempt to recover from further humiliation. But it's too late. I continue to word-vomit.

"I'm not sure I'll ever have kids." I pick up a piece of bacon and take a bite. Extra crunchy, just the way I like it. This guy cannot be for real. Polite, kind, generous, and a fabulous cook?

Green flag, green flag, green flag, and green flag.

"No? Why do you say that?" Scott stabs his fork into his eggs.

"My parents had only me, then divorced when I was sixteen. I never want to go through what they did. I love both my parents, but my mom and I have never had a close relationship. After she left, I went through a really dark period over the next few years. I wouldn't wish that on my kids."

I hesitate and then ask carefully, "Do you think you will ever remarry and have more children?"

Scott pops a piece of freshly sliced golden pineapple in his mouth. He chews and swallows before responding.

"I really don't know. Sometimes, I feel like Christine has been gone for decades and other times I feel like she died yesterday. I think I'm open to it, but the idea of having a life with someone else—"

"Makes you feel guilty?" I finish his thought.

"A little, I guess. I just never imagined myself with anyone else but her. She was my high school sweetheart. I know no one is perfect, but she was pretty damn close."

"She sounds delightful." I could never compete with that, with *her*. Not that I would want to. Out of respect for him and his family, I probably shouldn't act on this attraction. I keep going back and forth on what to do, but the more he talks about her, the less I feel he's actually interested.

Gah, but I want to kiss him so badly!

"So, tell me something no one knows about you." Scott takes a gulp of coffee.

"That's a great question." I contemplate before responding. "It's not a huge secret or anything, but most people don't know my name isn't actually Billie. It's Belinda. I just go by Billie."

"Your name is *Belinda Carlisle*?" Scott says emphatically and eyes me suspiciously. "You don't look like her."

"Ha, my mom was obsessed with her in the '80s and was so stoked they shared the same last name after she married my dad that she just *had* to name me Belinda. My dad has always called me Billie, and I like it, so I kept it."

"*Billie* or *Belinda* suits you well." Scott smirks as he takes another drink of coffee.

"And what about you? I mean, your last name is Bennington," I comment.

"Yeah, so?" Scott appears confused.

"Hello? Chester Bennington, you know, the lead singer from Linkin Park?" I scoff, pretending to be offended.

"Huh, I suppose you're right. I never listened to them much. I'm more of a classic rock or hip-hop kind of guy, and a little punk too. Hence the Green Day shirt."

"Linkin Park is probably one of my favorites of all time. Their music got me through my parents' divorce. When I found out Chester passed away, I cried for weeks and binge-listened to every one of their songs. I still get choked up thinking about it." I clear my throat to prevent myself from breaking composure. How the death of someone I don't even know affects me so deeply, I will never understand. His voice is my siren, capable of luring me to my demise.

Scott and I continue small talk through the rest of our meal. When I finish the last bite of my pancake, I sit back in relaxed satisfaction.

"That was spectacular. You know how to hit a home run with breakfast foods."

"It was my pleasure, Billie." He stands up and takes our plates to the sink. I think we both know it's time for me to leave.

"Thank you so much for the hospitality, but I should probably get going. I need to get back to my dad. Breakfast was five stars." I back up slowly and turn to exit the kitchen. It's then I realize my car isn't here. It's at the cemetery.

"I think you're going to need a ride." Scott says, amused.

"Yep," I reply, closing my eyes and nodding. "I definitely need a ride."

CHAPTER TWELVE

SCOTT

Those. Breasts.

I can't stop thinking about them—about *her*. I tried not to stare too long, but whoa, I couldn't help but take in what I could. Her body is mouth-watering: so curvy, so voluptuous, so... juicy. Her hourglass figure does something to me. I actually feel emotions other than dejection. It makes me think about all the things I want to do to her body...all the things I want her to do to me.

I sure hope she didn't notice my sudden surge of teenage hormones bulging from those gray sweatpants. Apparently, gray sweatpants drive women nuts. I don't know what my intentions were when I put them on. I've barely even spoken to a woman since Christine passed, yet I feel so drawn to Billie. Physically, yes, she's a ten. But the comfort she showed me earlier was nothing short of amazing. I was a complete disaster and she...she held me. She kissed my head. She stayed with me. I don't think I've even hugged someone other than her in over a year—not even my parents.

I haven't been able to get Billie out of my head since we parted ways at the cemetery. Should I ask her out to something more formal than breakfast? Her dad's dying, so I doubt she's emotionally available. She didn't reciprocate when I attempted to flirt with her earlier.

Is that an invitation?

That line was so cheesy. Maybe she's ticked off that I ghosted her over the weekend. Claire assured me to shoot my shot, but my sly attempts to flirt or hint that I'm interested don't seem to be working.

If I wait, will she even want to see me while she's grieving? I didn't want anyone near me for months after the funeral—the second one in a year—and everyone felt so incredibly sorry for me.

Once the last guest left Christine's funeral luncheon, I closed myself off entirely. The food stopped coming. The check-in texts slowed down, and I was left in utter darkness. I wanted it that way, honestly. A part of my soul died with Christine and sweet little Maggie. No matter what happens in this life, I will never get that piece back. It's forever with them, hopefully in a place much better than here.

After I finish cleaning up breakfast, I shower, get dressed, and take Bruno for a walk. The skies have cleared, and it looks like a storm never passed through this morning. I need to walk off this energy. I feel alive. Maybe I'll make an extra trip to the hospice center today. I normally don't pop in during the day on Tuesdays, but I know Billie will be there, and maybe I can offer some comfort back to her. I took the day off because I couldn't get my composure, so I'm free to do whatever I need.

Besides, on our way out the door, I completely forgot her clothes in the dryer. That'll be my excuse. That way she doesn't think I'm trying to take advantage of her fragile emotional state. I shouldn't assume she's fragile, but I know what death and grief feel like. Some days I feel like I can shatter as easily as glass.

"Come on, Bruno. Do you want to go see Billie?"

Bruno wags his tail with excitement and barks in agreement.

"Let's go, boy."

I grab her clothes and off we go.

CHAPTER THIRTEEN

BILLIE

I practically waltz into my dad's room. Claire is taking his vitals and gives me a thumbs up. I really like Claire. She's been a wonderful caretaker. I'm happy we've befriended each other. My life has been work and taking care of my dad for two years. There's little capacity for anything else. I don't regret any of my decisions. But it feels nice to have someone else to talk to in a reciprocated conversation. That is one thing I deeply miss about my relationship with my dad. He can hardly communicate with me. Can't write anything, type anything, say anything. It's so very sad because I've been grieving pieces of my dad for two years. My grieving won't begin when he dies because I'm already in it.

After Claire leaves, I sit down and grab my father's hand. I scoot the chair close to his bed and lean in toward his face. "Dad, I have to tell you something. I met this guy. Okay, it's Scott. He is *sooo* hot. I probably shouldn't even be telling you that. He's a pediatric oncologist at a children's hospital. I had breakfast at his place this morning. It wasn't a date or anything, but...let's just say he had a rough morning and we got caught in the rain. I wish you could talk back so you could tell me what to do. Normally, I would go for it, but his wife died of cancer and he lost his daughter right after birth. He's grieving, deeply. I'm getting mixed signals. I'm not sure if I should pursue this or not."

My dad blinks twice.

"Yes? Really? He is so kind. He makes me laugh. I'm incredibly attracted to him. I can't...I can't stop thinking about him."

"Thinking about who?"

A familiar voice startles me from behind, accompanied by the jingle of Bruno's collar tags. I turn my head slowly, bracing for what's waiting for me. My face constricts, flushing bright red. "Hiiiiiii," I say through gritted teeth. Bruno trots over to my dad and places his head on my dad's lap.

"Why, hello, Billie. Good to see you again." He looks fine as hell sporting his typical garb: a hoodie and fitted joggers. His hair is still damp from showering. I inhale a whiff of his fresh soapy scent when he nears my side. My insides melt, my head dizzy with desire.

"It's Tuesday. What are you doing here?" I ask curiously. Scott takes a seat beside me and hands me my bag of clothes.

"Well, I experienced a brutal wave of grief this morning, and out of nowhere this beautiful woman showed up, brightening my day. I can't...I can't stop thinking about her." He mimics my previous tone.

"Stop. You're such a goof." I attempt a playful swat, but he catches my wrist and then laces his fingers through mine. My breath hitches and my heart flutters uncontrollably. I gaze into his eyes and lean into him.

Kiss him, Billie! Kiss him! Do it now!

He glances at my lips and parts his. I can't help but close my eyes and swallow back everything within me to refrain from jumping him. He leans toward me so close that I can feel his breath tickle my lips. I have two choices: kiss him or bail.

My moral instincts take over yet again. I whisper, "My dad can see us."

You fucking wimp, Billie.

Scott tucks a stray piece of hair behind my ear. Then he runs his thumb across my lips and murmurs, "I know."

I glance over to my dad. The right side of his mouth is twitching, his eyes blinking repeatedly. I assume that's a good sign. His vitals are stable.

The moment is gone again. We were right there! By the same token, I do not want my first real kiss ever to be in front of my dad. I'm an open book to him, but anything intimate is reserved for behind closed doors.

I break away, stand up, and pace around the room. I can barely breathe because my body aches to be fulfilled. I try shaking my wrists to release the pent-up energy, but it doesn't work. Scott sits there, with his hand propping up his chin, smirking. It's like he gets a rise out of making me squirm. Yet, he's not doing a damn thing about it! He could have kissed me just now and didn't. How can he stay so calm, so unaffected by our encounter?

I'm not sure how much more I can take of this wondering, waiting. I've heard that, for women, intimacy is a slow burn. Ha, I feel like I'm engulfed in flames. When I sit back down, Scott leans toward me, but not too close this time, and chuckles, "Are you okay?"

No. No, I'm not fine!

I'm desperately trying to hold it together. It's impossible. My head is no longer in charge. My body and emotions have taken full control.

"I'm fine," I lie. He knows I'm not being honest, yet he sits as cool as a cucumber.

The moment simmers, and we continue conversation until the noon bells chime. That's my cue. I pull out my rosaries and begin praying. I've been praying the rosary every day since Dad was admitted. Sometimes at noon, sometimes at 3 p.m. If I really need an extra boost, I pray the Chaplet of Divine Mercy afterward. If I didn't have my faith and deep spirituality, I wouldn't be sitting here praying right now. I'd be dead in the ground because I couldn't handle this. I have to believe that there's a higher power and a paradise. If not, life is a total waste.

During the fourth decade of the rosary, Scott begins praying the words with me. Either he memorizes quickly or he's prayed a time or two. When we finish praying, I make the sign of the cross, kiss my father's hand, and continue to hold it. I feel calm, at peace. My attention remains focused solely on my dad.

"You know, I don't actually hate God," Scott admits. I don't look back at him, but I entangle my hand in his and reply reassuringly, "I know." I squeeze his hand. The room becomes uncomfortably silent when the anxiety of death creeps in as an unwelcome guest.

"What's it like?" I ask him.

"What do you mean?"

"Grief. What's it like grieving someone you love so much?"

Scott sighs heavily. "It's like....Hm, this is tough," he ponders. "Imagine being in the ocean where the waves are unpredictable. That's the grief. You have to wear a life jacket to keep yourself afloat because the ocean is so vast and drowning is inevitable without one. The life jacket is hope. But, you see, the life jacket is weighted down, heavy and restricting. It helps just enough to keep you above water when the waves are calm. Just when you think things are going to be okay, the big waves rage, and nothing can keep you afloat. Not even the life jacket can save you. With or without the life jacket, you're just...drowning."

I wince as my chest tightens from the description. "So...how do you get out of the water?"

"If that ever happens, I'll let you know." He gives my hand a squeeze back.

"Where are you now?" I ask carefully.

"Drowning," he whispers.

The burdensome conversation takes us a while to process. "I hate to leave, but I think I've overstayed my welcome," Scott says reluctantly and stands up. The hours felt like minutes.

"I enjoyed today, Billie. I appreciate all your kindness. Truly." He opens his arms for a hug. I naturally move into him, my body electrifying. We hold each other longer than a friendly hug. I'm not sure how else to describe the emotion, other than it feels like home. I nuzzle myself into his chest, his heart beating rapidly against my cheek. I feel comfort, safety, peace—and undeniably turned on. I don't break from him until he releases me. He pulls my chin toward his face and murmurs, "See you soon."

He and Bruno walk out of the room, and I swoon onto the couch. That was the most amazing thing I've ever experienced with a man. Now I yearn for him.

"Billie? May I come in?" It's Claire. She has a grave look on her face. I sigh in dread.

"Yes, absolutely. Please."

"I was hoping you had time to discuss some things about your dad's care," she says carefully. I've been avoiding this conversation, but it has to happen now. It's time.

"Certainly. Give me a few minutes. I'll meet you at the front desk."

"Take all the time you need."

CHAPTER FOURTEEN

BILLIE

I haven't left the hospice center since I arrived earlier today. I can't even begin to process the conversation that took place with Claire. I don't want to think about the end yet. Unfortunately, I have no choice. My dad is asleep, and I am beyond drained and defeated. I debate whether I should text Scott or not, but I could really use some company, a friend, *someone.*

Screw it.

ME
Are you awake?

SCOTT
Yeah, what's up?

ME
I'm coming over.

SCOTT
Okay. Door is open.

I didn't even ask him if I could come over because I can't take it any longer. I need to know what's going on with us, and I cannot stay here tonight after my conversation with Claire. Roberta assured me that my dad will be fine and told me to go home and get a full night's sleep in my own bed, but I don't want to go back home alone either. There's no way I'll be able to sleep. Worse comes to worst, I'll sleep in my car in the parking lot.

I drive slowly and cautiously because I'm gloomy. The last thing I need to add to the list of life's bullshit is a car accident. When I get to Scott's house, I practically drag myself to the door and place my head against it. I know he said to walk right in, but I need a min—

"Whoa!" I shriek. Apparently, he saw me coming and decided to open the door. I fall into his arms, which sends him backward onto his back on the floor, with me directly on top of him. We gaze into each other's eyes, laughing nervously.

Then I say the words that change everything.

"You know, if we keep meeting like this, someone's gonna think there's somethin' going on between us."

Without hesitation, he takes his hand, grips a handful of my hair, and says in a low, husky voice, "Something *is already* going on between us."

His lips crash into mine, and fireworks explode within me. My restraint is over now that he has finally kissed me. There's no way I'm stopping whatever is about to take place between us. My body is feeling things it has never experienced before, and I'm here for all of it.

I'll admit, I've never even kissed a guy before, unless you count Jerry Kuhns, who had to plant one on me during the school musical in the tenth grade. But that wasn't a *real* kiss. That bozo Brad tried to kiss me toward the end of the date we had, but I declined, and that's when he admitted I was *just a stupid bet anyway*. And I always thought I'd save myself for marriage, being

Catholic and all, but I'm about to change all that. Do I tell him I'm a virgin? What a pitiful thing to admit at thirty-six years old.

You're not here for it, Billie. Get back to reality! You need to be present for this!

When he goes in for a second kiss, he opens his mouth and I follow his lead.

How hard could this be?

I hear him groan in the back of his throat, and my sex begins pulsating, hungry for him to satisfy me. I go in for another kiss with more urgency. Again. And again. I am desperate for more as I feel him harden beneath me. He places his other hand on my hip and moves it slowly up my stomach and onto my breast.

Thank goodness I put on the lace pushup bra.

My breath hiccups as he gently squeezes me. That's when he sits up, stands up, and pulls me up with him without breaking from my lips. He then picks me up and carries me to his bed, practically throws me onto it, and pounces on top of me.

He straddles me and sits back on his heels. He pulls up my shirt, and I lift my head to let him remove it. I go for his, but he's already tearing it off.

My, oh my. His body is like one of a Greek god. I can't help but gape and put my hands all over him. He smiles and bends down to kiss me again. Before I know it, he's caressing my stomach right at the line of my jeans, gripping my panties. I feel like a lioness about to capture my prey, and my instincts take over. I grab onto him and roll with him so that I'm now straddling him.

I unbutton my jeans and begin sliding them down. He lifts me up off of him and sets me on the carpet so I can remove them. I then grab the waistband of his thirst-trap gray sweatpants and slide them off as he lifts up his hips. I take off my panties, then release and remove my bra, the last of my clothing...and innocence.

He props himself on his elbows and admires me from head to toe. I've never been particularly in love with my body, given society's ridiculous beauty standards. Right now, however, I feel secure and confident. He pulls me toward him and says, "You are stunning. I can't tell you how much I've been thinking about this, craving you. Come here. I want you so badly. I need you."

We begin wildly kissing, touching, and exploring each other.

I whimper.

He moans.

My breath hitches.

He sighs in pleasure.

I didn't know that this is how all of *this* feels: desire, intimacy, sex. Had I known, I don't think I would have waited so long, but it was absolutely worth it.

We change positions so that he's on top of me again. He kisses me down my neck while he's massaging my left breast. My nipples pucker at his touch, and I shiver. I yearn for his mouth on them.

He moves his head up next to my ear and whispers in a seductive voice, "You really do have great boobs." He caresses me lightly, and my body breaks out into goosebumps. I bite my bottom lip and place my hand over his, indicating to squeeze harder. He lowers his head and slips my nipple into his mouth, gently suckling. It feels sublime.

My entire body burns in desperation when he moves his erection back and forth over the top of my folds. What pure, unadulterated ecstasy.

Scott is a smokeshow. His curls. His silhouette. His muscles. All the nerves in my body are shooting off pleasure signals like firecrackers. I can't believe this is actually happening.

He continues to move against me while kissing me fiercely. My body is beginning to squirm because I am aching for him to be inside of me. I grab hold of his arms and move my hips in sync with each of his waves.

He then takes a condom from the nightstand drawer. He rolls it down his penis. Before inserting himself, he looks into my eyes, searching for something.

Consent, maybe?

I eagerly nod my head *yes*. I'm mentally ready. I can feel I'm physically ready because I am on fire with desire. I've been waiting my whole life for this moment.

He eases himself inside me, and I suck in a deep breath.

"Oh, God!" I cry out.

"What? What? Are you all right? Am I hurting you?" he stutters and stops moving.

"No, I'm fine," I assure him. "That feels so damn good. Don't you dare stop now." I pull him closer to me, and he begins to move in slow, steady waves again. I follow his lead. I hear several breathy *ahs* and *ohs* escape him, so I know I'm doing something right. We're in a rhythm together. It's indescribable. It's like my body was missing something, and I didn't realize it until now.

He relishes my body, grabbing my ass and then my thigh, pushing my leg up so that he can thrust even deeper.

Pressure forms within me, growing more intense each time he glides inside of me.

Is this good? Is this bad? It feels good, I think. Oh my, yes, definitely good.

I want to scream, but I don't think I should.

Am I about to orgasm?

My breathing becomes labored, and I release several moans with "don't stop" mixed in. I think he knows what's coming because he starts to intensify his thrusts.

And then it happens. The most breathtaking, glorious physical response I have and probably will ever experience. I cry out in satisfaction, Scott slowing his rhythm to a stop. He remains inside of me and laughs.

He laughs!

I panic inside.

Was I that bad?

"Did I do something wrong?" I ask meekly.

"No, no, no," he pants and smiles. "That was unbelievable. You feel amazing."

"Oh. So do you." I relax my stiffened body.

Is it over already? If so, I need more.

I shyly ask, "Did you...?"

"Oh, no," he huffs. "I'm just getting started."

He kisses me as his rhythm picks up again. Soon after, he turns us over so that I'm straddling him again. The only thing I know to do is move back and forth. I must be doing something right because Scott moans loudly, saying things like, "You feel so good. Oh my, you're so wet. Keep going just like that."

As I do, the intense pressure builds within me again. I move quicker, harder. I know he's about to orgasm when he sighs lustily and firmly squeezes my hips.

We climax in unison.

I have no words.

None.

I collapse on top of him. Time stands still, as if I'm in this warm bubble of euphoria.

After we recover, I giggle. "I thought you said you were just getting started," I jest. He chuckles.

"I can't help myself. You are sweet perfection. Besides, the night is still young." He gives me a seductive grin and a quick peck on the lips as I crawl off of him, basking in post-coital bliss on his bed. I no longer feel sad or tired. In fact, I feel energized and invigorated.

"I'm going to get us some water. Don't even think about going anywhere. I'm not through with you yet," he flirts and winks before heading to the kitchen.

And I don't leave that bed the entire night.

CHAPTER FIFTEEN

SCOTT

My eyes open ten minutes before my alarm is set to ring. I don't normally work the morning shift on Wednesdays, but I need to make up some work since I unexpectedly took yesterday off. This is the first morning since Christine died that I'm not full of despair.

Last night with Billie was remarkable. I haven't been with anyone besides Christine, and we made love for only a few weeks after she received her cancer diagnosis. We thought her feeling ill was due to the pregnancy, but it was undoubtedly the cancer overtaking her body. At that point, neither of us was interested in bonding sexually. It's been years since I've had sex.

It wasn't just the sex that was mind-blowing. I mean, the sex was out of this world, but Billie is...incredible. I don't know how else to say it. Everything feels natural with her. And that body? I'm looking at her right now as she sleeps, awestruck with her beauty. I wish I hadn't waited so long to make a physical move. I've been wanting to kiss her, fantasizing about having sex with her, but every time I went to initiate, something tugged me away.

And how we went from a kiss to sex in a matter of minutes just goes to show how much we've been holding back from each other and how much we've both wanted it to happen.

We didn't fall asleep until well after 2 a.m. It's barely six now. Even with only a few hours of sleep, I'm wide awake and ready to tackle the day. With a few minutes to spare, I write Billie a note.

I'm sorry you couldn't wake up in my arms. I wanted nothing more than to be next to you this morning. I have to go in early since I took off yesterday. Stay as long as you'd like, and help yourself to anything you want. I will be done working at 7. I'll pick up dinner and meet you at Bellevue. Text me what you're craving...other than me.

- Scott

I give Bruno a pat on the head before I go. I blow a kiss into the house and drive into the city to start my twelve-hour shift.

"Good morning, Miranda!" I singsong. "Here is a grande caramel macchiato with whipped cream and a dash of cinnamon." Miranda is my secretary, receptionist, and administrative assistant extraordinaire. She could retire at any time, and I dread the day. Her style and sass are what I love most about her. Miranda is always well-dressed. Her wardrobe accentuates the beauty of her ebony skin and shoulder-length curly hair. She doesn't take shit from anybody—especially insurance companies —but she is kind and compassionate. My patients and their families adore her.

I place the coffee on her desk, walk into my office, and flip on the lights.

"Scottie Matthew Bennington." She comes storming after me, sans coffee in hand. She's one of the few people allowed to call me Scottie—and use my middle name, for that matter. She never calls me Dr. Bennington unless we're in front of patients.

"What can I do for you on this lovely morning, *Miranda*?" I ask, accentuating her name.

"You can start by telling me who she is." She folds her arms and taps her foot, waiting for an answer.

Miranda knows. There's no point trying to hide it. I'm grinning ear to ear, and I think I'm standing a little taller this morning too. I'm also floating on cloud nine. I'm never this chipper in the mornings. "Now, that wouldn't be any fun, would it?" I joke.

"So there *is* a lady. I better clear your meetings for the day because you aren't leaving this office without dishing out all the details. And I'll make sure of that." She points her finger directly at me.

She isn't kidding either. I have a deep respect for, and a healthy fear of, Miranda. She's old enough to be my mother. Even though I'm her boss, she's *really* the one in charge.

"Her name is Billie. I met her at Bellevue. Her dad is dying and I'm there to...comfort her. Bing. Bang. Boom. Done." I dust off my hands.

"Now, hold on just a second," she says with a slight southern drawl. "Billie, huh? Okay...Hmmm."

"What?" I say exasperatedly. She's eyeing me up, thinking intently about what she wants to say next. I break the silence instead.

"Are you going to ask if I slept with her?" I fold my arms across my chest.

"You don't have to. It's written all over your damn face." She waves her hand at me. "You look like a thirteen-year-old boy who just discovered porn."

I feel like one, too.

"Fine, but last night was the first time. She's kind, intelligent. She's funny and a little quirky. She's *gorgeous.*" My eyes glaze over, envisioning our sexual escapade.

"I see. Well, you better find a reason to get her over here so I can meet her. You can't start dating just anyone."

"Oh, I can't?" I ask, amused. "Last time I checked, I was a thirty-nine-year-old man."

"You know how protective I am of you. Get her over here this week or I'll track her down my damn self," she orders.

"Yes, ma'am," I answer, indulging her. Miranda swivels on her heels and exits my office sternly, but I notice a momentary smile.

I don't stop smiling the rest of the day.

CHAPTER SIXTEEN

BILLIE

I cannot believe I lost my virginity last night. Holy shit!

About damn time, Billie!

Our bodies, our responses, the passion, the sensations. Have mercy! I mean, sure, I've been turned on from time to time, but I had no perception of hopeless desire, uniting with a man, and... *the orgasms.* Two of them, to boot!

Deep down I feel like a harlot waiting to be stoned to death in front of the church congregation. I failed the pre-marital sex test miserably. But I've been leading a chaste life since birth. If this is the worst thing I ever do, so be it.

Ugh, how am I going to make it through the day without wanting to text Scott incessantly?

First, a shower. I throw the covers off me and thoroughly check the sheets for any blood. I don't see any, so that's relieving. I'm surprised I wasn't all dried up and shriveled down there from lack of attention. Being such a devout Catholic, I've never even masturbated or experimented with myself. I'm starting to regret that decision.

Bless me, Father, for I have sinned...and will probably sin again later tonight if I have any say in it.

Once I'm dressed, I make a cup of coffee and debate taking Bruno for a walk. I've never handled a dog as big as him, but I'm well-versed in dog-walking because I used to walk my neighbor's dog every day during the summers for extra cash.

Oh, what the hell.

"Come on, Bruno! Let's go for a walk." We stroll around the neighborhood for a solid twenty minutes before navigating back to Scott's house. I can tell Bruno knows the area well because he anticipates every turn home.

Once Bruno is settled, I write a little note on the back of the one he left for me and place it by the coffee maker.

I need more.

P.S. I took one of your travel mugs. I guess you'll have to come get it.

– Billie

I grab the coffee and my belongings, which I think are only my keys and cellphone, and lock up. I make a pit stop at home to check the house and pull up the trash can. When I get home, the trash can is already lined up on the curb. It must have been my neighbor Rashaad. He always looks out for me.

I piddle around for a bit before I change into some fresh clothes, switch over the laundry, grab a few books, and venture back to Bellevue.

At 6:30 p.m., I text Scott. I haven't messaged him all day, and he hasn't messaged me either. I've read an entire novel, most of it aloud to my dad when he was awake. Dad hasn't changed since yesterday, thankfully. The repetitive nature of each day, though, is weighing on me mentally. I haven't told him about last night. I figured there are just some things I shouldn't share with a parent.

ME

Cheese pizza and Pepsi from Santino's?

SCOTT

Boring, but sure.

ME

You said anything I wanted!

SCOTT

I'm just teasing. See you around 7:30. ;)

I smile to myself, seeing his wink emoji.

When Scott walks into the room an hour later, my dad is awake and alert. We are watching the end of *Wheel of Fortune*. He blinks twice when he sees Scott. I'm thinking that's his sign of approval.

"Hey, Billie." He leans down and kisses me on the cheek. He's still wearing the black scrubs.

Take me right here, right now!

"Hey, Mr. Carlisle," Scott greets my dad, who blinks twice in response.

"Dinner is down in the common area. Would you like to join me, my lady?" He bows and holds out his hand.

"Why of course, kind sir." I give him mine, curtsying as I stand. "Dad, I'm going to grab something to eat. I'll be back." He blinks twice again, and I see the smallest twitch of a smile. I squeeze his hand and smile back at him.

"Mmm. I love cheese pizza. No toppings. Just dough, sauce, and cheese. My favorite is when the cheese has those burnt bubbles on top. Those, and pizza boobs. Yumfest in my mouth!" My stomach growls from the aroma as we fill our plates.

"What are pizza boobs?"

"Pizza boobs are the dough bubbles that don't have any cheese. I've always called them pizza boobs." I shrug.

"Interesting, your boobs are my favorite, especially when you're topping me," Scott replies in a raspy tone.

That was totally cheesy, all puns intended.

He's wasting no time getting down and dirty with me. I would fuck him in a linen closet right now if he asked me to.

"I think that can be arranged," I reply, chewing a bite of pizza. "I wasn't planning on leaving tonight, but if I have a reason to...." I keep my gaze on the slice of pizza. I pull off a long string of cheese and put it in my mouth, licking my fingers as I slide them out from my kiss-deprived lips. I meet his ogling expression.

"If you keep doing that, I'm going to whisk you into an open room," Scott replies, his eyes burning for me. I'm so turned on that I'm ready to say screw the pizza and actually go screw him.

Naturally, I do the cheese thing again because I enjoy a good tease. Scott closes his eyes and sucks in a deep breath, forcing a smile while he painfully groans through an exhale. He chews and swallows his bite of pizza, then takes several large gulps of his soda.

"You need to come back tonight, for sure. I won't deny it, Billie. Last night awakened something within me, something that I thought died a long time ago." Those words bring relief and make me feel at ease.

"You really mean that? I feel something for you I've never experienced before. This is crazy. We practically just met!" Saying it out loud like that kind of scares me. What we have going on is moving insanely fast, even though prior to last night everything seemed to be moving at a snail's pace.

"Whatever you're feeling, I'm feeling too," Scott confesses.

"I'm starving right now, so I'm feeling like I need to eat this pizza." I take a healthy bite.

"Yes, please refuel yourself. You're going to need all the energy you can get."

After dinner, I spend a little more time with Dad. Scott left right after we finished eating to unwind and settle Bruno. When my dad is ready for bed, I ask him if he cares if I leave for the night. He blinks once.

ME

I am on my way. You better be naked when I get there.

SCOTT

Ready and waiting.

I bid my dad a good night and practically sprint out of the automatic doors. I rush to Scott's house as quickly and safely as I can. When I arrive, the door is unlocked, so I walk right in.

"Scott?" I call out.

"In the bedroom," he hollers back.

I head down the hall and Bruno follows me. Scott is lounging in bed shirtless, wearing reading glasses, engrossed in a book. I drop my keys and phone on the floor and rip my clothes off. He wasn't kidding when he said he was ready. We consume each other again into the wee hours of the morning.

I open my eyes just in time to see the sun peek over the horizon. I'm still processing how I've gone from being a virgin with zero experience to this woman with intense sexual desire in a little over twenty-four hours. I feel empowered, revitalized.

I roll over to face Scott and kiss him on the cheek. He stirs, sliding me toward him. He doesn't open his eyes, but he smiles and murmurs, "Good morning, my beautiful wife." I'm taken aback by the response.

"Wife? Proposing already? The sex is that good, huh?" I giggle.

"Christine, I would marry you every day." My stomach drops and the color drains out of my face.

Red flag! Red fucking flag!

"Scott, I'm not Christine," I choke out in a panicked voice. His eyes pop open, and he shoots up into a sitting position. He looks genuinely confused.

"Billie, I am so…I don't even know what to say. I am so sorry. I was dreaming. I thought it was a dream. You believe me, don't you?" he implores.

"Yes, of course I believe you." I force a smile. "It was just a dream." He kisses me repeatedly on the shoulders, apologizing profusely.

What have I gotten myself into?

CHAPTER SEVENTEEN

SCOTT

I called her *Christine*, Miranda. *Christine,* for Pete's sake!"

"Who's Pete?" Miranda asks.

"It's an expression. *Fuck!*" I yell.

Miranda eyes me scornfully. "You better lower your voice and wash that filthy mouth of yours before the next patient arrives."

My body is in peak distress. I'm pacing back and forth the length of Miranda's desk because I'm so flustered. My mind is racing faster than I can speak. Billie acted fine this morning, but I know she cannot be all right with what happened.

I groan, "What am I gonna do, Miranda? What if she never wants to see me again?" If I ruined this thing with Billie before it even starts, I'm going to be devastated.

"The first thing you need to do is send her flowers. You need to break the ice because hell just froze over. Then you need to wait."

"Wait? How? What if she never responds?" I'm still pacing back and forth, and now I'm starting to sweat.

"I hope you brought your credit card because you aren't sending a dozen carnations, *Dr. Bennington*. She will respond.

Trust me. You just tell me what you want and where to send it, and I'll take care of it."

"No, no. That's kind of you, but I need to do this myself."

I call nine florists before I find one that has what I need and can deliver today.

"Eighteen dozen yellow roses? Are you sure?" the shop owner asks, bewildered.

"Yes. Eighteen dozen. I need them delivered ASAP to Room 218 at Bellevue Community Hospice Center. They're for Billie Carlisle. If you can get them there before 5 p.m., I'll tip an extra hundred dollars." I'm not messing around. I need to make this right.

"Deal."

"Don't forget the note," I remind the owner.

"We won't, sir. We appreciate your business."

The day crawls painfully. I listen to the ticking of the clock, waiting anxiously for my phone to ping. It's after five. Still nothing.

Screw this.

ME

Did you get my gift?

BILLIE

Yes

ME

Do you forgive me?

No response. I march out to reception.

"Look at this. That's it. That's all she said. You said she'd respond." I hold my phone to Miranda's face. Miranda lowers her chin so she can see over the top of her glasses.

"She did respond," Miranda gestures to the phone. "I didn't say it was going to be a *good* response. How would you feel if the situation were reversed?" Miranda presses her lips together contemptuously and gives me the side-eye.

"Angry. Enraged. Just as I am now. Except I'm not upset with her. I'm mad at myself." I cover my face with my hands and scrub up and down like I'm washing away the veil of shame I'm currently wearing.

"Give her some time. She'll come around," she assures me.

"What if this is over?" I lament. "I don't want to screw it up. I need to go over there tonight and explain to her how unintentional that was."

"Easy now. You don't want to scare her off. Just wait."

So, I wait.

CHAPTER EIGHTEEN

BILLIE

Eighteen dozen yellow roses arrive just as I finish my noon rosary. I have been vehemently praying for my sins because Scott and I have been doing unspeakable things to each other.

The Catholic guilt is brutal.

The delivery driver hands me a note after she places the last vase in the room. There's no space for any more flowers.

"I hope this brightens your day, ma'am," the driver says.

"Wait. Please let me tip you," I insist.

"Not necessary. We were generously compensated." She tips her hat and leaves.

Of course they were. Who the heck has eighteen dozen yellow roses in stock?

I wince when I open the note, bracing for impact. Part of me wonders if the name *Christine* will dazzle me from across the top of it.

I pry my eyes open one at a time and read:

Dearest Billie,

You mean so much to me already. I chose yellow roses because you have brought so much light back into my life. Please forgive me.

Scott

I'm a realist, but my emotions are getting the best of me. I know he didn't mean to call me *Christine*, but he needs to grovel a little bit.

I get the brilliant idea to surprise him, after making him sweat it out a bit, of course. I look up his number at work and dial. I assume it'll go to a receptionist, but I feel nervous that he's going to know it's me and answer. Once I get through a string of automated prompts, I hear a woman answer, "Dr. Bennington's office. How can I assist you?"

Phew. Not him.

"Um. Hi. My name is Billie Carlisle, and..."

The woman cuts me off, saying, "Billie. Oh, I know exactly who you are, and honey, you have this man in all sorts of a mess."

I groan into the phone. "What do I do? I'm hurt, but I'm falling for him so fast. I'm sorry. Please don't tell him that. I shouldn't be unloading onto you."

"Why not?" she laughs. "Scottie does it to me daily."

"Scottie, eh? Did you know sweet innocent little Scottie sent me eighteen dozen yellow roses today?" I say dramatically.

"Who do you think gave him the idea? But eighteen dozen? That sounds like a pretty expensive apology."

I don't know her name, so I awkwardly say, "Virtual high five, receptionist lady."

"It's Miranda, and you're welcome."

"Thank you, Miranda. So you think I should forgive him?" She knows him well. I'm sure she has sound advice to give.

"That's up to you, but this poor man has been through hell and back, and this profession isn't exactly sunshine and rainbows. Not on this floor of the hospital."

"You're right." I think for a moment. "Listen, do you trust me?"

"Absolutely not. I've never even met you, and I told Scottie he needs to get you over here so I can approve—or disapprove, for that matter. I can't have him getting his heart broken. He's had his head in the clouds since he met you. He's been smiling again. He's been...happy."

My heart flutters with excitement.

"Touché. Well...here's my plan. I want to surprise him by taking the roses and making a petal path to the bedroom. Then I want to shower his bed with petals, have him find me in bed waiting for him, and—"

"Say no more. Give me your number. I'll call you right back with his passcode."

I'm already at Scott's house when he texts me. I shouldn't be making him squirm for so long, but it serves him right. I'm deeply sympathetic to what Scott's going through, but I also have my feelings as a woman. Truthfully, I am jealous. I can tell Christine is someone I will never measure up to, and that sits in the forefront of my head every time I see Scott's face. Hearing him call me the wrong name made me feel insecure, and that's my issue. I need to remind myself to discuss that in therapy tomorrow.

The rose petals are placed exactly how I want them, and I've set several vases on the night stands. The comforter is decorated with petals, and I am covered in them under the sheets. Naked, of course. I went so far as to park my car around the block after I unloaded. I even locked the front door so that he wouldn't get suspicious.

I hear the door creak open. Scott mutters, "What the...?" I can hear Bruno's panting and nails clacking. I'm pretty sure Scott is tiptoeing because I can't hear him moving. As soon as he walks through the bedroom door, his expression softens from defensive to relieved.

"Billie, I am so so so so so so sorry," he repeats as he rushes toward the bedside.

I survey his regretful eyes. He caresses my cheek, and I nuzzle my face in his hand, kissing the softest part of his wrist. He pulls me toward him and kisses me so purely I can feel that I—*me, Billie*—am the one he wants to kiss, not her. It's crazy how a kiss can make all my fears subside.

He pulls back the covers to discover me naked and covered in petals. He flashes me a look of desperation and kisses me again, this time with yearning and relief. He then strips off his clothes and crawls into bed with me. Naked, we spoon for a while. I can tell Scott is feeling apprehensive about what comes next, so I guess I need to let my guard down. I don't like being vulnerable, but I will for him.

I break the silence when I figure out how I want to say what I want to say. "When you called me *your wife* and then *Christine*, it scared the shit out of me. I know it was an accident. But...." My voice trails off. I stare at the wall in front of me because I'm not sure I can face him without breaking down.

Scott droops his head onto my shoulder. "I know, and I am beyond sorry. I couldn't feel more terrible about it, really. I didn't mean to scare you."

"I was never angry with you, but I'm feeling jealous and insecure, knowing I will never be her. That she's the one you wish you could be with. Not me, if you had the choice. I don't know what's happening between us. Scott, I like what we have. I do. It terrifies me though. Other than my dad's illness, my life has been pretty static for longer than I want to admit. Feeling all these emotions so intensely is overwhelming. I suddenly feel like I don't even know who I am anymore." I shrug my shoulders and pull him closer to me.

"I'm scared too. I don't want you to feel jealous or upset, Billie. I don't want you to be like Christine or replace her. This is all brand new to me. I haven't been with anyone since her. And please do not feel insecure about yourself or compare yourself to her. I like you for being you. Billie, you are a beautiful person, inside and out...especially the inside." He chortles and cups his hand around my ass cheek, giving it an endearing squeeze. Then he kisses me gently on the shoulders and tickles my arm, grazing his hand up and down it lightly.

"We will figure this out. Let's just take things a day at a time. I can assure you, though, I'm not going anywhere." Scott's saying those words makes my heart leap... and my pussy wet. I work my hips so that my ass strokes his now semi-hard cock.

Pussy and cock? Your mouth is filthy, Billie!

I don't even care. I'm going with it. My body gets the hot, burning feeling of desperation.

"I need you in me right now." My breathy words barely escape me.

Scott whispers in my ear, "Get up on your knees and lie with your stomach on the bed. I want to try something."

I move into position without question. He kneels behind me, and I can feel him staring at my ass.

"You know, I thought I loved your boobs the most. Now that I get a full view of this ass, my heavens. I'm in love with it! It's the best one I've ever seen." Scott's voice is gruff. Heat flushes my face and I giggle nervously.

"What are you going to do next, now that you have my ass in your face?" I am curious but captivated. He laughs a mischievous chuckle, rolls down a condom and slides into me gently from behind. He reaches around me, placing his finger on my clit. My body stiffens in surprise.

This is...new. What in the hell is he doing?

He enraptures me with slow thrusts and a light massage. My legs involuntarily tremble. I'm on the brink of orgasm within seconds. His being inside of me this way causes a rush of new sensations, starting from my center and dispersing down my legs and up through my belly, into my chest and down my arms. He picks up speed and force, hitting what I think is my g-spot with his dick as he massages my clit more firmly. I'm not quite sure how it happens, but I detonate all over him. My body convulses and I'm heaving for air because—what the fuck was that?!

When I regain enough wits to speak, I blurt sheepishly, "Uhhh, yeah, sooo, I promise you I didn't pee all over your bed...." I'm confused because my other orgasms were nothing like this before. Granted, I've only had a few, but still.

"That," Scott announces, "is a whole new type of orgasm, and I fucking love it. Don't move." He moves out of me and grabs a towel. I stay as still as I can, considering my body and legs are still quivering. He places a towel underneath me and then rubs himself on me a few times before easing into me again. His breath hitches, which provokes me to grab and hold onto the bed sheets for dear life.

"There's no way I'm going to last long like this." Scott's breathing is heavy and deliberate. I can tell he's desperately trying not to come. I still have no idea what I'm doing sexually, but he clearly seems to be enjoying it.

"Now it's your turn not to move," I say seductively, as I begin to rock slowly. I take a tighter grip on the sheets. This sensation is downright indescribable.

"Baby, that is so hot. Please keep doing that. Your ass is phenomenal."

He called me *baby*, which prompts me to pick up speed because I feel another orgasm coming on already. Rose petals are flying in the air and off the bed like confetti. Scott moans loudly, and I can't help it anymore. I let out a scream. I'm slamming myself into him when he releases and promptly slumps on top of me. My orgasm is so intense I naturally push him out of me, and then even more liquid escapes. I see why he got that towel.

I topple over and close my eyes so I can regain composure from all the stars I see. Scott lies down facing me. We look at each other in disbelief.

"What just happened?" I croak and then laugh.

"That was mind-blowing," Scott sputters, trying to stabilize himself. "Holy mackerel."

"I can't believe I've been missing out on this all my life," I blurt without thinking.

Fuck. Shit. No.

"What do you mean all your life? When was the last time you had sex?" Scott asks skeptically.

I grimace and don't answer. Well, I guess the expression is the answer.

"Wait, don't tell me you were a *virgin*." Scott sounds alarmed.

"Okay, I won't," I squeak.

"Billie, are you serious? I took your *virginity*?" I nod with a guilt-ridden face. Scott props himself up on the bed. "You're lying. I don't believe it. Your mouth, kissing me...what you did with your hips!" he exclaims while swirling his hand around me.

"I'm not lying. You were my first kiss, too." I can feel my cheeks blushing with embarrassment.

"But we had sex the first night we kissed." Scott muddles.

I nod guiltily again.

He sinks back into the bed, stupefied, staring at the ceiling with his arms behind his head. "You mean to tell me that no man has ever loved you. Not one?"

That strikes a harsh chord within me, resentment building. Because what he just said—is true.

"No, Scott. Not a single one. It's not like I had suitors lined up outside my door. I was an awkward teen whose parents were going through a divorce. The only date I ever had was because someone bet a guy that he couldn't get me to kiss him. I went to college and kept to myself. No one showed interest in me. I got a job and focused on my work. Still, no one showed interest in me. My dad got sick, and I lost the very few friends I did have because all I've done is work and take care of him since. So, no, Scott. No man other than my father has ever cared about me in *any* capacity."

My lips start quivering. That's actually quite sad now that I've said it out loud. Scott stirs so much emotion within me I didn't know I had. Hot tears trickle down my cheeks.

Scott uses his hands to move the stray hairs from my face and catches one of my teardrops with his finger. His gaze burns into my eyes and he murmurs, "I care about you, Billie." He kisses me tenderly on the lips.

He continues to explore every part of my face, repeating *I care about you* each time he kisses me. He then moves down my neck, to my chest, to my stomach. I slide my hand into his curls and pull. Scott moans with yearning and desire, and I give into him once again.

CHAPTER NINETEEN

SCOTT

I feel like a teenager. My sex drive went from dormant to hyperdrive in a matter of days. Sex with Billie is out of this world. It's different. New. Passionate. Hot as hell. Just thinking about her gives me a semi. In many ways, I feel alive again, like the gray haze that's fogged my world for the last few years is gradually dissipating.

I pull Billie toward me in bed and wrap myself around her. I begin kissing her shoulders and neck. She gets goosebumps down her arm and snuggles in closer to me.

"Good morning, Billie," I whisper in her ear. Billie groans faintly, like she's trying to pull herself out of the night's slumber. I will never, ever mistake her for Christine again. I'm still reeling with guilt about it, because I truly was dreaming. I've never had another woman in my bed before. My subconscious had to have assumed the woman with me was none other than Christine.

God, I miss Christine. I miss her so much. She and I had our moments, as every couple does, but our relationship was damn near perfect. We grew up together, shared all our first moments

together. It would be unfair—and rather cruel—to have any
expectations that Billie would "replace" Christine and our
relationship would be similar to what I had with Christine. Both
are phenomenal women, so different from each other. And I love
that.

I also feel some type of way about Billie sharing all her first
intimate moments with me when I am not sharing all my firsts
with her. I can't believe she didn't tell me she was a virgin. Heck,
she'd never even been kissed before! I guess we never really had
an opportunity for conversation about it though. Things just
happened when she fell into my arms, and it felt like I was living
in a scene from a movie, almost surreal.

It's an odd feeling—missing Christine so much yet being
infatuated with Billie. This beautiful woman right in front of me,
gazing at me with such happiness in her eyes, makes me feel
differently than the way I felt with Christine. I can't explain it. It's
good though. So, so good.

I caress her hair and give her a tender kiss on the head. "I'm
going to brush my teeth and make some coffee." Billie yawns an
"okay" as I drag myself out of bed. I hear the shower start as I
feed Bruno and get the coffee brewing. I step outside to grab the
newspaper, breathing in the crisp morning air.

Yes, I still get the newspaper and read it daily.

Since today is a late day at work, I scan the first few pages
and indulge in my cup of hot coffee.

"Good morning," Billie smiles as she walks into the kitchen.
Her long, wavy brown hair is wet and combed out. She has on a
pair of red joggers with a worn blue hoodie that reads "Robert
Morris University" across the front in red-and-white lettering.

"Did you go to Bobby Mo?" I inquire, breathing in the sight for
sore eyes.

"I did, actually. This hoodie is eighteen years old. My dad
bought it for me the day he moved me to the Robert Morris

campus. He got a matching one as well. Hard to believe that was half my lifetime ago."

"You look good in red," I wink, tilting my head to peek at her ass. "Have a seat." I gesture to the booth. "Your coffee awaits. Would you like something to eat?"

"Oh, no. I'm going to run home after I leave here to check on the house and switch out the contents of the duffel bag I've been living out of since Dad arrived at Bellevue. Thanks, though. I will take the coffee to go, if you don't mind."

"Sure thing. I'll get it ready for you now." I stand up and grab a coffee mug.

"Wait! I have your travel mug in my bag. Hang on." She returns with the mug in hand and her duffel bag hanging from her shoulders. I feel the spark of attraction between us as soon as my hand touches hers when I take the mug from her.

"I don't think you're getting this back," she laughs.

"That's okay. I'll just have to find *another* favorite travel mug...I guess." I huff sarcastically.

"I'm sorry. I didn't realize it was your favorite," she replies playfully. "I'll get it back to you when you visit today, if you're still coming."

"Billie, I'm just kidding. I have plenty of other mugs, and this one isn't particularly my favorite. And of course I'll be there." I hand the freshly filled mug back to her.

"Thank you." She reaches out to grab the mug, but I set it on the counter and pull her in to kiss me. That tingly magic is growing more intense by the day. I wish I could crawl right back into bed with her. When she pulls away, I lace both my hands in hers.

"So, do you think you can get away later?" I look at her nervously because I'm feeling anxious about asking her my next question.

"I should be. I mean, as long as my dad is stable I can come over again if you want." She gives me a mischievous smile and a peck on the lips.

"Actually, I wanted to see if you could stop by my office. See where I work. Meet Miranda, my secretary. She insists I invite you to meet her. I'm sure she'll ask you twenty questions, but she's harmless...mostly."

"Is that so, huh? Well, after talking with her yesterday, she seems pretty harmless. But I can tell she cares about you." Billie looks away, embarrassed.

"You talked to Miranda?" I ask, surprised. I'm not sure why she would call the office and not talk to me.

"How else do you think I got in your house? I needed the passcode, so I called her and gave her a sob story—a truthful one —and she got it for me."

The lightbulb illuminates in my head. "So *that's* why she needed to know! I thought it was odd that she'd ask, but I wouldn't dare question her. She's great, but she also scares me a little," I chuckle.

"Ha, maybe I should take a rain check for the rest of my life then," Billie scoffs, taking a swig of her coffee. "You know, this coffee tastes much better when it's not burning my chest."

We bust a hearty laugh. We meet each other's gaze, and the mood turns serious.

"Are you sure you want to do this?" Billie gives me a wavering smile.

"Sure about what? Meeting Miranda?" I take my hand and tuck a damp strand of hair behind her ear. I lean in and give her a soft but passionate kiss. "Yes, I'm sure."

CHAPTER TWENTY

BILLIE

As soon as I arrive at Bellevue, I track down Claire and pull her into an empty room, shutting the door and frantically closing the blinds. Claire appears concerned yet pissed at the same time.

"What happened? Do we need to ride at dawn?" she queries in a loud whisper.

I pace the room, trying to gather my thoughts. I've never talked to anyone about sex before, and I'm not sure I know Claire well enough to trust her with something so personal. But I know I need to talk to *someone* about what happened between Scott and me because I'm a little freaked out myself.

"Okay, listen. I need to tell you something, but you have to promise not to breathe a word of it to anyone." My tone is serious, even though I'm mildly hyperventilating and shaking my wrists, attempting to stimulate some feeling back into them.

"Just tell me already! Who am I going to spill to? Dorothy in Room 210?" Claire playfully smacks my arm, and I roll my eyes.

"So Scott and I—" I no sooner begin speaking than Claire interrupts me.

"Oh...my...God...you two fucked, didn't you?" She gives me a shocked but expectant look.

"Well, yes, like a few days ago, but that's not the problem...I mean I'm not sure there is a problem," I continue.

"Does he have a micropenis? No, that can't be it. I've seen him packing pretty stealthily in his jeans before. Does he suck in bed? He looks like he'd be a phenomenal lover." Claire starts fanning her face, imitating that she's overheated and attempting to cool herself down.

"Just...shut up and let me talk!" I shout, then cower and lower my voice. Claire mimes zipping her lips.

"So, I need to know about orgasms. Have you ever, like, soaked the bed?" I chew my thumbnail, hoping that I don't regret what I just said.

Claire smacks my arm again. "Shut. The. Fuck. Up. You're a gusher?" She places her hand over her gaping mouth.

"What the fuck is a gusher?" I've never heard that term before, but I am also a former prude.

"I'm so jealous right now. I've never been able to achieve that type of orgasm. How did you do it?" Claire places the balls of her hands under her chin and bats her eyelashes at me.

I'm not sure how to answer that question, so I shrug my shoulders. "Honestly, I don't know. Scott just...well, his hands... and then he, like...well, you know...."

"No, I don't know. That's why I need all the details." Claire is still fully attentive, so I let it all out and detail-dump on her. I tell her about my first kiss and how that kiss turned into losing my virginity, which turned into Scott calling me the wrong name, and the flowers, then the hot, steamy make-up sex that has resulted in my questioning my ability to have amazing sex with someone. When I finish word-vomiting, I exhale audibly, waiting for Claire to respond. Surely, she has some kind of wisdom and is more experienced than me.

"Wow, this might be a first," she says slowly. "But I think I'm speechless. Like, genuinely, utterly speechless." The room remains quiet until I can't take the silence any longer.

"So this would be the time where you give me sisterly advice and tell me I didn't pee everywhere." I sit down beside Claire on the couch, which is identical to the one in my father's room, chewing my thumbnail again and jiggling my foot up and down.

"I think...you've hit the jackpot," Claire declares. "I mean you've hit the pinnacle of pleasure. I think the fluid comes from the Skene's gland. Could there be piss in with it? I mean, I suppose so. Did Scott like it or was he freaked out?"

"Oh, he *loved* it! He looked like a kid on Christmas morning."

Claire closes her eyes and smiles, shaking her head slowly. "Then what's the problem?"

"What? Stop," I whine, smiling and giggling. "I guess I never had anyone to talk to about this before, and I really was afraid I had pissed all over him." We both break into girlish laughter. "Can you walk me through the whole sex thing? I mean, I know the basics. Beyond that, I'm clueless. I've pretty much moved back and forth, and then I come and he comes. Is that really all there is to it?" I look at Claire skeptically.

"Honey, you could lie there motionless and a guy would come." Claire rolls her eyes. "Trust me, that's pretty much all you have to do. Sure, there are lots of positions, and oral, of course, but the basic premise is a hard cock in and out of a vag and presto, he comes."

"Ha, that seems too easy," I say, furrowing my brows. Claire nods emphatically.

"It really is, for men. For women—except for *cum queen* over here—" Claire hitches her thumb toward me. I blush. "It tends to be more challenging."

"To your point," I argue, "I am a thirty-six-year-old woman experiencing sex for the first time with the hottest guy I've ever laid eyes on in my life. I can imagine my insides have been so deprived that any type of stimulation sends me over the edge."

"What about your own two hands or toys? Surely you've been able to get yourself off that way." Claire sinks back into the couch and crosses her arms and legs, so I follow suit.

"About that...I've never done any of that either," I squeak out sheepishly. Claire shoots up into a sitting position and cups her face in her hands.

"Good grief, Bills! You're the prudiest of the prudes!" she shouts.

"Shhh," I say, swatting the air down with my hands to calm her. "I know. That's why I need you to be like...my informant." Claire's devious smile tells me I may have made a mistake.

"Your sexual advisor," Claire says seductively. "Next week, we'll talk oral. Same time, same place?"

"Same time, same place." We exchange smiles of appreciation. Claire glances at her watch.

"Well, I have to get back. Dorothy needs her meds in five." We stand up from the super-comfortable couch, and she hugs me tightly.

"I'm really glad we're friends," she whispers in my ear. I squeeze her back, letting myself feel the affection safely from another woman.

"Me too, Claire. Me too."

CHAPTER TWENTY-ONE

BILLIE

I'm navigating my way through the hospital, trying to find Scott's office. Twists, turns, corridors, elevators. It's like a maze. When I finally reach the floor I'm supposed to be on, I text him to let him know I'm close by.

My heart pounds involuntarily from nervousness. I'm not sure why I'm anxious. It's not like I'm meeting his parents. From our conversation the other day, Miranda does sound a little terrifying. Before I left Bellevue, I put on some makeup and straightened my hair, finishing the look with dark jeans and an olive sweater. I want to look presentable but not like I am trying too hard. When I reach the entrance, I walk through the double glass doors that welcome me to the reception and waiting area. Scott is waiting for me at Miranda's desk.

Damn it, those scrubs. He's wearing all-black fitted ones that just instantly make me want to jump him. I smile with relief when I see him beaming at me with an open embrace. After a brief, friendly greeting, we stand side by side so she can give us the once-over. She is standing behind her desk, wearing a pastel-blue top decorated with large purple hydrangeas that bring out the depth in her dark-brown eyes. Her curls are voluminous, perfectly defined, and her rose-taupe lipstick ties the look together.

"Hi," I blurt, holding out my hand to greet her.

"Hello, Billie. I've heard so much about you." Her handshake is firm, but her voice is warm and welcoming.

"Same." I grin. Scott lightly squeezes my shoulders and places a quick peck on my cheek.

"See, Miranda, I told you she was great," Scott announces. Miranda rolls her eyes toward him with a tight, closed-mouth smile.

"Why don't we have a seat on the couch so we can get to know each other better," Miranda suggests, stepping out from behind her desk and ushering us to the black leather couch against the far wall in Scott's office. The three of us get comfortable. I'm trying desperately not to fidget, but I can't help it. God only knows what's about to come out of her mouth.

The conversation doesn't go as badly as I thought it would. Contrary to her sassy, yet frightening, demeanor, Miranda is a very lovely woman. We talk about my growing up and about my dad. She flat-out asks me my intentions with Scott, which makes me tremble slightly. I've never been asked such a thing before. All I can say is that they are "pure." I don't even know what I mean by that, but she accepts it and doesn't press further.

We talk about my dreams and aspirations (*not sure*), if I want to get married (*yes*), if I want to have kids (*yes*). She asks me if I hope that man is Scott. I hesitate because I'm still getting to know him. But he looks at me so tenderly and genuinely that I reply with an honest "definite possibility."

I learn she has three grown boys and five grandchildren. She will be marking forty years of marriage next July, and they're planning a Caribbean cruise in the summer with the entire family. She also jokes about retiring next year. I see beads of sweat form around Scott's temples. She then tells me about how long she's worked for Scott and how she's basically a second mother to him, like her fourth son. The mutual love and admiration they have for each other is special. Though they work professionally, I know their relationship is familial.

It's very sweet to see those two. It's also a sharp, painful realization that I don't have that anymore, not in the sense of a reciprocal relationship, since my dad can't really do anything physically but make it through another day. Until recently, I thought I was fine emotionally, but it turns out I've buried my emotions. The longing for love and desire for a relationship is consuming me. No one can or will ever replace my dad or the relationship we have, but maybe it's God's way of showing me that I won't be alone once my dad does pass. And I don't want to get too far ahead of myself. This thing with Scott may not last. But I don't want to look at the "what-ifs" right now. I just want to enjoy what is happening, which is helping me get through every gut-wrenching day at Bellevue.

Watching my father die renders me helpless. I think about whether I should even be doing anything other than sitting by his side, but I know my dad would not want that, especially since he's in and out of consciousness. If the situation were reversed, I wouldn't want someone sitting next to me twenty-four-seven, watching me, waiting for me to take my last breath.

At the same time, I feel guilty. I feel such guilt having fun and spending time with Scott and Claire. I'm not sure why. Maybe it's because I've spent the last several years of my life dedicated to my dad. Perhaps it's because I know time is ticking on his life, and I feel like I'm abandoning him.

But he and I have had these conversations. At least he blinks at me, which indicates it's fine that I leave. He does sleep more often than not, and there's nothing I can do while he's sleeping. I just feel like it's selfish of me to be pursuing anything for myself right now.

I could try to balance this seesaw, but the fact is, my father's dying sucks, and I don't know how to deal with it. Who knows if I'll have regrets later in life? But right now I'm full of emotions. Claire and Scott make each day bearable.

CHAPTER TWENTY-TWO

BILLIE

The next few days feel pretty routine. I arrive at Bellevue by 9 a.m., visit through my noon rosary, and then Rick or another co-worker, friend, or family member comes to visit in the afternoon. I head back after dinner and stay until my dad falls asleep. Then I go straight to Scott's place. I've been sleeping really well in his bed. I wonder what the thread count on those sheets are. Plus, the fluffy comforter and down pillows are simply fabulous.

Sleeping at the hospice center anymore is impossible and makes me feel incredibly anxious. I'm afraid that if I don't stay, though, I could miss him passing away, and I don't want him to be alone when he goes. The nurses assure me every night before I leave that, if his status changes, they will let me know.

Thanksgiving is only three days away. The dread of what is to come is building inside me. I would never, ever leave my father, but I am petrified of helplessly watching him die. I am trapped in a space of anticipatory grief that's enveloping my entire being. I'm not sure how to describe it, other than it's like in a movie when someone sacrifices themself to save the planet or a crew of people. One of the main characters shuts another main character into a "safe place." The explosion happens, the main character dies, but the other character is saved. It's like I'm the person who is saved. I'm the one who's watching from behind a bolted door, waiting for my dad to succumb to the illness.

I just finished therapy, which I've bumped up to twice a week, and arrived for the evening shift at Bellevue. When I enter the corridor toward my dad's room, I hear crying. I sprint in a panic the rest of the way. Just as I'm about to bust through the door to Room 218, I see Rick crying over my father and kissing his face. The monitors and ventilator are showing he's alive and stable, so I'm confused as to what's going on.

Why is Rick kissing my father?

I mean, sure, they've been best friends all their lives, but I've never seen Rick and my father kiss on the lips or reveal any indications of a relationship.

Rick straightens himself up, sniffling. "Rick?" I query, barely audible.

"Billie. Hi. He's fine. I'm just—"

"No, it's ok. I'll come back," I reply, bemused, as Rick wipes his sullen eyes with the sleeve of his plum crewneck sweatshirt.

"Please, no. Come in." Rick clears his throat. "I was just about to leave."

I walk in and set my phone, backpack, and travel mug full of chamomile green tea on the coffee table among the vases of remaining yellow roses.

"Billie, do you have a minute to talk?" He asks, his tone filled with apprehension.

"Sure." I gesture him toward the plush brown couch.

Now I've at least figured out that Rick and my dad have some sort of relationship. I'm a bit upset with myself that I never saw it before now. But neither of them has ever mentioned anything. I had no inkling my father could be gay until a minute ago.

Rick nervously entwines his hands like he's lotioning them, contemplating what he wants to say. He then brushes his hands back and forth on his dark-wash blue jeans.

"You and my dad are together, aren't you?" I start.

"Yes, Billie. We've been together for a very long time," Rick admits, hanging his head through a heavy sigh. I lean in and give him a hug. I've never had anyone come out to me before, so I don't really know what to do or what to say, but I figure a hug is a universal sign of acceptance.

"It's okay," I whisper in our embrace. "You don't have to hide anymore. I accept you both." I'm feeling some sort of way right now about not knowing, but I'm not sure I know how to label the emotion.

Rick releases me and looks at me squarely. "Are you sure?"

"If anything, I love you both more for trusting me to know." I give Rick a reassuring smile. "I guess I can't believe I didn't pick up on it before. I'm sorry."

"Please don't be sorry. I'm sorry we didn't tell you. Your dad and I agreed to keep our relationship quiet. I know how religious your dad is. If the church knew, he may have been ostracized or mistreated. He spent years trying to figure out why he is the way he is. He tried fighting it. Hell, I tried fighting it. He married your mother and had you. I focused on my work and building Steele's into a respectable company, not just a corporate machine. I wasn't sure if my employees would be accepting of me. Being gay and out of the closet, particularly in the '80s, was a scary time once HIV started to spread. I didn't want to lose the company."

I put my hand on his and squeeze gently. "Rick, it's ok. You don't have to explain anything to me." My tone is genuine and sympathetic.

"I know, kiddo," Rick says resignedly. "We wanted to tell you eventually, but once his disease started progressing, we didn't want to put any more stress on you."

"I understand." Now that the initial shock has worn off, I'm enthralled. I want to know everything. This is a whole different side of my father I never knew. And it breaks my damn heart that he's been closeted his entire life because of faith and fear of society. People deserve to love who they want to love. Period. And for that, maybe I would be ostracized from the church too.

Jesus spent much of his time with the marginalized. He flipped the tables of the religious elite.

Not to mention the despicable amount of child molestation incidents that were brushed under the rug by highly revered and respected bishops and cardinals. I vividly remember when the monumental scandal broke five years ago. One of the cardinals in the diocese admitted to keeping molestation incidents tight-lipped and reassigning priests instead of reporting them to law enforcement. I deeply respected this man my entire life. He was so beloved that a prestigious elementary school in the area was named after him, which, of course, was quickly changed as soon as he admitted what he did. Imagine that: a Catholic school filled with small children was named after an accomplice to sexual abuse of small children! Then the man suddenly "retires."

Insert eye-roll.

He fooled us all, yet he's not in jail. Hasn't been charged or persecuted either. What a disgrace!

And then the church wonders why people are fleeing in a mass exodus. The scandal was precisely when my view of religion changed drastically. My faith was shaken, and my trust in humanity was shattered. I will never leave my Catholic faith. I know that. It's the people, not the faith, that are the problem. It's also the unattainable religious expectations that make people feel ashamed and afraid of going to hell. The way in which I practice my faith now no longer falls in line with the strict manmade rules that don't seem to take into account basic human decency.

To think we get one chance on Earth that makes or breaks eternity for us. Ultimately, that seems cruel. Not everyone is granted a long chance at life to develop themselves or their souls, so how would their eternity be fairly judged? I guess that's a question to ask at the pearly gates. I believe God is all-loving, so my inner conflict is a constant battle.

The double standard boggles my mind. Why is it that members of the clergy can molest children, particularly little boys, and it's so quick to be covered up and kept quiet? Yet my dad engaging in a loving, long-term homosexual relationship is so wrong that he would be sentenced to eternal damnation because the Bible says so.

Hypocrites, much?

Here's the thing: some versions have the word *homosexual* in them and others don't. It makes me wonder what else has been altered in translation in order to frighten people into behaving in a particular way to keep order and control of a culture.

Being with Scott has made me realize I've been stuffed in an emotional closet all my life. I feared that my feelings and actions were so sinful I would be cast into hell on Judgment Day.

Are we actually judged at pearly gates when we die? Maybe we judge ourselves. Does anyone *really* know what happens? No.

I digress.

"How long have you been together?" I probe.

"We snuck around as teenagers," Rick continues. "When we both graduated college, your dad got a job with Steele's, and I knew I would be taking over for my father, so we ended things. After Teddy and your mom got divorced, we rekindled our relationship. We've been together ever since, nearly twenty years." Rick becomes lost in a reverie.

The more details he gives, the more everything starts to make sense and the more irritated I become that I missed the signs. The weekly dinners together that I thought they had just because they were best friends. The weekends I spent with my grandparents because my dad had a "work trip." The weeks in the summer I spent with my mom. The elaborate birthday and Christmas gifts for my dad and me from Rick.

Up until two weeks ago, though, I was a Puritan, one who had never so much as experienced a real kiss. No exposure to being in love, intimacy, desire, sex—any of it.

"I'm glad my father has had you. I'm so happy to have you as part of my life too. Please know that I appreciate your willingness to share something deeply personal. I need to be clear that I am fully supportive of your relationship with him and feel blessed to know that you two have found lifelong love together."

I hope Scott and I can have what they have one day.

I give Rick another hug. He whispers, "Thanks, kiddo" into my hair as he hugs me back.

Monitor alarms blare and, within seconds, two nurses rush in.

I fly to my father's bedside.

"What's happening?" I cry out in fear. My father is a DNR. If this is it, there's no stopping his passing.

"Teddy, it's Claire. It's okay. I'm just going to give you some medicine to relax you. You're all right." She preps a shot of some sort of medication, then slides it into his IV. The other nurse checks his pupils with a flashlight. A wave of terror and nausea crash into me.

I hope this isn't it. I'm not ready.

Not like this. Please, God, not like this.

The next hour is a blur. As of now, he's alive, slipping in and out of consciousness. I don't think he's going to make it until Thanksgiving.

I cannot let him continue to live like this. It's time to begin the final stage.

It's time for my father to die.

Since the incident, I have not left the hospice center. Not once. I will not let my father die alone. I'm surprised he held on this long. Claire removed the feeding tube once my father calmed down the other night, and the nurses are making him as comfortable as possible. My dad has been alert for only brief moments throughout the day today.

The end is close.

I am going to miss this man so much. I'm not sure what I will do without him in my life, how I will function. All the things he will miss. If I ever get married, he won't be there to walk me down the aisle. If I ever have children, he won't be there to dote over them. There's a stabbing pain in my stomach where the grief is festering.

On Thanksgiving morning, I feel a sense of peace that we've made it to today, to share one last holiday being thankful for what we have. Meanwhile, I'm feeling the exact opposite of thankful. Peaceful, yes. Thankful, no. I'm indignant, sullen. It always seems to be the good people who get cancer and disease, then die tragically. How unfair!

And while that snooty, pearl-clutching Betty Ann Barber believes people's suffering is to "pay for our sins and those of our ancestors," I tend to feel differently.

It's in suffering that we learn compassion, for without suffering there would be no compassion. Maybe I'm wrong, but that's how I justify the pain. Why else would children get cancer? They're the most innocent of us all. And I can assure anyone who asks that an illness, loss, or traumatic event is not punishment from God. I'm so tempted to make that hypocritical woman a Minny's homemade *chocolate* cream pie, if you know what I mean.

I spend the day praying, singing hymns, and stroking my dad's hand. I hug and kiss my dad so many times, because I need him to know I'm here and that I love him fiercely. I know soon that I will not be able to do this, so I'm soaking in the feeling of him, embracing him so that the memory lasts the rest of my life.

Late in the afternoon, I give Rick time to say goodbye before I say my final words. I'm an anxious mess, pacing the common areas, fighting back the tears. When I walk back into his room, I know it will be the last time I ever speak at length to my dad. I'm not sure he will be able to hear me, but I convince myself he can.

Scott brings Rick and me a plate of Thanksgiving dinner from his family's gathering. He offers to stay, but I wouldn't make good company right now. Plus, I'm feeling particularly vulnerable and I'm not sure I trust Scott that fully just yet.

I force-feed myself because I don't think I've eaten more than two meals in the last three days. The food is spectacular. I hope to meet his family some day. He's said such wonderful things about them. The idea of a large family scares the heck outta me, but I can see how happy sharing the holidays together would be. Besides Scott, I will have Rick, my mom, and Claire. I will have very few people surrounding me that I feel comfortable around.

Rick comes out to the common area to heat up his dinner, which is my cue. I drag myself to Room 218 to bid my final goodbye before we wait until my dad leaves this life. I take a seat next to his bed and scoot as close as I can get to him. Everything is quiet. I can tell he's not in pain and that he's ready to go. He looks to be at peace, physically and spiritually.

"Hey, Dad, it's Billie." I choke out. "I'm sorry that this is how your life turned out and that this is how we have to say goodbye. If it were up to me, I would spare you the suffering and lead a parade from here straight to Heaven." I envision my dad laughing at the suggestion, but he is unresponsive.

"I need you to know that I am so proud of you. I am honored to be your daughter. You were always there for me. You treated me with such love and respect. I will treasure all the memories we made, especially that time we went fishing when I was twelve, and I capsized the boat. And the time I nearly peed my pants during our road trip to Bethany Beach, so you handed me the emergency empty mayo jar and told me to have at it." I chuckle and sniffle.

"I will cherish all the holidays we spent together. The singing, the food, the love, the laughter. The memories you leave me with will carry me through the rest of my life. You are the best person I have ever met. I love you so much. And, as much as it pains me to say this, go to God. He's ready for you."

I hug him and kiss his cheek, clinging to what little time I have left with him.

CHAPTER TWENTY-THREE

BILLIE

I didn't sleep a wink last night. Rick asked if he could stay, and I would never deny him time with my father. I didn't tell Scott what was happening, just that I was going to stay here for the night again. I'm sure he has an idea though. All night I prayed for a peaceful passing for my dad, that God would welcome him into Heaven with open arms. My dad has a heart of gold. I don't care what anyone says. He is a saint on Earth. I'm sure there were many closeted saints before him too. I pray that his soul is healed and that he can enjoy his eternal reward in paradise, free of pain and restriction.

I pray for him.

I pray for him.

I weep in my prayers for him.

It's the wee hours of Friday morning, and it's clear that my dad will be passing anytime. I call Father Pete, and he buzzes over to give my dad last rites. My dad cannot receive Communion, so he is anointed instead. Father Pete, Rick, and I pray over him a series of traditional prayers. After Father Pete leaves, I ask the nurses if we could face the bed toward the window to watch the sunrise together. I would have loved to go out to the gazebo with him, but it's too cold. I don't want to make his passing any more painful for him.

I've had a playlist on my phone for a while with all my dad's favorite religious songs, some of which include "How Great Thou Art," "Amazing Grace," "Let There Be Peace on Earth," "You Won't Relent," and our personal favorite, "Oceans (Where Feet May Fail)." This man will die with his faith and love for the Lord stronger than many other religious people I know. He's my dad—the only man who's ever loved me.

I am crushed to say goodbye, but I've had a peace about me since last night, so I know it's time. I'm finally ready to let go. He's finally ready to let go.

The nurses get everything set up for us. We turn off the monitors and remove the ventilator. I then begin playing the music. My dad is unresponsive, possibly unaware of what's happening, but I can't be sure. I crawl into his bed like a five-year-old child and hold him. He is so gaunt, so frail. Rick sits in a chair beside us, holding my dad's hand.

We wait, not anticipating, not wishing for it to be over, just waiting.

Other than the music, it's silent.

Peaceful.

My dad is surrounded by only love, and he deserves this after all he's been through.

Tears sneak down my face, a steady stream that continues to flow. The sun begins to rise, its rays warming our skin through the window.

In a soft whisper, I feel my dad's soul leave his body. I let out a cry of anguish and cling to his body tightly. Rick cries with me.

Now, my father can rest and rejoice in his eternal reward, one that should be as brilliant as the man he was because he is so deserving of it all.

CHAPTER TWENTY-FOUR

BILLIE

Within a few hours, the funeral home has collected and transported my father's body. Room 218 is now bare, cold—empty. I'm probably in a little bit of shock. I have to tell my brain to tell my body to move. My heavy eyes are bloodshot and puffy, and my emotions are numb. I'm gathering up the last of our belongings when I hear a soft knock on the door.

"Belinda?" The familiar voice sends a chill down my spine. No one other than my mother calls me Belinda. I brace myself as I peer toward the door.

"Mom? What are you doing here?" I'm surprised and maybe a little confused. I turn away to continue putting my toiletries in my duffel bag.

"Rick called the other day and said things were happening soon, so I hopped on the first flight I could. I'm sorry I wasn't here." Hearing her apologize angers me instead of soothes me. *I'm sorry I wasn't here* is the one thing she needs to repeat about everything she missed in my childhood when she up and left. Her apology comes off disingenuous, but I'm not really in the mood to argue.

"I see. How long are you staying?" I don't look at her and continue packing. My mother walks into the room and sits down on the couch. She smoothes her pants and leans toward me with her elbows on her knees.

"Well, that depends on how long you want me here." I stop packing and glance over to her, her eyes filled with some kind of emotion that I can't place. Her brows are furrowed. She looks hopeful and maybe a little sorrowful. I'm trying to craft an answer that isn't filled with rage because I've wanted her here for the last twenty years. Now that she's sitting here, offering to be here for me, I don't even want it. At the same time, I want to sob in her arms.

I take an unnoticeable deep breath and utter, "However long you'd like to stay." I pack the last of the toiletries and zip up the duffel bag. My mother gently places her hand on mine. Her touch alone nearly sends me into an emotional tailspin, but I'm burying it all within me because I can no longer be vulnerable with her. My guard is high and reinforced. It has to be. I pat her hand with mine, forcing a small smile before I heave the bag off the coffee table and head out to load my car. Just as I'm ready to leave, my phone pings.

Scott

How are you holding up? I'm thinking about you…

Shit. I didn't tell him my dad passed yet. It's been such a whirlwind of a morning. I call him because I cannot text him about a death. That's just weird and impersonal. He answers on the first ring. "Hey, beautiful. How are you?" he says tenderly.

My body still cannot register emotions properly. My brain is not functioning clearly, so I don't waste any time in saying, "He passed a little while ago." The phone is silent for a minute. I hear him subtly clear his throat before offering a response.

"Billie, I am so sorry. What can I do? I'll take the day off and do whatever you need me to do. I'm here for you."

"I'm not sure how to answer that," I say, and I mean that wholeheartedly. I want him to be here with me, but I don't know what he can do. "You don't have to take the day for me, Scott."

"It's already done. I texted Miranda. She'll take care of it. Are you going to be at the center for a while?"

"I'm actually packed up and about to go home. Want to meet me there?" It's probably not a bad idea to have someone else around because I'm fully expecting my mom to tell me she's staying at the house.

"I'll meet you there. I'll be waiting for you," he assures, and I feel a sense of warmth knowing someone will be there for me when I get home.

He was right. As soon as I pull into the driveway, I see Scott sitting on the porch swing. My mom isn't far behind. This isn't how I had imagined Scott meeting my mother, but now is as good of a time as any. He pulls me in for a hug as soon as I shut the car door, his chest scented in musk and male pheromones. My entire body gives out, granting permission for the weeping that follows. Scott affectionately caresses my back and kisses the side of my head. He's absorbing all the pain as I'm releasing it. Soon I hear two voices making conversation, one my mother and the other who must be her newest boyfriend because that man is not Chuck. By now, I've been able to slow my sob to a whimper, and Scott hands me a tissue.

"Your shirt is soaked," I notice as we separate from our embrace.

"I'm not even worried about it, Billie. It's really cold out here. Let's get you inside."

I don't do any formal introductions. Scott handles everything perfectly. He introduces himself when Mom and Pierre, I learn, get out of their rental car and offers to help carry in their bags. I head straight for the kitchen to put on a pot of coffee. Everyone gathers around the small island.

"Are you staying here?" I ask forwardly. I know maybe I should feel a little more excited or welcoming, but I can't do anything else other than what I'm doing in this moment.

"It's up to you, sweetie. We can, or we can get a hotel." It's probably not a bad idea to have company here the next few days, just to keep me sane. I'm not sure where Scott falls in all of this, but I can't expect him to drop everything for me.

"You can stay here. I don't mind. Dad's room is off limits. There's a queen-size bed in the guest room you two can share." The idea of my mom being back in this house with another man, in my father's bed, no less, makes my stomach churn. The last thing I need is for my mother to be boning her boyfriend in the same bed she shared with my dad. I shudder at the thought.

"That'll be just fine, honey," my mother says as she reaches for several coffee cups.

Honey. Sweetie. All of a sudden she's acting like she gives a shit. Maybe she does, in some way, I don't know. But I'm not feeding into it or letting my guard down around her.

For the next hour or so, we drink our coffees and talk about the details of the viewing and the funeral. I solidified everything weeks ago, so now we wait for the funeral home to let us know his body is ready for viewing. Because my dad was well-known at work and in the community, we will need two days of viewings, with four showings. I really don't want to have that many, but it is necessary because there's no way we will be able to have everyone see him in the time allotted. Most likely, the funeral Mass will be Wednesday morning, with the viewings Monday and

Tuesday. I'm hoping over the next several days I can rest and mentally prepare myself for what's to come. I know I am going to be a wreck and, once everything is settled, then what?

Do I go back to work right away? Do I take some time to relax and travel? Do I move away and never come back? Start fresh? The possibilities are endless, and it's incredibly overwhelming. But today—today is about finding some peace.

CHAPTER TWENTY-FIVE

BILLIE

Would you like me to stay with you tonight?" Scott's words are everything I need to hear right now. Scott wraps his arms around me from behind and kisses my neck. I lean into him and let him envelop me.

"I would like that, yes. And bring my Bruno boy. He obviously can't stay there the rest of the day and all night by himself." There's something really special about Bruno. He brought comfort to my dad and continues to bring it to me. Dogs are special creatures. I believe they really do help people heal, both physically and mentally.

"Okay. I'll run home real quick and be back in a bit. Is there anything I can get you? Are you hungry?" Scott is still holding me, and we've started swaying slowly. It's very soothing.

"No, I'm good. I've already had six messages from people saying they're bringing food over, so bring your appetite back with you." I kiss Scott's arm and nuzzle my head against his neck. He gives me a squeeze and a kiss before departing. Mom and Pierre are upstairs settling in, so I sit at the kitchen island, refill my coffee for the third time, and stew in my thoughts until I'm met with surrendering exhaustion.

I feel robotic all weekend. I wake up, make coffee, stare at the yard, and wait for the doorbell to ring because people are dropping food off on the hour, more or less. I stay in leggings, a sweatshirt, and a messy bun. I know most people don't expect me to be guest-ready, but I force a smile on my face, graciously accepting the food and thanking them for their kind words. The cards get thrown in a pile on the counter. I don't have the bearings to read them right now. Emotionally, I'm barely holding it together. I still have the viewings and the funeral to get through.

All the food goes in the fridge and freezer because I have zero appetite. The only thing fueling me right now is adrenaline, coffee, and menthols. My mother thinks smoking is a disgusting habit, but I tell her that leaving me when I was a teenager to bang an undisclosed number of men was too, and she shuts up after that. Pierre hasn't said much, as his English is quite broken and heavily accented. I learn that he lives in France, and my mother has been living with him—in FRANCE!!! Didn't know that.

I watch my mom and him talk into her phone, which translates back and forth. Knowing what I know now makes me realize how wrong my parents were for each other, but I am glad they were together long enough to make me.

Later I overhear my mother make the obligatory phone calls to family about my dad's passing and the details of the arrangements. Not like many of them will come, since most are scattered across the country. But whatever. I have been sitting on the couch watching trash TV and cuddling Bruno. This is exactly what I need right now. Scott's been great—practically waiting on me hand and foot. Not that I can't or won't do things for myself, but he wants to do it. Honestly, I think it's helping immensely to have someone care for me for once.

Last night, Mom suggested I come to Europe with her for a while to "rebuild our relationship." If I could have rolled my eyes any harder, I would have. I mentioned it to Scott, and he thinks I should go. Although, I don't know if I *want* to go. I'd love to travel through Europe, but I always thought I would do that on a honeymoon or middle-aged girls' trip. Definitely not with my mother and her European boyfriend. I told her I would think about it and let her know once things are settled. I really shouldn't be making big decisions right now. I can barely force myself to shower and brush my teeth. If Scott weren't around, I probably wouldn't.

I'm well aware that I'm depressed and actively mourning, but I also feel peace and relief—solace in acknowledging my dad is no longer suffering and a prisoner in his body and comfort knowing he will be watching over me. In a way, I've been grieving him for two years. Now that he's actually gone, everything seems so final. I fully understood he was never going to recover and the circumstances weren't going to change, but his passing reinforces the idea that I will never see him like I used to, talk to him like I used to, bond like we used to. I hope he knows just how much I love him and will long for him every single day for the rest of my life.

And maybe that's why I'm so alone and lonely. Grieving is such an intense and painful process, one that never ends, one that changes and moves in waves. I hate feeling this depth of pain, so to avoid the agony, I tend to remain disconnected from people, refusing to be vulnerable with the possibility of being emotionally shattered.

All my grandparents are gone. They passed before I was thirty. My mom left when I needed her most, and now my dad is gone. I have aunts, uncles, and cousins, but we're not particularly close. Again, because we live so far away from each other. The only cousin I keep in touch with is Abbey. We were born the same year and spent the first decade of our lives together. That is, until her dad got a hefty promotion at a fancy accounting firm and relocated to Dallas, Texas. I was heartbroken when she left. Back then, we didn't have wifi. I was in high school before my parents finally decided to get AOL dial-up. Abbey and I would chat on AIM. We naturally grew apart when we went to college because of our busy lives. She used to visit once a year until she started her master's degree program. We occasionally video chat now, but she's really the only one out of fourteen cousins that I regularly—and I mean that term loosely—keep in touch with. It would be nice to see her again though. Maybe I could add Dallas as a detour before or after my European excursion, if I decide to go.

The viewings begin at two this afternoon. I arrive an hour early at the funeral home to have some time alone before the condolences and tears begin. I dress in typical mourning garb—a black knit dress, black pantyhose, and black flats. There was no way I was putting on heels to be standing all day. My hair is slicked back and perfectly crafted into a severe ballerina bun. My ears are adorned with two simple gold studs. My necklace is a plain gold cross that hangs just below my collarbone. My makeup is minimal and waterproof, as I know I'll be shedding tears. I finish the look with a deep crimson matte lip stain. Hopefully, my hair and makeup will stay put for the day so I don't appear as haggard on the outside as I feel on the inside.

When I walk into the funeral home, I do not see anyone, so I meander to the small chapel located between the two viewing rooms. The setup reminds me of an old-school movie theater. The doors are labeled "Viewing Room 1" on the left, "Chapel" in the middle, and "Viewing Room 2" on the right. My dad is being laid out in the first viewing room. However, because we are anticipating such a large crowd, Viewing Room 2 is set up with chairs and light refreshments, all sponsored by, of course, Steele Manufacturing.

The chapel is simple but inviting. There are four oak pews on each side, with a small aisle dividing them. The front of the chapel contains an elevated white altar, with a crucifix hanging on the wall behind it. The altar contains an assortment of colorful flowers and tall votive candles. I bless myself with the holy water from the font, making the sign of the cross as I enter. I choose the front pew on the left side and kneel down. I close my eyes and wait for the prayers to come, but they don't.

Everything in my head is silent.

Peaceful, I suppose, but static.

I can't bring myself to start the rosary, so I wait. For what? I'm not sure. It isn't long before I feel a hand on my shoulder, which jolts me from my meditation because I didn't hear anyone walk in. I open my eyes and bless myself with the sign of the cross, looking up to see Father Pete.

"I'm sorry, Billie, I hope I didn't startle you," he says in a soft, tender voice.

"Not at all," I reply, sitting back onto the pew and scooting down for him to take a seat beside me. "I just didn't hear you come in. Please, sit with me." He indulges and we both stare at the altar. The chapel is a beautiful room. The wall against the altar is a glittery gold and the surrounding walls are ecru. There aren't any windows, but the ambience is light and airy. We sit in quietude for a while because I don't really have much to say.

Eventually Father Pete asks sympathetically, "Is there anything you need or that I can do for you?" I can feel him looking at me, but I can't bear to look at him because I'll lose my bearings. Instead, I look down at my fingers, which are picking at my cuticles. It's a nasty habit I gave up long ago. Every once in a while when I'm under a lot of stress, I'll pick until I'm raw and bleeding. The memory sends shivers up my spine. I steady my hands and place them on my thighs.

"I don't think so," I answer. "I appreciate your being here for me and especially my dad at the end." He nods in understanding. I see his eyes water in the corners, which sparks my waterworks. He leans in and hugs me, but I don't hug him back. Not because I'm uncomfortable, rather because I think at this moment I just need to be held. It's as if I'm that five-year-old little girl again, and I need a nurturing hug to regulate my big emotions.

I hear Father Pete sniffle after releasing his hug. "Your dad was a wonderful man, Billie. He never lost faith, no matter what life handed him. I admire him greatly. There's no doubt he's enjoying his eternal reward in Heaven." I stop and think for a moment, because my dad wasn't out of the closet. Would he still feel the same way if he knew? Isn't practicing a homosexual relationship punishable by eternal damnation? I guess I'm about to find out.

"Would you still admire him the same if you knew he was gay?" I suck in my breath and avoid releasing it until he answers. I don't know how he will respond to such a question. Father Pete looks at me quizzically.

"Are you *telling* me he was gay?" His tone isn't condescending or judgmental, but I can tell he's taken aback because of his loud exhale and widened, surprised eyes. "Was he having relation-ships with men?" In his eyes, I see instant regret that he asked that question. I think he's more curious than anything, but the

Catholic Church does not condone homosexual relationships, so knowing this information about my dad could easily change his views of him, and I want everyone to think of my dad in the highest regard. It's a shame people would feel differently knowing his sexuality, but that's "just life and society these days," am I right?

"Would that change the way you look at him? At me?" I keep my tone steady, but I'm bracing for the worst. Father Pete thinks for a few moments.

"Doesn't change my view at all, Billie. Heaven isn't filled with good people. It's composed of forgiven ones. Teddy was a virtuous man. His sexuality is only one part of him. Whether I or the Church agrees with his lifestyle or not, it's not anyone's business unless he were to make it so, and he did not. I'm a little surprised, simply because I never had thoughts that he could be, but it doesn't make me feel differently about him." He squeezes my hand. I let out a relieved sigh, but I'm still curious about more of his thoughts regarding homosexuality and the Church.

"Do you really think God would send my dad to Hell because he loved another man, given how devout he was to the Church?" I feel myself holding my breath again. He responds without missing a beat.

"I sincerely hope God wouldn't do that. But I'm not God. Even though I believe in Heaven and the afterlife, I really don't know what happens after we die. I think Heaven is a concept that humans can in no way explain or understand because it's beyond our ability as humans to comprehend its magnificence. When we die, everything will become clear. I do think that Jesus loves us more than his commandments. After all, he died for us because we as humans are made to break at least some of those rules throughout our lives." I nod my head in agreement when I hear the main door open and several people walk into the lobby.

"You're a very wise man, Father Pete. Well, I guess that's my cue to head over to the viewing room," I say resignedly. I'm not sure who's here, especially since there are still thirty minutes until the viewing actually begins. As Father Pete escorts me out of the chapel, he whispers, "I won't say anything about your dad." I respond with an appreciative smile.

In the foyer, I spot a cascade of auburn ringlets belonging to a woman who looks like my cousin—

"Abbey?!" I ask, flabbergasted. She rushes toward me for a hug. Her parents, my Uncle Bum (his name is John, but I will forever call him that) and my mom's sister, Aunt Marlene, walk briskly behind her.

After a long embrace between the four of us, I manage to ask, "What are you doing here? I mean, I know what you're doing here, but how did you get here so quickly? I didn't think you'd be able to come."

My Aunt Marlene gently rubs my back and says, "Your mom called after Teddy passed and we booked the first flight here. We would have come regardless, but she was the one who made it possible on such short notice."

Of course she would. She'll bend over backwards for her sister but can't fly in to see me once a year. Typical. But now isn't the time to let my rage consume me. I'm so glad they're here.

"How nice of her," I respond, hiding a tight jaw. We proceed to the viewing room. I immediately spot the dark cherry casket, decorated beautifully with a spread of various colored roses and other wildflowers. Dad's wearing a navy pinstriped suit with black velvet lapels, the one we picked out for this occasion at Brooks Brothers while he felt fairly well. We knew he would be very thin when he passed, so we had the suit custom-made for a much smaller frame. It still looks quite big on him, but buying a suit that fit his pre-diagnosis stature would have made my dad look silly now, and that was the last thing I wanted for him.

Come to think of it, that was our last fun shopping trip together. We destroyed an entire pizza at Santino's afterward and polished it off with some Ben & Jerry's and a movie, cozied on the couch. The undertone was solemn, but it really was a fun day.

He has a crisp, white button-down shirt underneath his jacket, which brightens up his face that has been masterfully done with makeup. I know my dad would be happy with how he looks. I know I am.

Flower arrangements, wind chimes, and plants surround him. It's heartwarming to see the outpouring of generosity from the community.

Oh, how my dad was loved by everyone!

"Billie, this looks beautiful," Abbey whispers, placing her arm around me. I lay my head on her shoulder and a tear drops onto her shirt.

"It really is. The funeral home has done a wonderful job," We stand there, taking in our surroundings, until we hear growing muffled voices in the lobby. "Well, I suppose I better get this show on the road," I say, shrugging my shoulders and cuing the funeral director that it's time to open the viewing doors for people to begin entering. I make my way to the foot of Dad's casket and wait for the first guests to extend their sympathies, hug me, cry with me, squeeze my hand, which is exactly what happens for the next several hours.

I reminisce about the times I went bowling late at night with my dad, when he was part of the club down the street. His teammates would give me quarters for the little arcade. The pinball machine was my favorite. Afterward, his buddy Mark would go out with us for pizza. Half the time I'd fall asleep in the booth.

I chat about the times we'd have a huge Independence Day bash at Abbey's house as a kid, with kegs that she and I would sneak sips out of when we were just seven years old. We'd go swimming half the afternoon, eat lots of delicious homemade food, and set off what I think were illegal fireworks. The house was so far out in the boonies that no one paid any mind to it. I really, really miss those days. Life was good. Everyone was happy, healthy. I felt so loved. It doesn't feel like it's been thirty years.

A steady stream of people from all over the community circulates for two and a half hours straight—and this is just the first wave. When I'm ready for a much-needed break, I signal to the funeral director that this viewing is finished and those still here will need to wait until the next time slot. There are probably still a good fifty people waiting, but I just can't do it anymore. I sneak out back to smoke a cigarette. Abbey follows me out. "Are those menthols?" she asks excitedly.

"Like they'd be anything else!" I scoff, handing her the pack. She pulls one out and lights up.

"These are so gross but so good. Reminds me of Tropic Heat," she grimaces as she blows out her first hit. Tropic Heat was the only worthwhile club in town. When she visited, Abbey and I would get glammed up and go there for a girls' night out. I frequented the club with several other girlfriends...when I actually had girlfriends. We had some great times there, followed by nasty hangovers. The club closed several years ago and is now an underwhelming discount furniture store.

"Oh, they're disgusting!" I laugh. "But they're helping me survive this entire ordeal." Abbey nods in agreement. "So, how's Dallas?" I ask casually. Abbey smirks and rubs her forehead with her free hand.

"It's...Dallas. I love Texas, but my heart just isn't in it. I miss it here." She looks at me sympathetically with her big brown eyes. Abbey and I resemble each other, so much so that we could be sisters. Her hair falls in ringlets, whereas mine is wavy, but our features and figures are similar. There's no denying we're related.

"You can always come back," I shrug.

"Actually...I *am* moving back," Abbey says, wincing but smiling.

"You are not! Are you serious?" I yell enthusiastically.

"Right after Christmas. I accepted a position as chief medical officer with Barney Health Network." I grab her free hand and jump up and down. The idea of having someone I love so close again overjoys me. We hold our cigarettes far away from our massive amounts of flammable hair, giddy with excitement. We finish the menthols, then hit the ladies' room to freshen up and rid ourselves of the smoke stench.

When we enter Viewing Room 2 for refreshments, I am taken aback.

My Aunt Noreen and Uncle Sal, my mother's other sister and her husband, are here, along with their kids. My dad's brother, Uncle Carl, with his girlfriend, Susan, and his kids are here too. Then there's my dad's sister, Katherine, and her husband, Stuart, and all their kids. I am so overcome with emotion I break down right there in the entryway. I am shocked yet grateful that everyone showed up for my dad—for me. Abbey ushers me to one of the long floral couches. Slowly, family approaches, sitting with me, hugging me, crying with me. I know I tell myself I don't need anyone. But I really do need my family right now.

More than ever.

CHAPTER TWENTY-SIX

SCOTT

This is the first funeral I've attended since Christine's. My stomach is in knots, and I can barely keep my wits about me. It's necessary that I get to the funeral home before the procession to the church. I examine my aging face and worn-out body, dressed in an all-black Hugo Boss suit, paired with a slim black tie. I take the time to finesse my curls and style my hair instead of running my hands through it and putting on a ball cap. I carefully groom my face to keep just a little bit of stubble. Before I leave, I spritz my favorite Tommy Hilfiger cologne, take a deep breath, and pray I can get through this day and be strong for Billie.

Memories flood me on the drive to the funeral home. The last time I saw Christine, as her casket was closing, it was like all the air had been sucked out of me. I haven't been able to breathe since. Except recently, with Billie. I feel hope rather than utter dismay.

When I arrive, the immediate family is already lined up to say their final goodbyes before the casket closes. The funeral director approaches me and asks if I would be the sixth pallbearer. I'm taken aback a little but honored at the gesture. This will be how I can be supportive today. I'll do whatever is needed of me. I can break down later at home privately if I need to.

Billie spots me and sighs heavily with relief. Her eyes and cute button nose are red from crying. She runs into my open arms, embracing me so tightly, so fervently. She begins sobbing, and my eyes start watering as well. I didn't know Teddy other than at the hospice center, but I can see the love Billie has for her father—the only man who's ever loved her. I hold Billie until she pulls away. She looks up at me with her golden-brown eyes and says hoarsely, "Thank you so much for being here. It means so much that you came."

"You're welcome," I respond. I can't say anything else because all my strength is focused on holding it together.

The family says their final goodbyes. Lastly, Billie approaches the casket. I walk up right behind her. For a moment, it's silent and peaceful. Then Billie lets go of my hand and throws a hug around her father, sobbing, weeping, wailing. She cries out in pain, "Daddy!"

I no longer see adult Billie. I see this small child wishing for her father to be here with her, aching for him to hug her back and tell her everything is going to be all right. It's a reciprocation that will never happen.

I lose my composure and begin crying too, as controlled as I can on the outside. On the inside, though, I am screaming. I hate seeing her in agony, an anguish that penetrates the soul. I gently place my hand on Billie's back to console her. She continues to weep for several more minutes before she inhales a hiccuped breath and begins to calm herself. Billie then gives a soft kiss on her father's cheek before walking out of the room. I escort her to the church across the street. Once she is seated, I take my place in the back with the other pallbearers and wait for the signal.

The funeral is a beautiful Catholic Mass, complete with traditional hymns. A harmonic a cappella rendition of the "Song of Farewell," which touches every single person, takes place with incense and Father Pete blessing the casket just before the procession out of the church. Father Pete delivers a top-notch homily, talking at length about how revered Teddy was, his accolades, and his unfailing love and dedication to his daughter and his faith. Billie remains quiet but streams tears steadily.

The rawness and realness of her grief is nearly unbearable to watch because I understand exactly how she feels and can't take that pain away. Once the funeral ends, the immediate family journeys to the burial plot, where Teddy's body is prayed over once more before he is laid to his final rest.

Afterward, everyone is invited back to Billie's house for a luncheon. The house is pristine, freshly cleaned, decorated, and catered, all thanks to Rick. I see how much he cares about Billie and what good friends he was with Teddy. I hope her friendship with Rick continues, as so many relationships fade post-funeral.

Billie appears drained. I know she's trying to hold it together, but I can tell she's had enough for the day. There's a sizable crowd at the luncheon, and space is limited. Between guests and the caterers, the house feels smothering. Servers maneuver through each room with appetizers, including stuffed mushrooms, fried cheese, and balsamic Brussels sprouts. The main dish includes Teddy's favorite meal—homemade fried chicken tenderloins (a family recipe), loaded pierogis topped with cheese, sour cream, bacon, and chives, along with roasted broccoli and a French baguette. For dessert, there is a donut ice cream bar, also Teddy's favorite, glazed donuts topped with a scoop of vanilla ice cream and a choice of virtually any topping imaginable. If anyone leaves hungry, it's their own fault.

"Have you eaten?" I whisper to Billie as she says goodbye to a few of Teddy's coworkers. She sighs forlornly and shakes her head.

"Let's take a break. I'll get you a plate." I lead her into the kitchen, where one of the servers pours a cup of fresh coffee for Billie. She doctors it up to her liking. After she takes her first long sip, she sighs again, this time in relief.

"Thank you," she murmurs, looking appreciatively at me as I set down her plate of food.

"You're welcome," I reply, taking a seat beside her at the island. "How are you holding up?" I affectionately rub her back.

"I'm really tired. I'm starving, but I'm not sure how much I'll be able to eat. Things seem a bit surreal right now." Billie takes another sip of coffee and several small bites of her food. God, she is beautiful. Even in this time of anguish, she looks angelic. The fact that I am having such strong feelings for her kind of scares me. What will happen once the fresh dust settles? Will she still want me? Will I be able to trudge through another grieving process with her? Can either of us handle it?

I don't know.

CHAPTER TWENTY-SEVEN

BILLIE

There are no words to describe today. I'm too spent to even try. I poke around my plate of food as the final guests leave and the catering crew cleans up. It's just my mom, Pierre, Claire, Rick, Scott, and me. Soon the house will be still again, quiet enough for me to succumb to my intrusive thoughts.

"Billie? Hey, you here?" Scott asks. I break my dissociated trance when he waves his hand in front of my eyes, trying to get my attention.

"Hiya. Sorry, what did you say?" The reality that my dad is gone and I've just laid him to rest is too painful to think about, unbearable to process.

"I asked if it's all right if I stay tonight or if you'd rather have the night alone." Scott lovingly rubs my shoulder.

"Please stay. I don't want to be alone." My voice quivers and tears well. On cue, Scott pulls me in for a comforting embrace. I inhale his masculine scent, his curls tickling my flushed, damp cheek. I hold onto him tightly, and he matches my intensity. Heat begins coursing through my veins, almost as if he's pouring his energy into me. I don't ever want to let go, but I suppose I have to for just a little while. When we release, I feel a little better, my stomach grumbling and begging me to actually eat something.

Just as I finish what I can tolerate, Rick walks into the kitchen, sighing heavily. His royal-purple tie hangs loosely around his neck. His slate-gray dress shirt is unbuttoned at the top, and the sleeves are rolled to his elbows.

"Heading out?" I ask meekly, looking at him with a mutual understanding of our exhaustion.

"Yeah, kiddo, soon I think. Hey, listen. I have something for you from your father. He made a video right after his diagnosis and made me promise to share it with you once he passed. I haven't watched it because he said he wanted you to see it first. I emailed you the file. There's no rush to view it. It's there for whenever you're ready."

My heart begins thumping so hard my entire body pulsates. I think it's impossible for my stomach to fall out of my butt, although this could be a first. I'm trying to remain calm, but my shallow breaths give my emotions away.

"Hey, you don't have to do anything you don't want to do. I just made your father a promise, and maybe you'll find it brings you comfort today, tomorrow, or anytime you're ready."

A message from my father? What could he have needed to tell me? Am I ready to hear what he has to say? I know if I don't watch the video now, though, I'll be thinking about it every moment until I do finally watch it.

My hands are shaking so badly I fumble through my phone to pull up the email Rick sent and click the link. There sits the dad I remember, paused on the screen. The healthy dad. My best bud. A warm smile crawls across my face, and I feel an intense rush of peace.

Dad is wearing his typical plain t-shirt, layered with a blue-brown-and-white flannel shirt, along with a pair of blue jeans. His hair is combed back, just like he always styled it in the mornings. Seeing the image brings back memories of how he used to smell, speak, and interact.

I press play.

Hey, kiddo. If you're watching this right now, then I've passed away. I'm so sorry I couldn't stay to watch your beautiful life continue to unfold. I would do just about anything to change this situation. I want this video to be a reminder and gentle message that I will always be here for you, watching over you, and protecting you. I encourage you to watch this anytime you want to see or talk to me. Know that I will be listening.

Billie, I need you to know how proud I am of you and how honored I am to be your father. You are the best thing I've ever done, and you continue to impress me every day. It pains me deeply to leave you alone in this world, but I will send someone for you. I don't know how I'll do it, but I promise you that you will find the love of your life. I know you don't need anyone to take care of you, but I want the perfect person to want to care for you. To love you as fiercely as I do. I know that's what you've dreamed of, to marry and have a family. But please remember, whatever you do in your life, I will always be supportive of you, even if it's not here on Earth.

When I'm gone, I'll be sending signs to make sure you know I'm looking after you. I just need to come up with them.... Let's see. Here we go. Anytime you see yellow roses, know that is me saying *hello*, guiding you, and validating that I see and hear you. And the time is...8:18 a.m. So anytime you see the number 18 or 8:18, know that it's me sending my love from Heaven.

You are and always have been my joy. When your time comes to leave this world, I'll be there to bring you home. I love you so much, Billie girl.

The video finishes and I stare at the screen, stunned. My father is amazing. I know how much he loves me. I will treasure this video forever.

Once the initial endorphin hit diminishes, I begin feeling so many emotions: shock, dismay, incredible sadness, and—suddenly—overwhelming rage.

Yellow roses.

Yellow. Roses.

I think back to the vase of yellow roses and orange tulips Rick brought shortly after Dad went to Bellevue. And how can I forget the eighteen—EIGHT-FUCKING-TEEN—dozen *yellow roses* Scott sent me? The yellow roses at the gravesite. The vase sitting right in front of me, filled with a dozen yellow fucking roses.

How in the world could this have happened? How could he send me these signs when he was still alive? No one saw this video. Rick said so, and I believe him. How am I seeing all these yellow roses?

This is impossible. Illogical. Inconceivable.

I snatch the vase of yellow roses off the coffee table and heave it against the wall without a second thought. Glass shatters everywhere. My mouth releases a shrill, pained scream. Never in my life have I ever made a sound like that. I couldn't describe it even if I wanted to, other than it was pure agony.

Scott, my mother, and Claire rush frantically into the living room. My hands are clenched, teeth gritted, and I'm blowing out enough heat to produce smoke. Claire approaches me cautiously, holding her right hand out in front of her, as if she's bracing herself for my wrath.

"Billie," she says carefully. "It's okay. We're here for you. Why don't you sit down? I'll make you a cup of tea."

"I...don't...want...to...sit...down," I mutter in between huffs, slamming my hand palm-down onto the coffee table. Scott walks over to me, unafraid that I may explode, and takes my hands.

"Billie...you're bleeding," he says in a low, calm voice.

I look down to see blood dripping from the palm of my hand and a shard of glass sticking straight out of it. I am in such distress that I don't feel any pain. I wish my entire state of being were numb.

"I need to get you to a hospital, babe. Please, let me take you," Scott says ever so delicately. I give him a faint nod and walk toward the door. I stare straight in front of me, my expression emotionless. I don't even care right now. I don't care about a damn thing.

I don't utter more than two words at the hospital. Scott does all the talking, explaining to the nurses and doctors what happened. I remember getting an injection at one point, probably to numb my hand that is now throbbing in extreme pain, cushioned underneath by a towel. I wish there were an injection to numb my heart. The anguish feels unbearable.

Scott holds my other hand the entire time, a calming and much-needed reassuring presence. A doctor carefully removes the piece of glass impaled in my skin and stitches up several spots that have deep gashes, the largest of which looks like a crescent moon directly in the center of my palm. I really did a number on my hand!

Several hours and a few prescriptions later, we return home. Scott drops me off and heads to the pharmacy to pick up the meds and a few other first-aid items. My mom and Pierre, who have settled upstairs, must have cleaned up because the glass and roses are gone. Claire is gone, but I have at least five missed text messages from her.

When Scott gets back, he finds me sitting on the couch, entranced by the fireplace.

"Hey, babe. I brought you a decaf white chocolate mocha latte and a pack of menthols." I accept the coffee and respond with a smile of gratitude.

"Let's sit on the back patio and relax. I'll get some extra blankets and turn on the fire pit."

I croak out an "okay" and follow him outside. He sets up a few camping chairs and lights the fire. It's quite cold out, but a little fresh air will do me some good. Plus, I'm not smoking in the house. I hate the smell, yet I am shaking at the anticipation of the instant calm that will rush over my body once I light that cigarette.

I take a deep first drag and hold the smoke in my lungs until I feel the calmness disperse throughout my body, then exhale toward the black, overcast sky. Scott wraps a blanket around my shoulders and takes a seat beside me.

"I get it now," I mutter in a static tone. "The pain you must be feeling, losing two incredibly precious people in your life. The gaping hole in your heart. I thought I was prepared for it. Clearly, I was not." I take another drag, followed by a sip of the latte.

Scott lights up beside me and thinks hard about what he wants to say. He examines his hands like he's looking for something, then takes another hit.

"It won't always feel like this," he finally responds. He doesn't look at me, but I can tell he's thinking about something more, so I probe.

"What are you thinking about?" I take a mouthful of latte this time and turn myself so that I'm sitting horizontally on the chair.

"I'm thinking that I feel so incredibly sorry you're going through this pain. I'm thinking about first losing Christine, the viewings, the funeral, the days and weeks afterward. Losing a loved one can be debilitating. I don't want you to feel that way. I'm glad I can be here for you." I'm happy he is here for me too. I can't imagine not having him here right now.

"Do you want to talk about the video?" Scott asks cautiously. I give it a moment of thought. I'm not sure if I should share the details. After all, all signs point to Scott being the one, the man my father sent for me, and the whole thing seems far-fetched and unbelievable. Plus, what if I scare him off? Instead, I choose to deflect the question and ask one back that's been eating at me since I watched the video.

"Why did you buy eighteen dozen yellow roses for me?"

"Hmmm," Scott murmurs. "Well, when I was a kid we had rose bushes on one side of the house. Every summer, my mother would pick the reds and pinks but never the yellow ones. When I asked her why she always left the yellow ones, she told me it's because she doesn't like the color yellow and it clashes with red and pink. So I grew to love the color yellow and tended to the yellow rosebush myself. One summer, she wanted to dig up that rosebush and replace it with a white one. I about threw myself on the yellow one, not even thinking about how badly the thorns would shred my skin." Scott laughs and shakes his head.

"She never did dig it up, and that bush has become an odd but special part of me. It's still there to this day. Yellow roses are my favorite flower. And the reason for eighteen? I don't really know, other than your dad's room number was 218, and I didn't want to send 218 dozen yellow roses. That would have been a tad over the top. I figured eighteen dozen would be sufficient." Scott chuckles at what he just said. I didn't even realize the connection of the number 18 to my dad's room. Nothing should shock me anymore. It's not like my dad picked that room number. Scott doesn't press me about the video further, and I don't offer any more details.

We continue to drink our lattes, chain-smoke menthols, and talk about fond memories of my dad and Christine. I thought I would feel awkward about it, but it doesn't bother me that he still talks about her. I want him to honor her memory, just as I will always honor the memory of my father. I do have concerns that if we get serious we may have some kinks to work out.

But right now I'm taking it a day at a time.

CHAPTER TWENTY-EIGHT

SCOTT

It seems like yesterday I was the one crying out in pain, grieving Christine. I was a complete mess for months. I was drunk the first month. I didn't eat. Barely slept. Wasn't functioning. Trying to survive each day. Some days the pain was so debilitating that my body throbbed from weeping, from exerting so much energy mourning that it had nothing left. Looking back, I'm surprised I made it through.

I hope I can be a comfort to Billie instead of a nuisance. It kills me to see her in so much pain because I know that pain. It's horrendous. Now, though, a lot of emotion is stirring internally for both of us. This delicate time is about Billie and her feelings, so I'm keeping myself at bay. However, I can already tell that the black portal of grief is about to rip wide open, and I was having a rough time before she and I met. There's a part of me that feels connected to Billie, but the other part of that connection is refreshing the affliction I thought I buried.

Last night, Billie and I fell asleep in emotional safety, wrapped in each other's arms. This morning, however, my alarm jolts me awake. I have that disoriented grogginess hanging over me. As much as I want to stay with Billie again today, I can't take any more time off work right now. One of my favorite patients, Layla, is due for a follow-up after her recent scans and lab tests. She's a mere six years old and in remission from leukemia. Hopefully, I will deliver another dose of good news this afternoon.

Billie is snoring softly, so I quietly slither my way out of bed and continue with my usual morning routine. Bruno has made himself quite at home here at Billie's. His dog bed is on the floor in her room, and his food and bowls are lined neatly in the mudroom. The backyard isn't big, but it's fenced in and flat. Billie's neighbor has a golden retriever, and the pair have been playing every day in the yard. He's going to be pissed when I finally go back home with him and he can't see his doggy girlfriend every day. I'm sure I can bring him here a few days a week when the weather permits. I don't need my dog depressed over losing the love of his life. It's really sweet watching them play. Bruno towers over Goldie, appropriately named, but she doesn't hold back her youthful playfulness. She gives him a run for his money, that's for sure.

I grab our usual coffee orders for Miranda and myself and arrive at the hospital right on schedule. We do our usual morning rundown before I start the day.

First, I pull up Layla's file. I normally run the tests myself, but I couldn't since I was away for the funeral and everything.

The results are not good.

The cancer is back with a vengeance. Based on her blood-work, the relapse is significant. Acute myeloid leukemia relapses aren't that uncommon, but Layla fought hard to get through her first round of treatment, which ended less than a year ago. My stomach feels queasy, and I'm beginning to sweat a bit. I hate this part of my job—the part where I have to deliver bad news. The part where I can't reassure a family that their child will survive. That this could be their last Christmas together. That they need to make arrangements for palliative and hospice care.

I walk out to reception. Miranda takes one look at my face, and hers turns pale as well. I don't have to tell her it's Layla. I know doctors are supposed to remain emotionally unattached to their patients, but sometimes cases hit me hard. I care about my patients, and in this line of medicine, it's imperative I do. Knowing that, though, does not diminish the angst I will feel over the next several hours until I tell Layla and her family what's next. I don't even know what's next yet, so I formulate a rough treatment plan before my first patient arrives.

The appointment with Layla goes as well as can be expected. Layla and her parents are devastated. We review some treatment options, remaining optimistic. They're not sure what they want to do yet, but they emphasize that they want to keep fighting as long as Layla wants to and can handle it.

I'm depleted of energy and leave work for the day as soon as I can. The drive home is solemn. I don't listen to music. I don't think about anything. I just focus on the road and stare blankly into the landscape. When I get home, I take a long, hot shower. After a lengthy stay in the steamy oasis, I check my phone to see three missed texts from Billie.

BILLIE
Hey, how was your day?

Just checking in, since I haven't heard from you today.

I'm usually not the clingy type, but I'm starting to worry...

The last thing I need is for her to worry about me, so I shoot her a quick text just to ease her mind.

ME
Hey, sorry. Long day.

Billie replies right away.

BILLIE
Do you want to talk about it?

ME
No. Not right now. I'm going to unwind and head to bed if you'll be okay for the night. Would you like me to come get Bruno?

BILLIE
I'll be fine. No, he can stay. He's been my cuddle buddy all day.

ME
Okay, babe. I'll see you tomorrow.

She doesn't respond, but I know she's probably upset. I mean, I would be. But I just cannot be vulnerable tonight. I have nothing left to give to myself, let alone to somebody else. Maybe a night by myself is what I need. Some time to sit in my thoughts. I've been alone for so long that I don't remember any other version of me. I'm good at being alone. I was good at being a husband too. But will I ever be ready for that again?

Time will tell, I guess.

Nope, I was wrong. I am not good at being alone. I slept like complete garbage, tossing and turning, in and out of slumber. It's like everything has hit me all at once. I miss Christine so much. I want to run over to Billie, but I don't want to smother her. Part of me doesn't want to see her because I hate seeing her in pain—it reminds me of my own pain I'm still battling. And Layla....I'm hopeful, but I need to be realistic that things may not go well this round of treatment. There's always hope, but there's also only so much her little body can handle.

I start the morning with a long, frosty run, blasting Linkin Park in my ear buds. I figure if Billie loves that band so much, I'll give them a try. And sure as shit, they're really good. Their songs are a blend expressing deep love, sheer sadness, and utter rage. My run time even improves by eighteen seconds. I feel refreshed after a shower and a cup of coffee. I check my phone and see Billie hasn't texted me. I don't know why, but I'm a little disappointed she hasn't.

Why do I even feel this way? Memories of Christine flooded my thoughts last night, yet I'm bummed out Billie hasn't texted me. I told her I had a long day and was going to bed. Why did I hope she would reach out and say she needs me? This is a tug of war, a guilty one. After battling the imaginary argument in my head, I text her.

ME

Good morning, beautiful. How are you today?

BILLIE

I slept like shit. It's nice having your warm body next to me. I miss you...

Knowing that she misses me gives me flutters of anticipation. I'm equally scared and excited. Thinking about it more, I do miss her. Seeing Billie grieve is just hard. It's all hard. I'm not sure how healthy it is to start a new relationship when both people are grieving devastating losses. Part of me feels like I'm about to fall head over heels in love with her, while the other wants to lock away my heart.

CHAPTER TWENTY-NINE

BILLIE

T he reception area is eerie at night. The overhead lights are dim. A lamp glows from Scott's office. Since the funeral last week, things with Scott have been off between us, and I'm not sure why. He's been distant. Just not himself.

He said he was working late tonight to catch up on some paperwork, but I miss him. The absence of my dad has left a gaping wound, and Scott distracts me from the bleeding. A very hot, sexy diversion from a gloomy week. I figure a mind-blowing office quickie would entice him to call it quits for the day.

I have been craving Scott. I cannot get enough of him, and...

I love him.

Madly.

Deeply.

I feel in my core that he's the one I'm supposed to live this life with. People have always told me, "when you know, you know." And after watching the video of my dad and how everything he said aligns with Scott, I know.

Tonight I want to show him just how much I want to be with him for the long haul. I want to keep things fresh and thrilling. My stomach is bubbling with excitement. I've never done this before, obviously, so I hope it's not awkward. I want this to be the hottest thing he's ever seen and done.

I mean, who doesn't want their girlfriend to show up unexpectedly to seduce and fuck the shit out of them? Come to think of it, he never actually asked me to be his girlfriend. Given what we have going on, it's safe to say we're together.

To-may-to, To-mah-to.

Under my classic tan trench coat, I have on a tight black dress with snaps in the front from top to bottom. It accentuates every sexy curve that drives Scott crazy with desire, easy to rip right off me. I will relish in it when he does. Underneath, I am wearing yellow lingerie, an allusion to the yellow roses he sent me.

Thankfully, Miranda has left for the night, so I walk past reception toward his office. His door is cracked open. I can hear he is on the phone. I don't want to eavesdrop if he's talking to a patient or their family. I stand far enough away so that I hear only muffled noises. Once he hangs up, I'll spring my naughty plan into action.

But his voice starts to get closer and clearer, and I catch him saying *Ryan*. My ears perk up right away.

"I'm really struggling, man. I care about Billie so much, but I'm not sure I'm ready to let go of Christine. I don't want to stop blowing a kiss to her picture every time I leave the house. I still love her and miss her terribly."

Silence.

"No, of course I don't want to break up with her, but I feel guilty. She's going through the stuff with her dad's passing, and I know grief can take a long time to process. I'm not sure how much energy I can put into dealing with my issues, helping her through her grief, *and* being a good partner."

Silence.

"I mean, yeah, I guess we're together. I don't know. We never really talked about where our relationship stands. I care about her a lot, but I don't love her the same way I love Christine."

He doesn't love me like he loves Christine? What does that even mean?!

My heart is pounding so hard I can feel it in every part of my body. I can't believe he's admitting this. After everything he's said to me, *this* is how he *actually* feels? After everything we've done together. After everything we've *been through* together. My dad is barely cold in the ground and Scott's already thinking about jumping ship. I didn't do that to him in the midst of his deep despair. I fucking held him instead. I kissed his forehead. I weathered the environmental and emotional storms with him.

I can't leave now. I need to address this. I move closer to the door so I can hear better. I shouldn't, but I do.

"Yeah, you're right. Maybe I'm just afraid. I'd be devastated if the situation were reversed. With Billie's dad recently passing, I feel this new wave of grief taking over, like it's getting worse, not better. Lately, the more time I spend with Billie, the more I miss Christine. "

Red fucking flag. I make his grief worse?! Fan-fucking-tastic.

Silence.

"Yeah, I know it's screwed up. That's what I'm saying. I don't know what to do. I don't think I can make a decision now. I think I just need more time to sort out my feelings."

Silence.

"All right, man, thanks for listening. You too."

I stand dumbfounded, with tears streaming down my face. I don't want to confront him, but I don't think I'll make it to the parking garage without collapsing. I hear shuffling, so I assume he's gathering his stuff. I still don't move. I can't.

He pulls the door open to exit, and the look on his face...the look on his fucking face. He's mortified.

"Billie, baby, let me explain." My expression turns from devastation into rage.

"Don't you fucking *baby* me, Scott! How could you? You blow kisses to your wife's picture while I'm sleeping in your bed? You don't love me like you love Christine? What in the actual fuck is wrong with you?" Scott looks like a deer in the headlights and shakes his head with disbelief.

"What are you doing here? I haven't heard from you all day and you just show up unannounced to eavesdrop on my private conversation?" Scott retorts.

"I wanted to surprise you because it's been a shit week, and I needed you. I thought this would lighten the mood. Apparently, though, I'm not the one who's occupying your thoughts these days." My voice is shaking. I'm not sure if I'm going to scream or cry.

Maybe both.

"You weren't supposed to hear that. I was confiding in Ryan because I'm struggling, okay?" Scott's nostrils flare in frustration. He's right. I shouldn't have listened in on the conversation, but this just goes to show he's been lying to me or pretending or just biding time.

Hot tears burn as they slide down my cheeks and my neck. "But what you told Ryan is how you feel, isn't it? You wouldn't just say all that to him if it weren't true!" My voice cracks as I attempt to avoid a complete emotional breakdown.

"You're taking it out of context," Scott says defensively.

"I heard every word you said." My tone is firm and angry.

"Can't we just go home and talk about this?" Scott groans and pinches the bridge of his nose.

"Home?" I explode. "Scott, I don't live with you. We don't have *a home* together. Our home? Our home exists in a cute, safe neighborhood with other young families. Our home has a wrap-around porch with a big wooden swing in the front. Our home is where we live when we get married and make babies together.

Our home is big enough to raise a family together, but not run by maids and butlers. Our home has a giant oak tree in the backyard so our kids can make forts and play pretend adventures. *Your* home is with Christine. So, if you want to be in love with a memory, go right ahead. Because I'm done."

"You're done? Wait a second. What's that supposed to mean? You can't be serious. Just give me time to—"

"Time to what, Scott? Blow more kisses back at your dead wife when you leave *your* home every day?"

Ouch.

I hit low with that one, and I know it. Guilt immediately flushes through my body, but I don't give myself permission to back down. Scott starts to breathe quickly and deeply. His eyes well with tears. But I can't stop what's taking over me. Everything pours out.

Word-vomit is worse than stomach vomit.

"You've been lying to me this whole time," I sputter through my fresh set of tears. "I trusted you. I felt safe with you. I gave you every part of me. I have loved you every single day since I held you in that cemetery, grieving *Christine*, and you can't move one step toward healing. Not one!"

"I can't just move on, Billie. She was my wife. You're rushing my grief!" Scott yells back at me. We're in an all-out verbal brawl. I'm surprised security hasn't come rushing down the corridor.

"Ha, you had no problem rushing me to your bed though!" I shoot back.

"That's not fair and you know it." Scott turns away from me and paces the length of his office. He's angry. I'm angry. And neither of us is holding back.

"I am well aware she was your wife. And I'm not asking you to forget her or stop loving her. But for the love of God and everything that is holy, I deserve better than this. Than to be your second choice. Than to be strung along until you decide if you want me or not."

I'm pretty sure he's having a panic attack because he's now standing still, hyperventilating and crying, unable to speak.

I soften momentarily to grab a bottle of water from the mini fridge and hand it to him.

Scott goes to the couch to steady himself and chugs half the bottle. I stand there with nothing else to say. I should just leave, but I can't bring myself to do it. I know if I do, it's over. And even though I'm saying I deserve better and I'm done, I'm so in love with him. I want him to fight for me, for *us*. But if he doesn't love me, then there's nothing left to hold onto, to fight for.

And I refuse to beg a man to be with me.

"I just don't know if I can be the man you need, and maybe you do deserve someone better, but I don't want to lose you, Billie. This is so hard for me." Scott finishes the bottle of water.

I am not backing down.

"Oh, please. That's a cop-out and you know it. I want to be with *you*. Not anyone else. Can't you see that?"

Silence.

Here goes nothing.

"Do you love me?" Scott relaxes against the back of the couch and closes his eyes. His tight facial expression tells me he's thinking about what he is going to say. If he has to think about it, though, the answer is *no*.

"I—"

"Do you love me, *Scott*?" I plead. I want the answer to be *yes*. I want to love him freely and not feel anxious or worried. He opens his eyes, sits up, and looks at me. He exhales, defeated, and shrugs.

"I don't know. I need more time." The words are crushing.

"Take all the time you need, then," I respond. "I am leaving to meet my mother in Europe for eight weeks, but maybe I just won't come back." Apparently, I just decided I am going on this trip. Because running away from my problems is the best thing for my mental health. Pretend nothing ever happened. Imagine my dad is still alive as I trek through Greek ruins, visit Spanish bodegas, and schmooze with the locals. Block Scott out of my mind. Erase our fling from my memory.

"Please don't leave me, Billie. Please. Let's figure this out."

"You want to figure this out," I say, my voice shaking, "yet you still can't tell me you love me, but I love you. Either you do or you don't." I take my hands and point them side to side. "Yes or no. It's that simple. I love you so much that when I'm without you it feels like a part of me is missing. I love you so much that I would stay with you and work through this if it meant what we have is worth saving. I love you so much that I'm standing here, hoping you choose to get your shit together so that *we* can be together."

I am weeping at this point, because reality is sinking in.

"I would choose you today, tomorrow, and always. If you don't already love me after all that we've been through and shared, then I won't ever be enough." I pause, trying to catch my breath. "Do you love me, Scott?"

"I'm afraid to say it, Billie. I'm afraid of this, of us. I don't want to say those words like this. Not when we're so upset," he pleads.

There's my answer. He can't say it.

"Have a good life, Scott. You deserve...*the best.*"

I can't believe I'm actually doing this, but I walk right out that fucking door. Then I stop, turn toward him, and blow him a kiss. Louder sobs erupt from me as I rush through reception to the elevators.

He doesn't follow me.

I guess this is it then. I'm not sure how I will endure this much anguish, but I will. I notice people throughout the hospital watching me cry. It's a children's hospital. Kids are sick and dying. Dying, just like my relationship. It's all sad as fuck.

I'm trying to navigate through wings and corridors, but I get lost several times before finally exiting the building toward the parking garage. I dart up two flights of stairs and start searching for my car. When I find it, Scott is standing there.

He did come after me. How did he find my car so fast? Never mind. He's here.

"Billie!" he begs. "Wait! Please don't leave me. Please. I'll fix this."

There is anguish in his eyes as he gasps for air. It's the same torment I saw at the cemetery when he was the most vulnerable I've ever seen him.

I feel like the wind has been knocked out of me from the emotional gut punch of our fight. I am attempting to process the fact he came after me.

What am I supposed to do?

My body has activated fight-or-flight mode. I'm not sure which to choose. Which way do I run? To him or away from him? Before I can talk myself out of it, though, I sprint toward him, leap into his arms, and kiss him. A jolt of electricity strikes when he catches me. I wrap my legs around him, my hands cradling his jaw.

His hands clench my thighs, cupping the very bottom of my ass. His lips crash recklessly into mine, unable to separate. I've never felt anything like this before. My body feels supercharged.

He grips me tighter and kisses me harder. I can feel his dick swell through his scrub pants, throbbing at my sex. I kiss him back feverishly, reciprocating his energy until he finally pulls away. Scott stares longingly into my eyes. I refuse to look away. I'm hungry for him. I don't want to leave him. I don't. But my fear of abandonment is powerful. If I run away first, he can't abandon me.

I can't stay here because of a *maybe*. I want him. I need him, but he apparently does not feel the same. Or does he and he just can't face the truth? Christine is gone and isn't ever coming back, and that's fucking painful. I don't know what it's like to lose the love of my life or my child. I cannot fathom that type of grief. But I don't want his grief to prevent him from loving someone else, from loving *me*.

Scott places me back on the ground and grabs my hand.

"Come with me," he growls, tickling my ear.

He briskly leads us back to his office. He shuts the door behind me and pins me up against it as he turns the lock.

He is so sexy when he's on a mission.

We're completely out of breath from the intensity of the last few minutes, so much so that I feel dizzy from the lack of air. I close my eyes and focus on my breath, fighting unconsciousness. He tilts my head toward his with his index finger. I open my eyes to find his lustful gaze.

At any moment, I have to decide what all this means for us. Am I going to continue this with a chance of getting my heart shattered? I wish I knew what he was thinking. This time, I wait for him to decide what he wants.

Scott finally lets out a deep masculine grunt, revealing he has made his choice, and kisses me passionately. His lips envelop mine. I whimper as he unties the belt to my trench coat, ripping it off me. He then tears my dress right down the front, exposing the sexy lingerie.

It was just as I had imagined—*glorious.*

"You're a naughty girl, hiding this little number from me. Goodness gracious, you're a sight for sore eyes." I let Scott admire me for a moment before peeling off his scrub shirt and tossing it on the floor.

He drops his pants, then grabs hold of me so aggressively that he rips my panties. He kisses me everywhere: my lips, my cheeks, my neck, down to my pebbled breasts, where he devours each one. I cling to him and savor the sensations.

Scott whisks me to the black leather couch, my hair whipping around us. He lays me down and pounces on top of me.

Before he satisfies the desperation pumping through my body, he whispers, "I don't have a condom."

What the fuck, Billie?! How could you come here and forget a damn condom when you planned on having sex with him?

"I'm not on birth control," I admit. It's silent for a moment. "But...I *am* past ovulation this cycle. What should we do?"

We pause. Our bodies are screaming for each other. My breath is more of a heave because the anticipation is intolerable. I cannot stop this. I do not want to stop this. I am desperate to feel him inside of me.

"I need you, Billie. I will do whatever it takes to make us work. I'm just scared, but I will work on it. I promise. I want you right now, completely as we are. I want to make love to you."

There's no question this is happening. Immediately, I pull him down so that our bodies are pressed together. I kiss him with everything I have to give. I feel him groan from his throat as our tongues dance some type of contemporary number.

He wastes no time moving the gusset of my panties to the side, ripping them further. I accept him with a gasp of delight as his rock-hard erection effortlessly glides inside of me. I grab a handful of curls as he kisses down my cheek, to my jaw, to my collarbone, to my left breast, penetrating me in steady waves. He takes my nipple in his mouth and sucks in unison with his thrusts. I release a loud moan, which sends shivers down his body. As he finesses my breasts, I dig my nails firmly into his shoulders. Scott inhales sharply. I whimper in response.

I then kiss his neck, sucking hard enough to leave my mark. My nails have surely left scratches on his back, another stake in my claim. This man is all mine.

Making love is ecstasy. It has to be. I wrap my legs around his back as I feel him intensify his thrusts. He kisses me with such urgency, like it's the last time he will ever do so. I exhale in relief, knowing that I'm safe with him. I can feel every part of him as the pressure within me takes hold.

"I'm gonna come," he breathes.

"I'm so close, baby," I whine. He moans and I cry out as I feel him burst inside of me the same moment I orgasm.

Oh, my God.

The pleasure of sex and orgasming without a condom is inconceivable. I feel him fill me, his seed spreading throughout my reproductive system. One that will reject every little sperm this late into my cycle because there's nothing in there to fertilize. Just a dead end. Sorry swimmers. Better luck next time.

We're panting for air. Several beads of sweat drip onto my neck from his forehead. When we're finished, he chuffs through a smile. I return the smile and roll my eyes.

"That was unbelievable," I marvel.

He remains inside me when he confesses, "I love you, Billie. I mean that with all of my heart. Please be patient with me. I'll get there, I promise you."

I am overcome with emotion because no man other than my father has ever said those words to me.

And he knows that.

I bore into his eyes, deep enough that I reach his soul, and murmur, "I love you too."

CHAPTER THIRTY

SCOTT

I almost lost her, my Billie. I was being honest with Ryan about my feelings, but seeing how that affected Billie when I opened my office door, I didn't have a doubt in the world that I am in love with her. I could see just how horribly I had hurt her and I just...froze. My panic attacks are getting out of control. I think it's finally time I do something about whatever is happening to me. I cannot imagine waking up tomorrow and not having Billie in my life. I have to get myself to a place where I am able to live my everyday life without wanting to join my wife and daughter.

Billie has been that source of light, of hope. And she's right. Christine isn't coming back. I can either hold onto a memory, or I can cherish and honor the time we had together while creating a life that's worth living, even if that's with someone else.

I miss being in love. If I had to choose between blowing a kiss to a picture every day or having a woman who loves me, who I come home to every day and sleep with every night, I choose Billie. Hands down. Because at the end of the day, that picture is not going to love me back and Billie will.

When she blew me that kiss and walked out of my office door, the pain of what I've been doing to her became real. I felt exactly how she felt standing at that door.

Humiliated.

Crushed.

Enraged.

Desperate.

I had to wait for my panic attack to subside before I could go after her, or I would have undoubtedly passed out. As soon as I could move, I sprinted. I unsuccessfully searched the hospital before scouring the parking garage for her, hoping I wasn't too late. Fortunately, her bright-blue SUV was easy to spot. I'm surprised I made it there before her, but I'm so glad I did.

When Billie rushed toward me, I knew in my heart that she's the one I need to spend the rest of my life with. The grief and loss that I deal with will become a minor part of my life versus my entire life. I know we haven't been together all that long, but I don't need any more time to decide. My feelings may not be as developed as hers yet, but they're there and only for her.

She's right. I do need to get my shit together.

Billie is still sleeping upstairs in her bed with Bruno, and I am searching for a therapist and grief counseling. I think a support group would be helpful and would welcome Billie if she wants to attend as well, since she's fresh and deep in the loss of her father.

I don't know how she does it, how she stays so strong. Last night was the most emotional and passionate I've ever seen her. It was kinda hot, if I'm being completely honest. When we made love, I could feel my soul bonding to hers. That's the only way I can describe the feeling.

We stayed at her place last night because going back to mine, especially right now, isn't an option.

I find a therapist I think may be a good fit and schedule my first appointment. Then I discover a grief support group that meets twice a week, one of which happens to be tomorrow at the Lutheran church in town. I'll stop in after work. If Billie wants to go, I'll swing by to get her on the way there.

While I'm at it, I pull up Zillow, just to see what's available. If I want to find happiness again, I need to stop holding onto something that's preventing me from accepting love and loving in return. I can still honor Christine and Maggie in other ways, but putting them above Billie will destroy our relationship and our hearts. And I know I can't stay in that house. It's time.

Here's one: Heartwood Trails in Bellevue. Ironic, of course. Four bedrooms, three and a half bathrooms. There's more than an acre of land that ends at a forest line. It's private but close enough to other neighbors that we could barbecue together. There's no fence for Bruno or a wraparound porch, but I can make those happen. I'll schedule a tour after Billie leaves.

I feel bubbles of excitement, no longer frightened by the idea of sharing my life with someone.

"Whatcha doin'?" Billie asks from behind me as she slides her arms around my shoulders. I immediately feel relaxed when she kisses my cheek.

Home. Billie is my home.

I turn off the phone screen to shield her from my recent house hunting.

"Oh, I was just catching up on some things. How are you this morning?"

"I'm okay."

"Just okay? Something wrong?" Whatever Billie is about to say pains her to say it. She hugs me tightly.

"I need to apologize for how poorly I reacted last night. I was emotional and irrational. I should have listened to you and given you time to respond. I was reactive because I was angry and petrified of losing you, so I figured if I ran away, you couldn't hurt me. I just felt so rejected, and I panicked. I didn't mean to say such hurtful things or pressure you into saying *I love you*. I am so sorry." She huffs in relief, her breath tickling my neck.

I place my hand on her warm, loving arms in reassurance. "I'm sorry too, Billie. I should have been more upfront about my struggles with grieving and my feelings for you. And I said some hurtful things too, and I recognize that. I've been doing a lot of thinking this morning, and I'm going to get my shit together while you're in Europe. I promise you that. I love you. I want to be with you. And I'll work every day to make you happy."

"I am happy with you, Scott. That's the thing. You don't have to *make* me happy because I am already happy, as we are at this moment." Billie nuzzles her face in my neck and gives me three soft kisses that produce goosebumps.

"I still need to work on myself though. I have two months. That'll give me some time to really dig into my issues and repair what's broken, at least some of it." I turn my head and plant a kiss on her cheek. She lets go of her embrace and slides onto my lap. She looks contemplative and sad.

"What's wrong, Billie? Are you upset about your dad?" I hope she's not still upset with me.

"Well, I was thinking about not going," she admits somberly.

"Billie, no, you should go spend this time with your mom and patch things up. It'll be good for you to get away. You've been through a lot. Take some time to decompress and process everything."

"You're right. I do need to get away. I wish you could come with me though," Billie groans.

"I know. Me too. But it's necessary I get myself into a positive space again. I've already made a therapy appointment with a woman named Shelly. I'll be seeing her next week. And there's a grief support group I'm going to check out tomorrow. You're welcome to come with me if you want."

Billie appears impressed.

"I would, but I have to get everything in order and pack for this trip. When I get back, we can go together."

"All right, now I'm jealous. I've always wanted to sip tea and eat crumpets," I say with a terrible British accent. I pout my bottom lip. She kisses it, then gently bites down. I get an instant erection, and I'm sure she noticed.

"I think you're going to find therapy very beneficial," she continues as if she's unaware of the stiffy in my pants. "I've been going since my parents got divorced, so it's been twenty years with the same therapist, believe it or not. She has helped me through so much. It takes time. There's no quick fix and you're done. It's a commitment."

"I promise I will commit to therapy, just as I'm committed to you."

Billie presses a long, sensual kiss on me, then moves a curl out of my face. "Would you like some breakfast? I'm cooking this time," she giggles.

"If by breakfast you mean you're going to sit on my face, then, yes, I'm starving." I wiggle my eyebrows up and down.

"Down boy. I'm not sure what you did to me last night, but I'm really sore." She stands up and gives me a mischievous grin.

"You know, you're sexy when you're fiery mad. It turns me on...badly."

"Well, you're going to have to wait it out. I want to eat actual food first. Would you like some coffee?"

"Actually, I think I'll take a walk down to the coffee shop and get us the fancy lattes. White chocolate mocha as usual?"

"There's no other latte that comes close to being superior to the white chocolate mocha. My favorite."

"I will be right back. I love you, Billie."

"I love you, Scott."

CHAPTER THIRTY-ONE

SCOTT

Eight weeks. I can handle this. We're not even at the airport yet and I already miss her. Being apart is going to be rough. I'm so in love with her it hurts. I feel confident she will come back, not leave me for someone else, or end our relationship (anymore). If she did, though, the loss would be just as devastating as losing Christine.

The moment I realized I fell in love with Billie, everything made sense. I was able to let go of all the anxiety and fear I have been holding onto so tightly. I was able to embrace the thrill of loving someone and being loved in return.

I place my hand on Billie's thigh and squeeze affectionately as we approach the airport. She laces her fingers through mine.

"Are you excited about the trip?" I ask nonchalantly, my sad attempt at small talk to prevent me from emotionally crumbling and begging her not to go. I'm glad she's chosen to work on her relationship with her mother. I'm supportive of her taking a much-needed reprieve from everything. I did the same thing shortly after Christine's funeral—except I ended up at an all-inclusive resort in the Bahamas and drank myself silly for a month straight. I will never drink a dirty banana again.

"Yeah, I am, actually. I feel this empowering sense of freedom, but I have some lingering conflicting feelings about leaving you." I can feel Billie looking at me. I can't turn to meet her gaze or I'll break composure. My entire body is stiff, trying to hold itself together.

"Don't worry, babe. I'll be here when you get back. Plus, we will video chat, even if it's 3 a.m. my time. I will message you every day. We've got this. The only thing you have to do is enjoy yourself. Drink some really good wine in Italy. Tour France. Eat your way through Spain. Admire Greek art."

"My mother loves to travel, so I'm sure she'll have everything planned to the minute every day. We're starting off in England, touring there for just a few days. Then we fly down to Spain. After that, I'm not sure where we are exploring, but we will finish in Italy. Maybe I'll fake food poisoning a few times just so I can watch trash TV in peace," Billie giggles.

Her laugh is infectious.

"I'm relieved I don't have to stay in France for two months straight," she continues. "I can't go to Europe and not see *Europe*. It might be the only time I get to go there."

"I've never been. Maybe we can take a trip there some day," I suggest.

"I would really like that." Billie squeezes my hand and smiles as she stares out her window.

My stomach churns as we pull into the airport. I really don't want her to go, but I need to put in the work to get past my commitment issues. She needs to grieve her father's death and make amends with her mom. It still doesn't take away from the fact that I'm going to miss her so much.

"Well, here we are," she says with a quiver in her voice.

I need to reassure her before I release the tears I've forcibly held back all morning. "Listen," I grab her hands and face her toward me. I close my eyes and kiss her hands, then cover them with mine. "I love you. I'll be here. Just message me when you land in London. I'll talk to you before we fall asleep tonight."

"You're right," she laments. "I'm just going to miss you."

We get out of the car and unload Billie's luggage. Before Billie heads into the airport, I kiss her forehead and pull her in for a tight hug. Her sweet floral scent intoxicates me. She always smells so good.

"I love you, babe," Billie huffs.

"I love you too, sweetheart."

We kiss several times, neither of us wanting the moment to end, until she leaves with tears in her eyes.

My heart already aches. But it's going to be okay. Everything will be just fine.

CHAPTER THIRTY-TWO

BILLIE

T he non-stop flight to London is about seven and a half hours. Earlier in the morning, I loaded my iPad with Season 3 of *Bridgerton*. After the plane takes off, I put in my earbuds and press play.

Colin better get his shit right with Penelope, or I'm done watching this show. Ugh, why do men do this "I-can't-love-you-because-I'm-scared" shit? So infuriating.

I binge the first five episodes before exhaustion takes over and I fall asleep. I awaken to an announcement from the pilot that we are descending and should fasten our seatbelts.

After the plane lands, I gather my luggage and find my mother and Pierre waiting for me outside the entrance doors.

"Sweetheart!" my mom squeals as she scurries toward me. She's wearing a floral sundress, with blue heels and a white raincoat. Why she's dressed for spring in the throes of winter is beyond me.

"Hi, Mom," I greet her with chipper sarcasm. She throws her arms around me. I pat her unaffectedly on the back. I haven't gotten a hug like that from my mother in more than ten years. This feels foreign and weird, and I'm not sure how else to feel about it. But I will accept it.

Baby steps.

Pierre doesn't say anything to me. I'm beginning to wonder if he speaks English well enough to hold a conversation. I should probably start learning some French. He opens the car door and pops the trunk. We load up my stuff and drive to the cozy English cottage.

Here goes nothing.

CHAPTER THIRTY-THREE

SCOTT

"Scott, welcome. Please come in." Shelly, my new therapist, greets me warmly.

"Thank you. I'm Scott. Nice to meet you." I hold out my hand to shake hers. She reciprocates with a firm handshake.

"Yes, I know that," Shelly giggles. "It's nice to meet you too."

"Oh, yeah, I guess so. Sorry, I'm a little nervous. I've never done this before."

"That's okay. We'll take it slow and see where we end up. Have a seat." Shelly gestures to a chair. There's no couch. I thought people who go to therapy lie on a couch and spill their ugly guts out.

If I had to guess, Shelly is in her early-thirties. She's definitely younger than I am. I'm not sure how I feel about that, knowing that someone younger than I am is going to be giving me life advice. But I'm open for anything at this point. She's dressed in a white blouse, a fitted blue blazer, black jeggings, and short heels. Her navy cat-eye glasses accentuate the outfit. She seems trendy.

"So, Scott," Shelly begins, "what has made you choose to start therapy?"

I have to think about that for a minute because there are so many reasons why I chose to come today. I blurt out the first thing that comes to mind.

"My wife and newborn daughter died a few years ago, and my new girlfriend says I'm stuck in a wave of grief and won't move forward."

"Wow, that is not exactly what I was expecting," Shelly says surprised, "and I am incredibly sorry for your loss. That must feel heavy to carry. Would you say you're here to process the loss you endured or to develop a relationship with your girlfriend?" She jots a few notes on her yellow legal pad.

"I don't really know. I think both. I mean, I agree that I am treading mud, so to speak, and my relationship with Billie, my girlfriend, cannot move forward until I get out of whatever is holding me back. Ever since I met Billie, I started getting panic attacks, and I have never had one before that. Not once in my life."

"Why do you think that is?" she inquires.

"No clue."

"Would you say Billie makes you feel scared or panicked?" Shelly eyes me intently.

"No, not at all. If anything, she's made me feel things I haven't felt in years, since I was with my wife, Christine."

"Bingo," she declares.

"I'm not sure I know what you mean." I eye her suspiciously.

"Being with Billie is making you feel a range of emotions, ones that are essentially foreign to you and not ones you've shared with anyone else since Christine. I don't think Billie is causing the panic attacks. I think the feelings you're having are triggering the reality and finality of your wife's death and your relationship with her. You may have been grieving her since she passed away, but you're just now starting to mourn her, which is intensified due to your feelings for Billie." Shelly nods her head and presses her forearms along her thighs, lacing her hands and waiting for my response.

"What's the difference? Isn't it all the same?"

"Yes and no. Grief is usually held on the inside, in our heads and hearts, and mourning is expressed physically, ergo the panic attacks." Shelly gestures by unlacing her fingers and using her hands to emphasize what she's saying.

This realization hits me like a ton of bricks. "Well, shit. I never thought of it like that."

"What do you think is preventing you from having a relationship with Billie?" Shelly clicks her pen and jots a few more notes on her legal pad.

"I feel guilty that I'm moving on. Because when I married Christine, I promised I would be with her all the days of my life."

"But—you were with Christine all the days of *her* life, so if you're concerned about breaking vows, you aren't. Logically, you're no longer sharing a life together. It's natural to have feelings for her that will never go away, but they won't be reciprocated in a human relationship with her. Is that what you want? To love one-sidedly?" Shelly asks skeptically.

"Damn it. Good point. No, it's not what I want. Maybe I'm afraid she will be mad that I've met someone else." I scratch my head in nervous frustration.

"How is she going to be mad though? She's not here." Shelly is speaking rationally. Clearly, I'm thinking irrationally.

"Well, wherever she is." Everything Shelly is saying and questioning is unequivocally accurate. This session is far from how I envisioned therapy. It became intense from the moment I stepped in the door. I wasn't quite prepared for things to get so deep during a first appointment.

"Regardless of spiritual beliefs, Christine *as a person* cannot be angry with you here on Earth any longer. And if you're assuming she will feel upset beyond the grave, you're creating a theoretical situation in your head that does not exist. Then you're stressing yourself out as your feelings for Billie become more intense, causing you to question whether you want to have a relationship with her because you're experiencing these negative emotions around her. Negativity can feel repelling when you're feeling hurt or sad."

What the fuck? I am mind-blown right now.

"How...how can you know all this stuff so quickly? You're spot-on," I say exasperatedly.

Shelly thinks for a moment, tapping her pen to her chin. "I would probably say the six intensive years of college and thousands of hours in clinical work, plus board certification."

I flush with embarrassment.

"Well, yeah, I guess that would do it. This is good. This is really good. I'm pleasantly surprised how insightful and enlightening therapy is. I was expecting to sob like a child for an hour and recount all the things I miss about Christine."

Shelly glances at her watch.

"We still have time. What do you miss about her?"

"Everything," I huff. "I miss the way she smelled. She always wore this perfume—pink something—and it reminded me of strawberries and pears. I miss how she woke me up in the mornings, our dinners after our long days at work. I miss seeing Christine healthy. I miss being intimate with her. I miss the excitement we shared when we found out she was pregnant. I miss...I miss her devoted, unconditional love the most, I would say."

For the next however many minutes, I continue to let out all the bundled emotions, feelings, and thoughts I've shared with no one over the past two years. It's like a huge weight has been lifted off my shoulders. And yes, I blubber through the whole damn thing. Shelly says nothing until I've said everything I needed to say.

"All of that is really touching, Scott. I'm sure Christine felt the love you have for her. Here's what I'm thinking for our next session. I want you to write a letter to Christine. Imagine you could talk to her one last time. What would you say to her? If Christine were still here and just living in a part of the world where it's impossible to see or continue a relationship with her, what would you like her to know about you and your life now?"

Interesting. There's so much I want to say but no idea where to even begin. "Okay, I can do that. And just bring it next time?"

"Yes, it may not be finished by then and that's okay. I really want you to take your time and reflect on your life with her. We can work through it in pieces if we need to."

Naturally, my anxiety spiral immediately takes over and my body doesn't hide it. I jiggle my leg and chew my thumbnail. Shelly sits there calmly, her legs crossed at the ankle, observing me. "What if I want to look at it every day? What if I find myself reading it incessantly?"

Shelly appears unaffected by my sudden change in emotions. "Do you think you will?"

"Undoubtedly, yes."

"Okay, then we will mail it."

"Mail it where?"

"I'm not sure, but we can figure that out too. Don't let writing this letter spiral you into a depressive grief episode. You may feel sad, yes, but it should feel cathartic." Shelly glances at her watch and looks back up at me with a genuine and caring smile. "Our time is finished for today, but I look forward to seeing what you come up with in your letter."

"Thank you for your time today, Shelly. I think these sessions are going to be very helpful for me."

We both stand and walk to the door. Shelly giggles as I depart. "Yes, that is the goal. Have an enjoyable rest of your day. I will see you Thursday, same time."

"Sounds like a plan. Thanks, Shelly."

CHAPTER THIRTY-FOUR

BILLIE

"Hello, my love!" Scott answers the video call on the first ring. It feels so good to see his face.

"¡Hola! ¿Cómo estás?" I ask in a very American accent.

"I...love you too?" Scott laughs.

"No, it means *hello, how are you?*" I chuckle back.

"Well, I just got out of my first therapy session with Shelly."

"Oh, that's great, babe! How did you like it? What'd you talk about? Wait, nix that. I don't need to know what you talked about." Scott's eyes light up for the first time in a while. It's good to see a spark again, even if it's just momentary.

"It's okay. I want to talk about it. First, she's really good at her craft. In the one-hour session, she helped me see so much that I've been struggling to find answers for during the past two years. It's crazy! Like, why did I wait this long?"

"Because your now-much-calmer-girlfriend lost her shit on you and basically forced you to go." I smile at him sheepishly and chew my bottom lip. Gosh, I miss his lips. His body. His warmth.

Everything. "I'm really glad it was helpful," I continue. "When's your next appointment?"

"Thursday. I'm going to go twice a week at first. I'll drop to once a week eventually. She already gave me homework."

"Oh, yeah? What's that?" I raise an eyebrow.

"I have to write a letter to Christine. I'm supposed to pretend she's living on an island on the other side of the world and write to her because I can't see her."

"What's the letter supposed to be about?" I'm trying to play it cool to hide my surge of jealousy. Jealous of what? I don't even know.

"She didn't say, actually. I guess I'll just write whatever comes to mind."

"Oh, okay." I shift in my seat. I know I need to be supportive, but I continue to feel particularly insecure.

That's a me problem, not a him problem.

"I can let you read it if you think it'll make you feel better," Scott offers, probably because my face expresses everything I'm thinking, even though my mouth is shut.

"No, I can't. I need to let you do this, and I need to work on feeling more secure."

"Whatever you need to do, babe. You're welcome to see it if you change your mind. Well, enough about me. How's Spain?" Scott plops himself on his bed and props his head up with his hand.

"It's beautiful here. I really love the culture. I had to dust off the cobwebs in the very back part of my brain to trigger what I learned in my high school- and college-level Spanish classes. I'm pleasantly surprised how much I remember. A lot came back to me pretty quickly."

"I like it when you talk Spanish to me." Scott gives me a suggestive smile.

"Oh, yeah? Well, then. Eres un tonto," I say in a sexy voice.

"I'm not sure what you said, but you can do that to me anytime," Scott answers seductively. I burst out laughing.

"I said *you are a goofball.*"

The hotel room door swings open. Mom and Pierre waltz in with handfuls of shopping bags.

"Hello, sweetheart! I got you some new clothes I think you're going to *love*," she says, greeting me excitedly.

"Hey, babe, gotta go. Mom wants me to give her a fashion show. Love you."

"Love you too."

I end the call and silently groan. My mom has no idea what I like. I'm dreading the runway strut she's going to make me do.

Spending time with my mom and her boyfriend hasn't been as bad as I anticipated. England was a lot of fun. We toured pretty much every historical landmark. I was able to meet with a penpal I've had since high school. Steffi and I have written back and forth many times and video chatted once technology became available, but seeing her in person was so special. We lost touch over the years, but we've been chatting more since my dad passed. She's hoping to make a trip to the U.S. next year. I'm already looking forward to it.

I'm glad I have friends again. I wouldn't trade a second of caring for and being with my dad. Now that he's gone, I've been longing for girlfriends to sip margaritas with on random weeknights. I've missed going to sappy movies and talking about the books we're reading. I miss shopping with them and having nights on the couch just to gossip and watch trash TV while sharing a bottle of wine. I miss true friendship.

Claire has been a godsend. She's so unlike me, but I love that she offers a different perspective. She's outgoing and brutally honest. She doesn't give a shit what people think of her. Her political and religious views are different from mine, but I like that she challenges me to think more critically about my views. Most of what I believe and know was fed to me since birth. Not that that's a bad thing necessarily. I consider myself an open-minded person but haven't had deep, fruitful, and constructive conversations about hot-ticket topics people argue about.

But not us.

I've always been very accepting but not knowledgeable or exposed to much, I suppose. Claire knows a lot about many things, yet she remains respectful of my opinions.

However, I don't know much about Claire's personal life. She keeps details pretty private. I know she was a traveling nurse, particularly during COVID, before settling back home in Pittsburgh and getting a job at Bellevue. She expressed working in hospice is her calling, and it truly is. She is a beautiful person inside and out.

Shortly after my dad's passing, she said we were going out and wouldn't tell me where. She took me to a gay bar in Lawrenceville, where we saw drag queens perform. Let me tell you, it was the best time I ever had at a bar. The atmosphere, the costumes, the makeup, the music—all of it made me feel so free and uplifted. The staff and patrons were friendly and fun, and everyone was there to have a good time and be entertained. It didn't matter what I looked like or the fact that I'm straight. Everyone accepted everyone.

Underneath all the makeup, hair dye, wigs, fake nails, and outfits, we are all just people trying to survive this life.

Here's the thing though. None of us makes it out alive.

C'est la vie.

CHAPTER THIRTY-FIVE

BILLIE

I woke up feeling *blah* today. By now, I assumed I'd be adjusted to the time changes and jet lag. I've been on European time for nearly six weeks, but I cannot shake the exhaustion. I slept twelve hours last night, yet I still can't seem to function. I'm lying on the couch watching movies on my iPad, and that's probably where I'm going to stay the rest of the day.

"Honey, why don't we take today off from our sightseeing and rest? You look worn out. Get some sleep. I'll get you some wedding soup from the café down the street." My mom grabs her parka and designer handbag before walking up to me and kissing me on the head. I don't know when my mom decided to become all "motherly," but it's nice to have her actually care about someone else other than herself and her boyfriend.

I look up and smile at her. "Sounds good, Mom. I could use the break."

"Pierre and I are going to run some quick errands. I won't see anything important without you. I'll be back with that soup in a little while."

"Okay, have fun," I call out as she and Pierre leave for another day of shopping.

As soon as the door closes, my iPad rings. Claire is video calling me. It's 5 a.m. there, so I wonder what's wrong. Or maybe she worked the night shift. I swipe my finger to answer the call and let out a huge yawn.

"Hey, Billie. Out too late partying last night? Drinking too much of that authentic Italian wine?" Claire asks, too chipper for the time of day.

"You're up early." I yawn again.

"I haven't been to bed. I was supposed to be done at eleven last night, but we lost a patient, so I stayed with the family until they were ready to go home."

The realness of that pain strikes my core, but I don't let her know it. I yawn again.

"Ugh. I'm sorry. I can barely keep my eyes open today. I've been tired the last few days, but today I don't even want to get out of bed. This jet lag is wicked."

"Maybe you're pregnant," Claire jokes.

Laughter.

Silence.

Panic!

I shoot up from my lounging position. I throw the iPad like a frisbee onto the couch and bolt for my phone.

"What's wrong? Billie, where'd you go?"

I always track my cycle on an app, but I haven't checked it recently because life has clearly been crazy. Scott and I used protection every time except during the hot, steamy office make-up sex, but I was on day twenty of my cycle. I normally ovulate between twelve and fourteen days. Like clockwork.

Where is my phone?!?

I abandon ship and dart to my suitcase to look for a box of tampons. I would have had a period by now. I pull out the unopened box.

Oh, no! Shit. Shit. Shit.

My hands are shaking as I look frantically for my phone. I can hear Claire calling for me from the other room, but I'm so petrified I can't respond. I snatch my phone from the nightstand and wince as I prepare for impact when I press the tracking app's icon.

You're 42 days late.

"Oh, God! Claiiiiiiire?" I shout, rushing back over to the couch. I grab the iPad, my face as white as a ghost.

"What's wrong? Where'd you go? Are you okay?" Claire looks worried.

"I think I *am* pregnant. I'm forty-two days late." I show her my phone screen. I hold my hand over my mouth because I suddenly feel nauseous.

"Oh, my...No way. You need to get a test! Like *pronto!*"

"What if I'm pregnant? How am I going to tell Scott? What if he's mad?" My mind floods with anxiety. In no way do I feel any sense of joy or excitement—only pure fear.

"Honey, why would he be mad?" Claire asks with concern.

"Because maybe he's not ready for all this. I was the one who forgot the condom when we did it in his office. Maybe he'll think I trapped him into staying with me. I'm not sure I'm ready for all this. We've been together, what, a few months?" I shake my head in disbelief. "I mean, I love him with all my heart, but a baby? That changes everything."

"Well, go get a test before you hop down the rabbit hole, and call me when you take it so you're not alone. Unless you'd rather do that with Scott."

"No, I want to be sure before I tell him." I pace the room, chewing my bottom lip hard enough to taste blood. I trace the crescent-shaped scar in the middle of my palm from the glass-throwing incident.

"Okay, I will buy a test and call you back as soon as I can. Please keep your phone next to you turned all the way up."

"I promise you I will answer on the first ring." Claire's tone turns sympathetic. "It's going to be all right. If you're pregnant, we can talk about your options."

I shake my head because I've already made up my mind, terrified or not. "If I'm pregnant, I will keep this baby whether Scott wants to be involved or not."

"It's settled then. But you know he won't abandon you, Bills."

"I don't really know. I left for this trip after the huge fight at his office that almost ended us, and we've slowly been working on our relationship. Things are going really well, but parents? We're not even married."

"You know, you don't have to be married to have and raise kids," Claire retorts.

"I know. Catholic guilt. But we haven't been together all that long."

"So what?" Claire shrugs. "My parents got married six months after they met."

"Claire, they're divorced!" I exclaim.

"Oh, shit. You're right. Bad example. But lots of other people stay together."

I take a deep breath in an attempt to calm my pounding heart. "I guess you're right. Okay, I'll call you as soon as I get back."

"I'll be here."

I end the call, then throw on presentable clothing. I grab my wristlet, phone, and room key and speed walk to the nearest convenience store. My mind is racing. I go through all the times when we were together, and none of them were near my peak ovulation days. The only explanation is that I ovulated late and conceived on his office couch. Or the condoms simply failed.

I missed a period entirely. I've never in my life skipped one, and I'm beyond belief I didn't realize it sooner. I have been religious in tracking my menstruation, ovulation, and sexual encounters with Scott. After I left for this trip, I didn't think of it because I knew we wouldn't be together.

I find a little corner shop and start scanning the aisles. I see two different types, so I grab two of each and take them to the counter.

"Buongiorno," the cashier says, welcoming me.

"Buongiorno," I reply politely but impatiently. She rings me up. As I try to pay, the coins drop onto the counter because my hands are shaking uncontrollably. I hand her several other bills. The cashier expresses concern, but she can tell I don't speak Italian. I don't wait for my change.

"Grazie," I say, grabbing the bag and rushing back to the hotel.

I call Claire back as soon as I open the door. She answers on the first ring.

"Do you think it'll be a boy or a girl?"

She doesn't even say *hello*.

"Oh, you're so sure I'm pregnant. Maybe it's stress from all the shit that's happened these last few months. Stress can throw off your menstruation."

"It can *also* throw off your ovulation," she warns.

"Fuck, you're right. Okay, I'm going to go pee on this stick. I'll be right back," I call out as I scurry to the bathroom.

"I'll be here."

I can't read the directions because they're obviously in Italian, but I'm smart enough to figure out the illustrations pretty easily. I pee on the stick for five seconds and wait a few minutes until something pops up on the digital screen. Easy enough.

Once I'm done, I set the test flat on the bathroom vanity, walk out to the kitchen table, and grab the iPad.

"My heart is pounding right now. I think I might pass out," I say. I'm hyperventilating and starting to feel a little woozy.

"Now, get yourself calmed down. No one else is there with you, so you can't pass out. You could hurt the baby."

"You're not helping, Claire!"

She seems amused by this, and maybe some levity is what I need. I pace back and forth and pour myself a glass of water. I take three large gulps. Fortunately, I don't feel like I'm going to pass out anymore.

"How long do I need to wait? Do you think it's done?" I ask impatiently.

"It's been six minutes. You can go check. Wait! Take me with you!"

"I'll cover the test and bring it out here. Hang on."

I inhale deeply to compose myself. I decode that a positive test will display *incinta*, and a negative one will show *non incinta*. I place my hand over the test, making sure I do not look without Claire.

"Okay, are you ready?" I ask, my eyes squeezed shut.

"Give 'er to me straight."

I relax and open my eyes. I look down.

Incinta.

Pregnant. No question about it.

Instantly, a warm wave surges through my entire body.

Oh. My. God.

I'm going to have a baby. Holy shit, I'm a mother. I huff out all the air in my lungs, place my hand on my chest, and smile.

"Well? What does it say, Bills?!" Claire asks eagerly. I look up at her with tears in my eyes and show her the test.

"I'm pregnant."

CHAPTER THIRTY-SIX

SCOTT

G ood morning, ladies."

"Good morning, Scott. Hi, Bruno!" Roberta greets us.

Bruno trots up to Claire and Roberta, who are sitting at the front desk at Bellevue, to receive his love and affection like he does every time we arrive.

"Scott, do you have a few minutes to chat?" Claire asks.

"Uh-oh. What did I do this time?" I jest. "Roberta, do you mind handling Bruno for me?"

"You don't even have to ask. Stay here, Bruno. You're going to hang out with Aunt Bertie." Bruno lies down on the dog bed Roberta pulls out from under the desk. That dog is well-loved, and it brings me joy that everyone around me treats him like a family member. He's my fur kid—possibly the only kind I may ever have—so he gets spoiled.

Claire leads me to the gazebo.

"Is everything okay?" I ask. Now, I can tell something is off because Claire is usually joking with me, but she's been quiet other than asking to talk privately.

"Totally fine. I wanted to check in and see how you're doing with Billie being gone and all." We sit down on the lounge chairs in the gazebo and take in the gorgeous view that I will never tire of seeing.

"I appreciate your asking." Maybe she is simply checking in with me. "I'm struggling," I reply, "and I don't think I can handle another two weeks without her."

"Funny you mention that because I know she's been missing you too. So...why don't you fly out to Italy to see her?" Claire asks matter-of-factly. She stands up and pretends to fluff fake snowdrops in the hanging basket at the entry of the gazebo.

"I'd love to, but I can't take off work. I'm booked solid for the next six months."

"Well, you better not book out much further than that!" Claire exclaims.

"Why? What's wrong?" I'm sensing an elephant in the gazebo.

"Nothing! Nothing is wrong. I mean, you two should take a trip together soon and enjoy each other's company. I just thought maybe that time could be now since she's already in the most romantic city in the world, but I understand. Work is busy. A doctor is always on duty." Claire moves over to another hanging basket.

She does have a point. "You're right. I'll talk to Miranda later today and see if I can get something on the calendar. Billie and I deserve it."

"You absolutely do. Are you doing all right otherwise?" she inquires.

"Yes, actually. I recently closed on the house. The renovations are already underway. Therapy has been going really well. I see Shelly twice a week. I've been going to grief meetings weekly. I think I'm finally getting my shit together, as Billie so gently suggested." I chuckle with amused sarcasm.

There's a brief silence as we look over the rolling hills of the landscape.

"Claire?"

"Scott?"

"What do you think about me proposing to Billie?" I hear a loud-pitched squeal erupt from her. "I take that as a *yes*?"

"Yes! One hundred percent yes. Do it." She claps her hands excitedly and jumps up and down. "Are you going to do it when she gets back?"

"Well, I was going to wait a while because everything is fresh. But maybe that trip I'll plan for us this summer will be perfect."

"No! You can't wait that long!" Claire shouts, making me jump in surprise.

"Why? We haven't been together that long. I don't want to rush into a marriage if we're not ready. Plus, I just bought that house. I figured that'd be enough of a surprise when she gets back. I mean, I know for sure she's it for me, but maybe she's not sure. I may end up selling that house before I move into it!"

The reality that Billie could hate the house or doesn't want to move in together turns my stomach. She wouldn't have to move in right away. Everything would happen when she's ready. Regardless, I know it's time to say goodbye to the house I shared with Christine and make a new home, preferably with Billie.

"Oh, no. She's sure. I mean, I'm sure she's sure too."

"Claire, is there something you're not telling me? Is Billie okay? She didn't meet some Italian prince and decide to marry him, has she?" Worry gnaws at my insides.

"Well, you can rest assured she hasn't because Italy does not have a monarchy. It's a democratic republic."

"Maybe she found one of those guys who leads the canoes down the river."

"You mean a gondolier and a gondola?" She laughs.

"How do you know so much about Italy?" I ask skeptically.

"I talk to Billie practically every day, you know. She tells me everything."

"Everything? In that case, what aren't you telling me?" I fold my arms and look at her expectantly. I know something is going on, but Claire isn't budging on any details.

"Listen, everything is fine. Billie is great. She's having a blast, but I know she misses you. I'm sure she would love to see you. Plus, if you're planning to propose anyway, why not do it now and start living happily ever after? You could propose on one of those canoes that those guys lead down the river."

Claire elbows me in jest. And maybe she has a great idea.

"*Miranda*. My dear, sweet, extraordinary Miranda," I sing-song to her, pouting my lips and batting my eyelashes, which gets her every time.

"Whatever you need, the answer is *no*." Miranda eyes me over her bifocals but doesn't stop typing.

Apparently, not this time.

"Fine. I want to propose to Billie, and I want to catch the next flight out of here and ask her to marry me on a gondola. Then, when we get back, I'm going to surprise her with the house of her dreams."

"What's a gondo—hang on! You bought a house? You want to propose? When did all this happen? Did you buy a ring?" Miranda sits back in her office chair and folds her arms.

"The house is a done deal, and the ring is with the jeweler. I picked it out this morning. Listen, can you make it happen that I can take time off? I need two weeks." I give Miranda the puppy dog eyes and pout my bottom lip again. It's worth another shot.

"Two weeks?! Come on, Scottie, I'm good, but I'm not...." She types feverishly on the keyboard and clicks aggressively with her mouse. "Oh, wait, I am that good. You're all clear, Dr. Bennington. Everything will be rescheduled. Enjoy your flight. And you sure as *hell* better let me see that sparkler on her finger when you get back."

I tackle her with the biggest bear hug and a dramatic kiss on the forehead.

"You're the best!" I squeal like a child.

"Scottie?"

"Yeah?"

"It better be one hell of a rock on that finger if she's going to marry your sorry ass," she says with her unmistakable sass, smiling at me warmly and winking.

"Thank you," I mouth to her.

I'm getting married!

"I'm getting married!" I call out to no one after I shut the door to my office, assuming Billie will say *yes*. I want to spend the rest of my life with her. I pull out my phone and book the first flight to Italy.

CHAPTER THIRTY-SEVEN

SCOTT

It's only for a day. Two days max. I'm sorry. Dr. Ross wants to take us on a golf outing. He said they don't get good cell service out there. I don't want you to be worried if you can't reach me for a while." I hate lying to Billie, but it's absolutely necessary if I'm going to pull off this surprise.

"I understand." Billie looks crushed on the other side of the video call. "I miss you so much. This trip has been fun and all, but I'm ready to come home. I was thinking of booking a flight out in a few days. I could be waiting for you when you get back from your boys' weekend."

"Aw, babe, no. You've got two weeks left. It'll fly by. Are you not enjoying yourself?" I ask, concerned.

I see tears welling in her eyes.

"Billie, hey. Honey, what's wrong? Did something happen between you and your mom?" She shakes her head and wipes away her tears.

"Nothing, babe. I'm homesick, and I wish you were here."

"I'll be right here waiting the moment you step off that plane, and we never have to be apart again. You hear me?" She nods her head and wipes away another tear.

"I love you, Scott. Please don't ever leave me, okay?"

"I love you too. Leave you? Why would I do that? I've been putting in the work. Therapy. Grief counseling. The whole nine. You were right. I needed to get my shit together, and I'm getting my shit together. I want to be the best version of myself so you get to have the best version of me. Shelly told me that last part," I say matter-of-factly.

"I know you are, and that's amazing. I'm so proud of you."

She's *still* crying.

"I'm committed to you, babe. I'm yours. We've got this," I assure her.

"I think...I think...." She tries to end the call, but I hear everything. She's heaving and vomiting. Then the call drops.

She must really not be feeling well. I hope she doesn't have a stomach bug.

Wait. Full stop!

She's tired.

She cried our entire call.

She's suddenly afraid of me leaving her.

And now she vomited.

Christine felt this way when.... It hits me like a ton of bricks.

She's pregnant!

I'm pacing the length of my living room while Bruno's head swivels back and forth. "She's pregnant. She's gotta be. That's why Claire was acting weird, and it explains Billie's unusual behavior." I'm talking out loud to myself but to Bruno too. I haven't told anyone about my suspicions, but I feel pretty confident. It all makes perfect sense.

"I'm gonna be a dad. Holy shit. Holy shit! A father!" I start hyperventilating because the gravity of it all is scaring the shit out of me. I bend over and put my hands over my kneecaps.

What if Billie loses the baby?

What if something bad happens to her?

The post-traumatic memories flood me, sending me into a panic attack. I need to get myself under control. My flight leaves in a few hours, enough time to pack, pick up the ring, drop Bruno off at Claire's, and attempt a last-minute therapy session. Okay, I don't know for sure if Billie is *actually* pregnant, but I would be surprised if she weren't, given her symptoms.

I pull out my phone and text Shelly.

ME

I need a session immediately. It's an emergency.

Just as I finish packing, my phone pings.

SHELLY

I'll call you in 15 minutes.

"All right, fifteen minutes. I can handle this. You're going to be okay, Scott. It's not going to be the same as Christine and Maggie. Everything is going to be fine this time. You're going to marry Billie. You're going to have a baby with her. You got her the house of her dreams. You're going to share a long life together as a family."

I continue talking aloud. Shelly says it's a healthy coping mechanism—a way to process what's happening and engage with the rational side of my brain when I'm feeling emotionally out of control. I think it's working because my heart rate is stabilizing. I no longer feel like I'm having a panic attack.

Once I'm composed, I become determined.

"Go get your wife, Scott."

I grab my luggage and Bruno and walk out the door. It closes behind me, and I don't look back this time.

Shelly calls me while I'm on my way to Claire's. Claire is dropping me off at the airport so I don't have to leave my car there for two weeks. I explain everything that's happening as fast as I can. Before I've finished emotionally vomiting, I have to pull over because there's no way we're going to be done before I get to Claire's condo.

"That's...a lot to take in," she soothes. I know it seems stereotypical to think all therapists have a comforting voice, but she really does.

"Please tell me everything is going to be okay." I'm trembling with fear. Not fear of Billie being pregnant or me becoming a dad or me marrying her—rather losing them and reliving my worst nightmare a second time.

"I can't tell you that because I don't know the future. But I will tell you that manifesting a good outcome goes a long way for finding peace and reducing anxiety. You have all your coping skills in place for when you're triggered or feeling out of control. Use them. You'll be just fine."

"Thank you, Shelly. I really needed this. You know, you're really great at this therapy stuff."

"Oh, Scott, I know," she laughs. "Now, good luck on your trip, and tell me all about it when you get back. Two weeks. You're on my calendar."

"You bet." I end the call and text Claire I'm two minutes away.

When I arrive, she's already outside waiting for us.

"Bruno! Buddy! Come here to Auntie Claire."

As soon as I open the car door, Bruno makes a beeline for her extended arms. When I finally catch up to him, Claire asks, "So, are you all ready for your big trip? You're welcome for the suggestion." She grins wide enough that I can see all her teeth.

"She's pregnant, isn't she?" I blurt out, foregoing a greeting and starting off our conversation strong. Claire freezes and her eyes pop.

"Wait, she told you already?"

Caught red-handed!

"So she *is* pregnant! I knew it. I just knew it. Everything makes sense now. Your acting weird, well, weirder than normal, and Billie feeling exhausted. On our call the other day, she cried and then threw up. I heard it all."

Claire grimaces.

"How long have you known?" I probe suspiciously. Claire's face turns a rosy shade of pink.

"Just a few days. Not long, I swear." Claire looks like a puppy dog who's been busted for chewing a pair of designer shoes.

"Well, I'm glad you didn't tell me. Obviously, that's something she should do. Is she okay with it? I need all the details. I don't want to walk into this blindly. I need to handle this well. I have to handle this well for the sake of our relationship and our future."

"She's afraid you're going to be mad at her and leave her and said she's keeping the baby whether you have anything to do with them or not, basically." Claire laughs because we both know I would never desert them.

"How could she think I would be *mad* at her for something like this? We both knew what we were doing. We never really talked about kids more than once a while ago, but I would never abandon my wife and child. Never."

Wife. I feel invigorated saying that again.

"Good, because I'd kill you myself if you did," Claire warns.

"Here, look. What do you think?" I pull out the engagement ring. It's a two-carat oval-cut solitaire diamond set in platinum. The band is dazzling, with smaller round diamonds halfway around.

"It's breathtaking. She's going to love it." Claire's eyes well up.

"Are you...are you crying, Claire?" I ask sarcastically. Claire isn't one to cry easily. In the time I've known her, I've never seen her shed a single tear.

"You guys are so...so...perfect for each other!" She pulls me in for a hug. "I wish I could be there to watch you propose, but I'm sure I'll get every single detail."

"Every last one. Now let's go. I have a flight to catch."

The journey to Rome is long and uneventful. When I leave the airport, I pull out the location of Billie's accommodations and hail a taxi. I don't speak a word of Italian, so I hand the driver the paper with the hotel's address. He nods in understanding.

When I get to the door of her hotel room, I'm almost too afraid to knock. I didn't even give her mom a heads-up that I was coming.

Do it already!

I knock three times.

No answer.

Shit, what if she's not here?

I knock again, a little louder this time.

"Coming!" I hear Billie's voice.

Phew.

The door opens and there she is. Simply stunning as always.

"*Scott!*" she cries, leaping into my arms. I kiss and hug her amorously, easing my grip when I realize I may squish the baby.

"Billie, my love." I inhale her signature sweet floral scent.

"What are you doing here? I thought you were golfing." She huffs in disbelief.

"I didn't want to lie to you, but it took me a day to get here. I didn't want you to fret if I didn't answer. I'm sorry. I didn't want to ruin the surprise. You're happy to see me, right?"

Tears fill her eyes and stream down her cheeks. Yep, she's definitely pregnant. Those hormones are wicked. She nods her head as she cries into my chest. I hold her until she releases me.

"I'm here now. Let's enjoy every second of this trip," I assure her.

"How long are you staying? I want to come home with you."

"I'm here until you leave, babe. Two weeks. The flight here sucked, but I was able to get on the same flight home with you. I made sure of that."

"God, I love you." She kisses me with such passion I'm hard instantly. She's been gone for six weeks, and I've missed my woman. She promptly leads me to her bedroom.

I feel whole, once again.

The next morning, I'm awakened by a soft kiss on the cheek and the smell of freshly brewed coffee.

"I'm glad I got to wake up beside you this morning, darling." I prop myself up and accept the cup of steaming coffee.

"Good morning. You slept like a rock last night."

"You did too, except for when you were snoring."

"I do not snore!" Billie protests.

"I can assure you, you do. And you drool too."

"Stop," she whines, giving me a playful swat.

"It's a cute drool." I give her a wink. "Where's your coffee?"

"Oh, I didn't want any this morning. I made some tea instead."

No coffee, probably because of the caffeine.

"Is it decaf?" I inquire.

"Yes," she says hesitantly, "it is. I've been trying to detox from caffeine. I was drinking way too much when Dad was at Bellevue. I was starting to feel paranoid."

Preg-nant.

I'm honestly surprised she hasn't told me about our baby yet. "So, what do you want to do today?" I ask.

"Well, how do you feel about going to the Vatican? I have to see it before we leave."

"That's perfect. I know how important your faith is to you. I would love to share that experience together."

"Are you sure? I mean, I don't want you to feel like I'm pressuring you or forcing you to do religious activities you're not open to or ready for."

"It was on my list of things I wanted to see too. Really."

She gives me an excited kiss on the lips.

"You're the best. I love you. Okay, I'm gonna go get ready!"

The Bridge of Angels is in the Vatican.

If that isn't a sign from our loved ones that today is the day to pop the question, then I don't know what is. I chug the rest of my coffee and prepare to propose to the most beautiful woman I've ever seen. The one who's carrying my child.

Our tour of the Vatican thus far has been beautiful. We start off at St. Peter's Basilica, followed by the Vatican Grottoes, which are conveniently located beneath the basilica. Then we take a guided tour through the Vatican Gardens. Pictures do not do any of them justice.

Next, we stop at a quaint eatery for lunch. Italian pasta, of course. Afterward, we visit the Sistine Chapel, which is as magnificent as everyone says. I get chills several times because the ambience is overwhelming.

Before we get to the Bridge of Angels, we explore the Piazza del Risorgimento. We listen to the street performers and purchase a few knickknacks from the vendors. When we finish our stroll, I ask Billie if she is up for one more stop. She tells me there is no way she is leaving without crossing the Bridge of Angels, after a detour for a gelato. I can't help but smile to myself.

We both indulge. It does not disappoint. Italian gelato is a ten out of ten.

The sun is just starting to set as we arrive at the Bridge of Angels. We take our time absorbing the breathtaking landscape.

Billie says, bewildered, "This view takes my breath away. It is absolutely mesmerizing."

I look over at her and reply, "Yes, it really is."

She knows I mean her, and she flashes a bashful smile.

Now's the time.

I turn my body toward her. I grab both her hands and pull them to my chest. "Billie, I need to ask you something."

"Anything." She offers me her full attention, and I'm positive she can feel my body shaking. I take a deep breath.

"Billie, I have been drawn to you since the second we smoked that cigarette together." She giggles briefly because that wasn't the smoothest opening line, but it's true. I clear my throat. "I know our circumstances of meeting weren't ideal. But you've been the best thing that's happened to me in a very long time. You have the most gracious heart. You're smart and funny and so damn sexy I can barely contain myself around you. I want to cherish you every day for the rest of our lives."

I see her body language acknowledge what is happening, her eyes glassy and lips quivering.

"Belinda Marie Carlisle, I love you body and soul, today, tomorrow, and always. And I will love you even after my last breath."

I get down on one knee and present the ring. She gasps.

"Will you please do me the honor of being my wife?"

I expect her to immediately shout *yes* and leap into my arms, but she doesn't move. I wait a few seconds before prompting a response.

"Billie?"

Hold on—is she going to say no?

"Scott, I need to tell you something before I answer."

The baby news. That's right. Here it comes. I'm ready.

"Please, tell me you didn't sleep with a gondolier!" I blurt. I blame the sarcasm on the nerves.

"What? No!"

"I was kidding. I'm sorry." I rise to her level, because being on one knee this long without a response is awkward. "What do you need to tell me?" I make my eyes smolder and try to change my expression to one that's more serious, but I'm still grinning.

"I...we're...well...I'm pregnant," Billie stutters.

Her expression pleads for a positive response. She must feel afraid because I feel her body shivering. Without delay, I cup her face in my hands and tuck a piece of hair behind her ear. I kiss her. I kiss her until she relaxes her stiff, quivering stance.

When we open our eyes, I murmur, "I know." I give her a toothy kiss because I can't stop smiling. She steps back, bemused.

"How did you know? Did Claire tell you?"

"No, I figured it out myself. You said how tired you were, and I could tell you weren't being honest about tasting all kinds of wine because Cortese is a white wine, not a red one. Plus, well, you've been crying on our calls, and I heard you vomit the other day when you thought you hung up on me. This morning you weren't drinking coffee, which is particularly odd for you, and the cherry on top was your craving for gelato. I put two and two together."

"I guess the signs were pretty obvious, now that you put it that way. So you're not upset? Are you all right with this?"

I'm terrified, but I'm certainly not going to tell her that. I'll work through it, nevertheless.

Manifesting.

"You're carrying life inside you. Billie, I could never be upset with you over something we did together. We made this child. I will be by your side every step of the way."

I can feel the fear dissipate from her body. Mine remains wound tightly from head to toe.

"I love you, Scott. I love you and this tiny little baby we've made." She places my hands on her belly.

"So, are you saying *yes*?" I ask optimistically.

"Well, actually, do you mind proposing again? This moment is super romantic and unbelievable and perfect and..." Billie looks around, taking in the scenery. "I want to give you the response you deserve."

I don't make a smart-ass comment this time because I would do anything for her right now, the mother of my child. I clear my throat and drop to one knee again.

"Billie, a few months ago we were strangers. Now look at us. You're my miracle. You've given me a purpose for living. You've given me hope, your trust, and this precious baby. With you, I'm not afraid of what the future holds. As long as you're by my side, I will adore you every day. I love you, Billie. Will you marry me?"

I present the ring again and she cries out, "Yes!" I slide the ring down her left ring finger and kiss her hand. I pull her into me and kiss her passionately. She reciprocates just as strongly. Time seems to stand still as we absorb this unforgettable moment. I then brush her cheek with my thumb and gaze into her glittery brown eyes.

"I love you, Mrs. Bennington," I whisper.

She blinks affectionately, looking back at me with heavy eyes, and whispers back, "I love *you*, Dr. Bennington."

CHAPTER THIRTY-EIGHT

BILLIE

I'm engaged! *Aah!!!*

I didn't have "getting engaged on my European trip" on this year's bingo card, but I daubed that fantasy. I stare wistfully at my ring finger and place my other hand on my belly. Scott picked out the perfect ring. It's more than I could have ever hoped for.

Scott is lounging on the terrace admiring the Italian landscape when the kettle whistles. I steep our tea and join him. He caresses my hand, which sends shivers up my arm. He slides his hand on my belly. Unexpectedly, a sob erupts.

"What's wrong, Billie?" Scott asks, tenderly wiping away my tears.

"On my way out here, I thought to myself that I should call my dad and tell him all the good news. It hit me just now that he's not here anymore. He's going to miss everything, Scott. He'll never see me get married. He can't walk me down the aisle. He'll never meet his grandchild. I'll have to live the rest of my life without him. Death is cruel for the living!" I bury myself in his chest, releasing one ugly cry, complete with snot dripping from my nose and onto his shirt. Scott doesn't seem to mind. He holds me, caresses my hair, and kisses my head.

This has to be what true love is. To love another man and to have him love me in return. I didn't know it could feel this intense yet comfortable.

"I think I'm ready for you to watch the video my dad made for me." I wipe my face with a tissue, then pull out my phone.

"I'm ready if you are." Watching the video this time is easier to digest, but seeing my dad again takes my breath away. When the video ends, I feel a teardrop land on my forehead and notice Scott wiping his eyes.

"That was a beautiful video. I understand why you asked me about yellow roses and the number 18. There's no way that was a coincidence. There has to be something beyond this life, where your dad, Christine, and Maggie are healed and happy. There has to be."

During dinner later this evening, we tell my mom and Pierre we got engaged. She cries happy tears, hugging Scott and me together and jumping up and down. Once she settles, we break the news about the baby. She freaks out—but excitedly. I don't remember ever seeing her this genuinely happy before. Part of me had expected her to rant about having a baby out of wedlock and condemning me for not waiting until marriage.

Meanwhile, I heard her and Pierre several times doing... whatever it was they were doing. Maybe she has finally accepted the fact that people can make choices and not feel embarrassed and ashamed about them all the time. Pierre is good for my mom, I will admit. He wishes us well and says he is very happy for us. I can see why my mom likes him. Besides Pierre's being a well-rounded person, there's something sexy and mysterious about a man who speaks a romantic language and attempts speaking English with that accent. It would make any woman swoon.

Things with my mom are stable for now. I do appreciate her trying. I know our relationship will never be what I have wanted or longed for, but I remain optimistic that things between us will continue to improve. After all, she's going to be a grandma later this year, and I would hate for our broken relationship to impact my baby.

The last two weeks with Scott in Italy are simply divine. And the sex? I don't know what happens down there with nerve endings and whatnot, but it has been out of this world. Everything feels different, more intense, more pleasurable. And since I'm already pregnant, no condoms ever, and I love it. He can't keep his hands off me either. He said knowing that I am carrying his child makes me even more attractive to him, and he always makes it clear how much he loves my body since the breakfast boob incident.

I do see a huge improvement in Scott, particularly with expressing his feelings. I can tell he's been working really hard in therapy to find joy with someone else—with me. And I've been putting in the work too. I'm going to therapy as I always have, virtually while I've been away. Lately, I've been focusing on my relationship with Scott and processing the loss of my dad in conjunction with the events of the past two years.

I am thrilled to be back on U.S. soil again. I'm dying to see Bruno too. I've really missed him. Claire just picked us up from the airport and is driving us back to Scott's house. I've been feeling particularly nauseated this week, especially since the flight. Consequently, I am in desperate need of a comfortable, familiar bed. When we get to town, however, she starts taking turns that don't lead anywhere close to where Scott lives.

"Claire, where are you going?" I ask, irritated.

"I'm taking you home, silly," she scoffs.

"Um, last time I checked, Scott's house wasn't anywhere near the plaza," I argue.

"Hold your horses, Bills," she snaps. I turn to Scott, who's sitting next to me in the back seat.

"Scott, what is going on? I don't want to stop anywhere right now. I'm whupped and, if I don't eat strawberry toaster pastries within the next fifteen minutes, I'm going to have a meltdown. Claire, please tell me you got some."

"Here." She tosses an entire box back to me. I tear open the packaging and begin devouring one. Toaster pastries are one of the only foods I don't immediately regurgitate.

"We're almost there. I promise," Scott assures me.

"Almost where?" I probe.

We turn into a beautiful neighborhood and pull into the driveway of a large house. Scott gets out of the car and opens the back door for me to get out. I'm utterly bewildered.

"Scott," I ask hesitantly, "what is this?"

"It's *our* home." I stand there breathless and in shock. It looks exactly like the home I described during the heated argument that likely resulted in this pregnancy.

"You didn't! Did you buy this house? When? How?" My thoughts are racing, trying to comprehend what's happening.

"I did buy this house. I bought it the week after you left and closed on it right before I arrived in Italy. It's mostly furnished, but we can change it to whatever you want. The wraparound porch isn't done yet, as you can see, but the contractors will be finished with it soon. The wooden swing is set up. The fence was recently installed, and I planted two oak trees in the middle of the backyard. Those won't be ready for pretend adventures for a while though."

"You remembered," I cry. There I go again with the tears. These hormones, I tell ya.

"Every word." Scott puts his arm around my shoulders and kisses me on the top of my head. "I hope this suits you. It's not a mansion, and there aren't any maids or butlers," he jests.

"I'll settle for a cleaner once a week. Deal?" I laugh.

"Deal."

"This is perfect, Scott. This is absolutely perfect."

CHAPTER THIRTY-NINE

BILLIE

O ver the next several weeks, we settle into our new home. The house truly is everything I could have hoped for— maybe more. The large kitchen has white cabinets with countertops of black granite with golden flakes. The counters look like they shimmer, even in the dark. The walls were originally white, but I told him I wanted to go bold, so we—*okay I* —picked mermaid green. It looks phenomenal. And the walk-in pantry...oh, it is fantastic. A far cry from the standing cabinet stuffed with snacks and the cereal boxes that line the top of the fridge at my father's house. Don't get me wrong, I *love* that house and all its character, but there's definitely a lot more room here.

The white oak hardwood floors create a spacious effect. The kitchen blends into the family room, where two oversized dark-gray couches sit across from each other. A recliner large enough to fit both Scott and me sits beside the couch on the right side of the room. The flat screen TV hangs above the gas fireplace. The mantel will be where I display all my favorite holiday decor. The speckled rug combines splashes of mahogany, blue, orange, and red, perfect for hiding future toddler messes. Giant sliding French doors on the far side of the kitchen open to a gorgeous covered deck. The flat grassy yard extends an acre to a tree line. I look forward to grilling and chilling out there this summer.

The entrance to the house presents a show-stopping crystal waterfall chandelier that dangles from the high ceiling, with a grand staircase to the right. The room to the right of the entryway is supposed to be a formal living room, but we're making it our office for when Scott comes home early but needs to finish up paperwork and I decide to go back to work, whenever that may be. The left side is the formal dining room, with a long table, large enough to host ten. The top half of the walls is navy blue. The bottom half is white wainscoting patterned with large squares the entire way around the room.

This house is five stars. How lucky I am that Scott has chosen to provide our family with this home! He has a heart of gold, and I am starting to feel guilty again about going off on him at his office. He's doing everything he promised, yet I'm responsible for hurting him deeply. I know I did. I would choose him with or without this house. As long as we are together, I couldn't care less where we live. I know our relationship is a bit unconventional, but I wouldn't have it any other way.

The weather has been gray, dry, and cold, typical for western Pennsylvania in late January. Now that the trip and holidays are over, I'm beginning to feel a new wave of grief. I don't have many memories of the holidays, my first ones without Dad. It's likely I subconsciously blacked them out because the pain is so raw. I'm fine with it though. I don't want to remember the pain.

The reality that I'm unable to tell my dad about getting engaged or having a baby is burrowing deep into my core. I hate that I can't show him the new house. He will never play ball or dress up with his grandchild. He will never attend sporting events or band concerts. We will never go for ice cream again or hit up a Pirates game in the sweltering July heat.

I miss him terribly. And while my future gleams, my entire being is overshadowed by the hazy fog of sorrow.

I'm sitting at the bay window in the office when Scott arrives home from work.

"Hey, honey! How was your day?" he greets me, with a kiss on the cheek. "Sweetheart, why are you crying?"

This crying is getting out of control, but I can't help it. Any little thing, whether it be sad, funny, or sweet, sets off the water-works these days.

"I miss my dad so much, Scott. I still can't believe he's gone." My sniffles turn into blubbering. He kneels down to wrap me into his arms.

"I know, babe. I saw how much you loved each other, and you know as well as I do that he's in Heaven watching over us. I know it doesn't ease the pain, but he's not missing a single thing. He just can't be here physically."

Instead of making me feel better like he anticipates, I start crying harder. "I'm sorry. I'm so very sorry."

"Sorry for what? You never have to apologize for mourning your dad." I shake my head, trying to get the words out between sucking in gulps of air and trembling.

"I should never have gotten so upset with you at your office that night. You were right, and I didn't want to hear you because I couldn't relate to how you felt. But the world appears dull now that he's gone. I'm sorry for being an insensitive jerk."

Scott pulls me in closer and runs his hands down my back. Once I'm able to get myself under control again, I sit back and see tears streaking his cheeks.

"It's all right, Billie. Grief sucks, plain and simple. I appreciate and accept your apology, but I forgave you that night. I regret not being more upfront with you. We're in such a good place now. I mean, look at us." I bow my head as fresh tears form in my eyes.

"Hey," Scott says as he places his hands on my cheeks and tilts my head up toward his so he can look into my eyes. His striking green eyes are filled with compassion. Instead of finishing his thought, he places a soft, heartfelt kiss on my lips, which begins to calm me.

"Are you hungry?" he asks.

"Yeah...I'm always hungry." I wipe my face with my sleeve. Scott hands me a tissue.

"What are you in the mood for? Do you want to get pizza from Santino's?"

My puckered lips curve into a smile. I nod my head *yes*.

"Cheese pizza and Pepsi. Got it." Scott picks up his phone to place the order.

"I also need a side of ranch dressing."

"For pizza?" Scott grimaces.

"Don't question it at this point." I shrug, surrendering to the craving. "It's the baby, I swear."

CHAPTER FORTY

SCOTT

I'm gathering up my things for the day because Billie has her first doctor's appointment and ultrasound this afternoon. I won't lie—I'm a nervous wreck. Everything is starting to feel real, petrifying if I'm being honest with myself. Being a husband and father doesn't frighten me in the least, but I continue to feel terrified that something will happen to Billie or the baby. I'm not sure I can handle another loss like that. Billie is around ten weeks pregnant, and Christine was only thirteen weeks along when we found out she was ill.

My stomach is bubbling with anxiety. I want to feel excited, but I feel like I might be sick. I walk out to reception to bid Miranda a nice day. "Enjoy the rest of your afternoon, Miranda. I'll see you tomorrow."

Miranda stands up abruptly, to lecture me, I'm sure. "Don't forget to bring me pictures of this little nugget. And I need all the details." She looks over her glasses and raises her eyebrows at me.

"I will. I promise."

"Uh-huh. You better or I'm retiring," she threatens.

"You wouldn't do that to me *now*...would you?" My heart skips a beat because Miranda's retirement would really suck.

"Just do what you're told and you won't have to find out." She really is something, that Miranda. She's a *fuck-around-and-find-out* type of person. Rest assured, I'll do what I'm told.

I'm meeting Billie at the doctor's office, which has a lab and imaging center in the same building. Having all her prenatal care except the delivery in one place relieves a lot of stress and anxiety I've been having, and I'm not even the one carrying the baby.

Billie is already parked in the lot, so I pull up beside her. She steps out, and her long, flowing chocolate hair dances in the wind. God, I love her.

"I think I'm going to pee my pants if I have to hold my bladder much longer," she groans.

"Let's get you to the restroom then." I usher her toward the entry of the office building.

"I can't. I have to have a full bladder for the ultrasound," she fake-cries.

"Oh, okay. Well, let's hope things move quickly and you don't pee yourself." We head briskly into the imaging center and check in.

"Fill out these forms and then sign here, Mrs. Carlisle." Billie takes the papers and turns to find a seat. *Mrs. Bennington. Mrs. Bennington!* I yell in my head. I know she's not my wife yet, but she's mine and has graciously agreed to accept my last name when the time comes. I don't want anyone calling her Mrs. anything else, but....

"Mrs. Carlisle?" an ultrasound technician calls into the waiting room. What I wouldn't give to say, *It's Bennington, for Pete's sake!* But I keep my mouth shut and follow Billie and the tech back to the ultrasound room. There's a bed, two chairs, an ultrasound system, and a television mounted on the wall across from the bed.

"You can have a seat. Billie, you'll need to take off all your clothes and put this paper robe on, with the opening in the front. We may need to do an internal ultrasound if we need clearer pictures."

"What's the difference?" Billie asks.

"For internal ultrasounds, I insert this transducer into your vagina. For external ultrasounds, I use this doppler over your abdomen where your uterus is."

"Sounds fabulous," Billie says sarcastically. The tech leaves the room, and Billie prepares herself for the ultrasound. I'd love to have my way with her right here on this bed, but that's probably frowned upon.

A few minutes later, the tech knocks lightly on the door. Billie and I say, "Come in" simultaneously.

"Alrighty, let's start with the external ultrasound, since you have a full bladder, and take a peek at this beautiful little baby, shall we? Go ahead and lie back on the bed. I'm going to put some warm gel on your belly."

Billie grabs my hand and I help ease her down. The tech squirts gel on her abdomen and places the doppler on top, wiggling and moving it back and forth.

"See, there is the baby." The tech points to the screen. There's our precious little baby, who resembles a kidney bean right now. Exciting nonetheless. I admire Billie, beautiful as ever, soaking in her first look at our child, which makes me feel *verklempt*.

"If you look right here," the tech continues, "do you see this little flicker? That's the heartbeat, at 168 beats per minute. That's exactly what we want to see."

The heart looks like it's twinkling. I can see the tiniest nubs for arms and legs forming. How incredible! I see a small tear glide down the side of Billie's face. She's so happy. I'm so happy.

The tech continues typing and clicking and moving the doppler across Billie's lower abdomen. When she's finished, she announces, "It looks like you're right on track at ten weeks and two days along. Based on your last period, your due date is August 18."

Of course the due date is 8-18. Thanks, Teddy. Yet it's so close to August 11, the day I lost Maggie.

Billie gasps in delight and squeezes my hand in reassurance. It's like she's reading my mind and knows exactly what I need. Meanwhile, I'm supposed to be the one supporting her.

"That sounds like the most perfect day to have a baby," Billie says tenderly.

"I'm going to give all this information to your doctor. Feel free to use the restroom, but do not get dressed. Keep this paper robe on and place this other paper blanket over your lap. The doctor will be in shortly to do your exam."

"Thank goodness! I am about to pee myself!" Billie laughs. I extend my hand to pull her up into a sitting position on the bed.

"Yes, that's probably the worst part of the first- and second-trimester ultrasounds," the tech sympathizes.

"Wait, I have to do this *again*?" Billie groans.

"Unfortunately. At least one more time, but you'll get to see a much better image of the baby around twenty weeks." The tech shuts the door as she leaves, and Billie bolts for the toilet. While she's doing her business, I pick up the ultrasound pictures of the tiniest little baby. Upon closer inspection, I can see the formation of the head and the arrow the tech added to the picture that points to the heart.

After the appointment, I ask Billie if she wants to grab lunch before we go home. She suggests Eats and Treats, a Pennsylvania gem with the *best* pastries and desserts, including my favorite massive chocolate chip cookies. Another thing I love about Billie is that she knows what and where she wants to eat.

When I was in my early twenties, before med school, a bunch of the guys would go out to the club and then hit up Eats and Treats for the all-night breakfast buffet. We used to sit in the smoking section that had glass dividers separating it from the non-smoking section and chain smoke. The buffet was filled with the tastiest and greasiest breakfast foods, which sobered me up many nights. I never left there without a chocolate chip cookie.

The building has since been torn down and rebuilt. There isn't a smoking section or buffet anymore, but the chocolate chip cookies are still as good as ever.

I hold out my hands to Billie as we sit across from each other in the booth. She places her hands in mine and relaxes her shoulders.

"I can't believe that's our baby." She looks over at the ultrasound pictures sitting on the table.

"It looks like you," I say sweetly.

"What, like a blob?" She seems offended, but she's kidding...I think.

"No, beautiful. I mean it." She smiles at me and releases her hands as our meals are placed in front of us. I got a turkey club and fries, and she ordered a buffalo chicken wrap with chips. We dig into our meals, as neither of us has eaten yet today, other than several saltine crackers and ginger ale Billie had shortly after she woke up.

"So..." Billie begins, as she swallows a bite of her wrap, "I'm struggling to decide when to go back to work. It's been a few months, so I should probably get back into the swing of things."

"You want to go back to work? Why?" I ask, with a mouthful of sandwich. I'm caught off guard a little. I guess we never had this discussion.

Billie furrows her brows. "Well, yes, Scott. Why wouldn't I?"

Shit. She seems offended for real this time, but I didn't mean it that way. I finish chewing and swallow before answering.

"I mean, you can, I guess...I don't know. I just assumed you'd want to stay home with the pregnancy and your dad passing away and getting his estate and house taken care of. It's a lot."

Billie seems even more irritated with me.

What's happening? What am I doing wrong?

"Do you not want me to work?" Billie eyes me firmly.

"It wouldn't make much sense to go back for a few months and then have to quit after the baby gets here." We've stopped eating and stare, gridlocked, at each other. I could cut the tension with a knife.

"Why would I quit my job after the baby gets here? I'd go back after maternity leave."

We're definitely struggling to communicate because I feel us both becoming increasingly agitated. "Well, who's going to take care of the baby all day?" I ask, clearly frustrated.

"Daycare, Scott, where many babies go while their parents work." She squares her jaw and presses her lips into a thin line.

I shake my head vehemently. "I do not want my kids in daycare. I have nothing against it for other people, but I don't want that for my family. Chris—" I stop myself right there. Nope, can't do that. I'm shooting myself in the foot here. Billie looks pissed.

Say something, Scott! Hurry!

"How's everything tasting for you two so far?" our cheery server interrupts. Billie sarcastically mutters, "fabulous," staring at me with daggers in her eyes.

Mayday. Mayday. I am going down.

"Do you really just expect me to give up everything to stay home, make babies, and raise them for the rest of my life?"

The server slowly backs away without saying another word. He flashes me a sympathetic glance before hurrying back to the kitchen.

"No...let me think for a second." We continue eating without conversation until I finish my sandwich and wash it down with a full glass of water.

It's time I attempt to dig myself out of this hole.

"What I'm trying to say is that I can take care of you on my income. You don't *have* to work. I thought you'd *want* to stay at home with the baby. If you want to work, I'll support that. However, I don't think we should send the baby to daycare. I would be open to a nanny."

Billie doesn't respond, but I can tell she's mulling over my suggestion. I wait patiently while she finishes the rest of her meal. She eventually meets my eyes and says, "I have never relied on anyone to take care of me in my adult life. My dad has been there for me, but I didn't need him financially. I have always taken care of myself. I have always worked, since I was fifteen." She picks up a remaining chip, dips it in ranch dressing, and pops it in her mouth. "Depending on you to take care of me scares me...a lot," she continues. "It makes me feel reliant and vulnerable, and I don't like how that feels."

"Billie, I promise you I am not going anywhere. I know we haven't really talked about our finances, but trust me when I say that I can provide for us without any issue. I don't have millions, but I'm financially secure. You and our kids, or one if that's what we decide, wouldn't want for anything. Please, *please* do not feel bad or guilty or nervous about relying on me financially. I will be relying on you for other things that aren't money, I'm sure. We're in this together, babe." Her eyes begin to water. I'm not sure if she's going to cry or not.

"You have to understand that I have *never* been in a relationship before. I don't know what I'm doing, what I should expect. I mean, I got pregnant within weeks of us being together. All of this is a lot. *It's a lot!* My life has been turned upside down." She nods her head and stares blankly out of the window.

"Are you...having second thoughts about us?" I start anxiously bouncing my leg up and down. I tend to do that when I'm worried or nervous. She sighs apologetically.

"No, not at all. I love our baby. I love you. I love our house. I love it all. It's new, and I'm frightened that something bad is going to happen because everything is wonderful in my life right now." I move to her side of the booth. I put my arm around her, and she rests her head on my shoulder.

"We can be scared together because I am too." I continue to console her.

"But you've been through all this before. A wife, a house, a pregnancy. I have no idea what I'm doing at all."

"Honey, *we've* never been through this before with *us*. This is all new to me too, just in a different way, I guess." I suddenly get a grand idea. "Hey, why don't we have a housewarming party? You can meet my family. You can invite Claire, Rick, and whomever else you want. We can share our wonderful news about the baby, our engagement, and the house. It'll be a great celebration."

"That's a really nice idea," she says as a smile creeps across her face. "Let's do it."

The server arrives back at our table, appearing even more chipper than his previous visit. "Can I interest you in a chocolate chip cookie or a slice of peach pie?" he asks.

"A chocolate chip cookie, please," Billie replies.

"Give us a dozen, if you wouldn't mind. We can take the rest home."

"Coming right up," he says, collecting the empty plates from the table.

CHAPTER FORTY-ONE

BILLIE

Twelve Weeks Pregnant

It's a snowy Sunday morning. I'm being lazy today. I went to Mass last night, so I don't feel the least bit guilty about lying in bed all comfy and cozy watching trash TV. I've been debating whether or not I want to go back to work, and the more I think about it, the more I want to stay home with the baby. I'm attached to this little person already. I can't imagine leaving all day a handful of weeks after he or she arrives. I cradle my belly and realize I need to pee badly. While I'm in the bathroom, I decide to take a quick shower, brush my teeth, and put on some fresh clothes. There's just one problem: I can't zip my jeans. I take a look at myself in the full-length mirror and gasp.

"Babe! Come here, quickly!" I call out. I then hear Scott racing from wherever he is in the house.

Crap, I shouldn't have said that with such an urgent tone. I forget how anxious he is about this pregnancy after what happened with Maggie.

"What? What's wrong?" Scott bolts into the room, frazzled.

"I'm sorry, honey. Nothing's wrong. Look at this." I pull up my sweater to reveal what is now clearly a baby bump. I swear that happened overnight. I know for sure it wasn't there when I had my ultrasound a few weeks ago. Scott's expression softens.

"You are the most beautiful woman I've ever seen." Scott's mouth drops open before the seductive smile peeks through. He marches toward me and plants a passionate kiss on my lips. "I absolutely love your pregnant body. I'm not sure how I'm going to keep my hands off of you." His hands move down my arms and onto my baby bump. He kneels down and kisses my belly, wrapping his arms around me and hugging my waist.

I feel myself getting emotional again. My body is going through so many changes, and I know this is the start of many that are possibly permanent. I acknowledge my body's getting bigger is par for the course of pregnancy, but it still shakes my confidence nonetheless. Besides, I'm only twelve weeks along. I have twenty-eight more to go. I sigh and place my hands in his curls.

"You do?" I ask, feeling relieved. Scott stands up and looks directly into my eyes.

"Yes, you are stunning. I mean it. I know I can't relate to what you're experiencing, but believe me when I tell you that I love everything about your body, and I will love it through this pregnancy and beyond. You're working hard to create and grow a healthy baby. Sweetie, you've got my baby in there. I'm honored that you're doing this for our family." He caresses my belly again. I place my hands over his. I nod at the reassurance and shrug. Scott always seems to know the right things to say when I'm feeling insecure.

"Well, I guess it's time to go shopping for maternity clothes. These suckers won't zip," I say, pulling at the waistband of my jeans, attempting to button them. I let out a hefty sigh and stop trying to suck in my belly. These jeans aren't happening, not even close.

"Do you want me to come with you? Or is that something you'd rather do with Claire?" I'm sure he'd suggest my mom, but she's living her best life in France with Pierre.

"If you want to come, I'm happy to go together. But I'm sure Claire would love to go shopping too."

"Okay. Well, I think Ryan is planning on coming over later to watch the basketball game, but I can cancel."

Scott's offer is sweet, but I'd actually rather go with another girl. I'm not sure how much fun he'd have sitting on a bench, watching me model clothes all afternoon. Claire can at least try stuff on with me.

"No, please don't cancel. I'll call Claire. We'll make a girls' day out of it."

"You're the best." After he leaves the room, I start pulling out the biggest, most comfy clothes I can find. Leggings and an oversized hoodie it is for today. I text Claire a picture of me in the mirror with my bump clearly showing.

ME

STOP what you're doing! It's an EMERGENCY!!

Operation Baby Bump has arrived.

We need a shopping date, stat!

Not surprisingly, she texts back right away.

CLAIRE

AHH! Stop it! Look at my little niece or nephew peeping out there.

I'm here for it. Be there in an hour to pick u up.

We have to hit up Caliente's. Mocktails for u, duh!"

She cracks me up with how she sends short texts back to back. It's contagious because I've started the same habit. Mmmm, Mexican food, get in my baby belly.

Claire and I are having a great afternoon. I needed this so much. Girl time. Bonding time. Baby time. We get lunch first to fuel ourselves before hitting up several department stores and boutiques in town. I get pants, shirts, leggings, sweaters, and a few stylish dresses. I also snag some maternity lingerie I plan on modeling later. Now that the morning sickness has finally lifted, I have a little more energy and desire to have sex again, for now at least. Knowing that Scott can't keep his hands off me makes the lingerie surprise better yet.

On our way back to my place, I muster the courage to ask what's happening between her and Ryan.

"Nothing, really, I guess," Claire shrugs as she keeps her attention focused on the road.

"Um, try that again. You don't make out with a guy casually and not catch feelings," I scoff.

"I absolutely can. Do you know how many guys I've made out with?" Claire responds, amused.

"No idea."

"Me either," she chuckles. "I like casual, easy, low-stress, no-maintenance kind of hookups. I don't like commitment. I don't think I'll ever get married. And I won't be having kids."

"If I'm being too nebby you can tell me, but why not?" I keep my eyes on the road so I don't pressure her to respond. From my periphery, I can see her chewing her lip, contemplating how much she wants to share.

"It's not something I like talking about," Claire huffs. "Maybe another time."

When I open the door at home, Claire and I hear Ryan and Scott yelling at the TV. Bruno comes trotting up to me as soon as he hears the door close.

"Hey, Bruno boy! I sure missed you today." I set my bags down and give him the ear massage he loves so much. Bruno groans in appreciation and paws at me for more when I pick up my bags again. I head toward the commotion in the family room.

"Come on, ref! That was a foul! Terrible call!" Ryan shouts at the television.

"Get with the program, ref! Jeez!" Scott adds. "Do you want another beer?" He collects two empty bottles from the end table and enters the kitchen.

"Sure, man," Ryan answers, watching the game intensely from the couch. When Scott sees me smirking at him, his face lights up. Claire plops down beside Ryan. She's practically drooling. He puts his arm around her, and she snuggles into him. I can tell she has feelings for him. He kisses the ground she walks on. He also has the patience of a saint. I'm not sure why she won't commit, but maybe someday she'll feel comfortable enough to open up to me.

"Hey, babe! How was your shopping trip?" Scott asks.

I lift up six bags from various shops. "I would say pretty successful, as you can see. I charged it all to your credit card, and I don't feel a damn bit guilty about it either."

Letting someone care for me is taking some getting used to, but he loves it and I kinda like it, too. It must be an ego boost for him, knowing that he's a reliable provider and protector over his family. His primal masculinity is such a turn-on, yet he cleans, cooks, and does whatever else needs to be done.

"That's my girl!" he cheers, retrieving two fresh beers from the fridge.

"I'm gonna let you three enjoy the rest of the game. I'm whupped and need to lie down. Try not to lose it on a screen. They can't hear you," I giggle.

"We'll keep it down. Go get some rest." Scott gives me a peck on the cheek.

I grab him by the shirt in his chest area and pull him back toward me. "I have a little something to show you later, big guy," I whisper so Ryan and Claire can't hear it.

"Oh, you do, do you?" Scott puts his hands on my arms and moves them all over me, settling on my ass and giving it a tight squeeze.

"You quit right now. It's for *later*." I wink at him and squirm free from his bear hug.

Within seconds of crawling into bed, I am sound asleep.

CHAPTER FORTY-TWO

BILLIE

When I open my eyes, I feel rested. I glance at the clock: 7:18 p.m. Of course it is. The number 18 is still popping up all the time, every day, several times a day, day and night. Instead of being angry about it, I embrace it. It's my dad saying *hello*, just as he promised he would in that video. It seems unbelievable that I notice this number so frequently, but it's true. Receipts, house numbers, game scores, clocks, and that's just a few instances.

I freshen up before heading downstairs to see what's happening. It's quiet, so I'm assuming Claire and Ryan left. I find Scott lounging on the couch in front of the TV, with Chinese food beckoning. My stomach grumbles.

"Hey, honey. Come sit. Have some dinner." He waves his hand to the spread of food on the coffee table. He's got all my favorites: egg rolls, garlic green beans, fried rice, chicken lo mein, General Tso's chicken, and chicken and broccoli.

"Are you sure you're not the one who's pregnant?" I jest, because that is a lot of food for just the two, well, two-and-a-half, of us. I get comfy on the couch and reach for the lo mein.

"I wasn't sure what you'd want, so I got everything I've seen you order before," Scott says with a shrug. "Hey, leftovers."

That was a good call on his part. I haven't felt like cooking much lately. In fact, I haven't felt like doing a lot of anything recently. I don't think I'm severely depressed, but I do think I'm deep in grief. Not to mention the sight of raw meat makes me instantly vomit.

"You're the best, babe." I dig in and we chow down while we watch a movie. It's late when the movie ends, but I really want to model that lingerie for him. I've been feeling spunky all day, and that nap just gave me the energy to have hot, steamy pregnant sex with my fiancé.

"Hey, I'm going to head upstairs." I stand up and let out a big yawn and stretch.

"You going to bed?"

"Yeah, I think so. I'm really tired." Little does he know I'm about to fuck his brains out. I give him a kiss on the lips and scurry to the bedroom. I brush my teeth and put on the negligee with the lacy yellow push-up bra and sheer veil that flows from the bottom hem of the bra and covers my bump. I can open it in the front so that the bump shows but the veil is still visible. The negligee also came with a yellow g-string. It's not remotely comfortable, but it's sexy as hell. I shake and mess up my hair enough to give it some volume and sex appeal. I crawl into bed and grab my phone.

ME

If you know what's good for you, you'll get upstairs right now.

SCOTT
Ummm…did I do something wrong? You okay?

ME

No

Yes

Now get up here before I fall asleep!

Scott takes his good old time. He's probably letting Bruno out, locking up, and turning off the lights—all the protector bedtime duties. I'm watching trash TV when I hear the door creak.

"Oh…my…God," Scott breathes, his mouth practically on the floor at the sight of me.

"It's about damn time you got up here." I throw off the covers, kneel down on the bed, spread my legs, and sit back on my calves so he can see the sexy attire. "Do you like it?" I ask, playing innocent.

"Are you…are you kidding me? Look at that baby bump. Billie," Scott says huskily, "I'm about to ravish you." He climbs onto the bed to admire me. "Did you get this today?" His hands explore the straps, cups, and sheer veil.

"Yes, I did. I couldn't try it on, but I'm pretty happy with how it looks." I bite my bottom lip and shimmy so that the sheer veil waves.

Scott pulls me down on top of him as he lies back on the bed. I straddle him so he can get a closer view. His hands move over my bump and onto my breasts. He squeezes both of them gently. I'm so fired up I moan in pleasure. I feel his dick harden as soon as I let out a whimper. I start to move back and forth over him. Even in sweatpants, I can feel he's solid and aching to be inside of me.

"Do you like me on top of you like this?" I whisper, breathy and seductively. Scott swallows a breath, nods, and murmurs an "Uh-huh." His fingers slide under the strap of my g-string, and then puts his hands on my waist, moving me harder over the top of him. The intensity of sex is still ecstasy, with all my nerve endings on high alert. I move off of him briefly just to pull his sweatpants off, then resume my place on top of him, moving back and forth so that his dick is poking at my folds and tickling my clit. I groan louder and move faster and harder because I'm about to get off something fierce without him even inside me. Scott uses his hips to move in rhythm with me. Seconds later, I release an intense orgasm all over his abdomen.

"Baby girl, what has gotten into you? You just soaked me." I huff a laugh because the intensity of the orgasm took my breath away. "Do it again," Scott demands. "I love when you come all over me."

I resume my position but, before I continue, Scott whispers, "Hold on a sec. I want to try something." He lifts me off of him and grabs a towel, laying it on the bed sheets. Whatever he's about to do I'm assuming is going to require cleanup. He instructs me to lie on my right side, and he spoons in behind me. I start to gyrate against him when he reaches around and down to my openings. He takes his hand and gently eases three fingers into me. He moves in and out slowly, the intensity causing me to gyrate harder against him. He puts his thumb on my clit and presses lightly. I cry out, instantly detonating like a grenade. I see now why he grabbed a towel.

Scott gives me only seconds to recover before he starts again. He kisses my neck and shoulders while he's fingering me. His breath becomes labored because I know he's holding back from pushing inside of me. It doesn't take long before I feel myself about to climax again. Since no one can hear us, I moan loudly and proudly.

There's no one to compare Scott to sexually, but he sure is talented. He understands how my body works and reacts. Clearly he enjoys pleasuring me. I'm not sure if it's normal, given the conversations I've overheard, but I orgasm a lot. I don't know why, whether it's the sensitivity in my body or if Scott deserves a medal for his foreplay and pleasure skills, but climaxing is quick, easy, and often for me.

I'm sure he revels in that fact too.

He makes me come again before I roll toward him, kissing him passionately, biting his lips gently and stroking his erection. He cups the back of my head with his hand and tugs a handful of my hair, which sends me into a tailspin.

"Fuck me hard, Dr. Bennington," I order him. A wicked grin creeps across his face as he climbs on top of me. He then growls while easing into me. Ecstasy, as always. He moves slowly and gently at first, but it only works me up even more. I grab onto his hips and pull him harder and deeper inside of me.

"I need you to fuck me harder, Daddy," I moan, unbearably aching for him to be rougher with me. His expression softens.

"I don't want to hurt the baby," Scott admits.

This feels like torture because I need to release another orgasm. "I promise you, and I mean this kindly, your junior is not long enough to poke my uterus in addition to my fully closed cervix."

Scott looks impressed.

"I Googled it just to make sure. Trust me, you can't hurt the baby. If it gets too rough, I'll tell you. Until then, I want you to dominate me."

His eyes smolder with desire as I place my arms on his biceps and dig in my nails. Scott obliges and fucks me harder, just like I've been begging for, and I let him know vocally how good it feels.

He flips me over into his favorite position—the one where my ass is practically in his face, and he fucks me from behind. I come again. And then again. Things become even more intense when I tell him to pull my hair and spank me.

Scott chokes out a nervous laugh but does as he's told. I whimper every time he smacks me and cry out "yes" when he tugs at my hair. When I feel him getting close, I beg him to come.

And he does not disappoint. I'm pretty sure he releases for a full minute. We collapse on the bed and snuggle up to each other until our breathing synchronizes. Scott wraps his arms around me and caresses my back.

"What got into you all of a sudden?" Scott croaks in disbelief.

"Did you like it?" I ask hesitantly. Normally I feel confident, but this is something new we've never tried.

"Are you kidding me? That yellow outfit. Your breasts. Did they grow overnight?" He gently squeezes each one, which makes me giggle but sends pleasure signals to my core. "Your bossing me around is such a turn-on," Scott admits. "Plus, this kinky side is really hot."

"I'm glad you enjoyed it. I love making you feel good, baby," I murmur back.

"Billie, words can't express how good you make me feel, every day."

CHAPTER FORTY-THREE

SCOTT

"Hi, Mom!" I greet my mother when I open the door. She gives me a warm hug. This is probably the first time I've hugged her in nearly two years. Not that she didn't want to, I just didn't want anyone touching me, mostly due to self-isolation. Sure, I've attended holiday gatherings, but I kept to myself or roughhoused with the kids to avoid conversation.

"Hi, Son! What a beautiful place! I can't wait to see the entire house," my dad comments, trailing behind her with a hot dish.

I give him a pat on the back and a "hello." Dad replies in his typical semi-sarcastic manner, "It's about time you got a bigger place, don't you think?"

"Ha! Yeah, I figured with all the kids, it was time," I joke.

He smirks with approval. My dad can come off as an asshole sometimes, but he's a softie at heart.

Ryan is just about to climb the front porch steps, empty-handed. "Hey, doofus," I say. "Where's the wine?" I hold out my arms and look around the porch artificially.

"Ah, shit!" Ryan mutters.

"Dude, you had *one job!*" I call out to him.

He jogs back to his 2001 white Toyota Supra, his side project since we were teenagers, throwing his hands in the air. "I'll be right back!" he calls.

Shortly after, Claire arrives, followed by Rick, and my sisters Elodie, Julia, and Scarlet, along with their husbands and kids. We do our formal introductions, and my family greets Billie with open arms. I have a really good feeling about tonight.

Billie is hiding the baby bump with an oversized brown tunic sweater and a pair of black leggings. Only Claire and Ryan know about the baby and the engagement, so no one has brought it up.

Once we finish formalities, my mom, sisters, and Billie prepare the table with all the food while the husbands wrangle the kids. In our family, the ladies prepare and the men clean up. I enjoy cooking too, so I took charge of the ham and potatoes.

Ryan still isn't back yet, but we're not going to wait to start the meal. Who knows how long he will be? The kids are running amok as usual. The atmosphere feels exactly like Christmas. We fill our plates, say grace, and begin the typical family chatter.

What's new?

How's Bruno?

What are the kids up to this school year?

Did you hear about my promotion?

Yada. Yada. Yada.

Billie and I keep eyeing each other nervously, trying to decide the best time to make our announcements. However, my mother asks a question that ignites a complete shit show.

"So, Billie, tell me, do you live in the city?" She cuts a piece of ham and daintily puts it in her mouth.

Billie flashes me a confused look and I shrug. I never flat-out told my family we were moving in together, but I figured they'd assume so because they at least knew Billie and I were dating. Why else would I buy a bigger house? My bad. I guess it's time to let the cat out of the bag.

"Oh, uh—" Billie stutters, so I interrupt.

"Everyone, Billie lives here. This is our home." I hear a few gasps and utensils clatter onto our brand-new plates. Everyone's eyes widen. It's painfully silent until Elodie opens her damn mouth.

"Don't you think that's too fast? You've known her, what, a few months?" Elodie questions. Billie clears her throat and furrows her brows.

"I don't think so, no. Not when you know you're with the person you want to spend the rest of your life with." I reach my hand out for Billie's and smile at her. She smiles tenderly back at me.

"Hold on a damn second! Are you *proposing*?" Elodie blurts out. She really needs to shut her trap. Billie didn't put her ring on today because we didn't want to spoil the announcement of our engagement.

"Elodie, zip it!" Scarlet pipes in. "Let him do it," she says with gritted teeth.

"Yeah, Elodie, Jeez," seconds Julia. My mom stares at us blankly. My dad and brothers-in-law shift uncomfortably in their seats, waiting for my next move. Claire looks like she's about to strangle Elodie, and Rick appears flustered.

"Actually," I begin, standing Billie up beside me. "We're already engaged. Billie and I are getting married." I look into her eyes and give her a loving kiss on the lips. I can still feel her apprehension, so I keep my reassuring grip on her hand. I'm expecting *hoorays* and hugs and pats on the back, but everyone sits there silently, except Elodie.

"Already? It hasn't even been that long since Christine died, and you're moving on to another marriage so soon? What, did you knock her up?" Elodie scoffs. Claire stands up just as I slam my fist on the table. Everyone jolts in their seats.

"That is enough, Elodie!" I growl. I must have frightened little Maren because she starts crying. Julia goes to comfort her.

"Now, let's all just calm down," soothes my dad.

"Can't someone just know who they want to be with and marry? Who says she's knocked up?" Scarlet comments.

Then Scarlet's husband, Tim, asks, "Well, did you knock her up?"

"*Tim!*" Scarlet swats him on the arm.

I can feel the blood boiling beneath my skin. This was supposed to be a housewarming celebration of all the great news in our lives, and my family—practically the only family Billie will have now—completely blew it. It's an absolute disaster. This is probably the worst reaction I could have anticipated. Billie releases my hand and steps away from the table, placing her hand over her mouth and taking off up the stairs toward our bedroom. Claire flies after her.

"What is *wrong* with all of you?" I spit. "Thanks for ruining the night for us. Rick, I'm sorry you had to witness this. I'm not sure what possessed some of my family members this evening with their rude, egregious behavior. Now, if you'll excuse me, I need to check on my *pregnant fiancée.* You may see yourselves out, and *you* better be gone when I come back down here." I point directly at Elodie and look at her with pure disgust. When I reach the staircase, the front door swings open. In walks Ryan, holding up several paper bags.

"I got the wine, everyone! The party can officially start!" He tilts his head, confused, as I stomp up the stairs. He can probably see the smoke radiating from every orifice of my body.

Ryan's excitement fades.

"Was it something I said?"

When I get to the bedroom, Claire and Billie are sitting on the bed. Billie is crying and Claire is rubbing her back, soothing her.

"Billie, baby, I am so...I am so sorry." I apologize, kneeling down in front of her.

"I'm going to let you two talk. Call me later, okay?" Claire gives Billie a hug and closes the door behind her. I go in for a hug next but she pushes me away. She stands up and darts for the closet, grabbing a large duffel bag.

"Honey, what are you doing?" She's thrashing around the room, opening drawers, pulling out clothes, and shoving them into the bag.

"I'm leaving. I need to get out of here. They hate me. I don't belong here. I need to go." She marches into the master bathroom and starts grabbing all her toiletries. Bottles crash on the counter and fall to the ground as she tries to add them to her clothes pile.

"Where exactly are you going to go? Everyone is leaving now anyway."

"Home. My old home." Billie continues overstuffing the duffel bag.

"The heat isn't even turned on over there. You'll freeze!" My fight-or-flight response kicks in, alerting me that she's actually going to walk out on me again. I don't move any closer to her because I don't want to get caught in the crossfire of her rage. I want to remain calm to prevent a panic attack. So far, it's not working.

"I don't care," she hisses.

"You're not taking our baby to a freezing-cold house!" I stomp my foot and point to the ground. The agitation is building, my emotions boiling over. I take a deep breath to get myself in check.

"It's my body, Scott! Mine! I'm carrying this baby, not you. The baby will be fine. I'll be fine." Her voice trembles.

"Sit down, Billie," I say calmly. I sit on the bed and pat it for her to join me.

"No." She huffs into the walk-in closet and grabs extra blankets.

"Yes. This is ridiculous. Sit down," I say with a little more authority.

"I don't want to sit down. I want to leave. I'll stay with Claire," she insists.

Calm. Calm. Stay calm.

"You are not leaving, Billie. I will not let you do it." Billie rolls her eyes at me, which provokes me to shoot back, "You really need to stop running away when something bad happens. You don't get to just leave when things get hard, Billie. This is our home. Screw what Elodie says."

"Ha! Easy for you to say. They didn't come for your blood tonight. She has nothing but disdain for me. And no one even tried to help the situation. They all must think I'm some kind of whore who got herself knocked up the first month to trap you and take your money and replace Christine." Billie cries through her words, but that doesn't stop her from packing.

"You know none of that is true. You're going to be my wife, the other half me. If anyone says something to you, they say it to me too. I will handle Elodie, but right now I need you to unpack that bag." Billie walking away from me again would be agonizing. It's making me feel anxious. It's making me feel angry. It's making me feel like I'm failing her.

"No. I need to go." Billie is sniffling and grabbing a few more items from around the bedroom.

Oh, shit. Here comes the word-vomit.

"You know, for someone who is hell-bent on not becoming her mother, you're sure acting like her right now. Are you just going to abandon me like she did you?" I spit in fear and anger.

I did it.

I said it.

I know I hit below the belt, but I don't know how else to get her to wake the hell up and realize that what she's doing is messing with my head and my heart. Billie freezes, her eyes meeting mine. I brace myself because I suspect she's about to release her fury. She softens her expression instead. Her eyes glaze over as she crumbles to the floor, erupting into the most painful cry I've ever heard from her, worse than at her dad's funeral. Tears of regret fill my eyes, so I go to her side. She lunges forward and clings to me for dear life.

I hold her and caress the back of her head with my hand. I whisper, "I'm sorry, Billie. I'm so sorry." She climbs up into my lap and nestles her head on my neck. I place my free hand on her baby bump, rubbing my thumb over it in an attempt to soothe her. Soon, she's no longer crying and her breathing hiccups.

"You're right," Billie rasps. "I am my mother. I'm just like her. Everyone leaves me, Scott. First, my mom. Now, my dad. My friends...gone. I don't know what else to do when I'm upset. I just don't want you to leave me too."

"I shouldn't have said that. You're not like her. I'm upset because the thought of being without you tears me to pieces. I'm never going to leave you, Billie. You need to realize that." I sniffle.

"You can't promise me that. You can't guarantee that nothing bad will happen to you that'll take you from me." Frustration builds in Billie's voice.

"You're right, to a point, I guess. But I'm never going to walk away from you—*ever*. I'm here, baby. I got you. I love you so much," I reassure her. She pulls back and looks up at me, completely exhausted.

"I'll never walk out again. I promise you that. Never. I'm sorry I scared you." She gives me a soft, heartfelt kiss on the lips.

Our lives have been a roller coaster over the past couple of months, and I think we're both having a difficult time processing it all. Six months ago, neither of us knew the other existed. Now we're engaged, we've moved into a new house, and we're having a baby together. It's enough to make anyone's head spin.

"Why don't you lie down. I'll take care of all this, up here and downstairs. Just relax, watch some trash TV. Nestle our sweet little babe. I'll get you whatever you want. Drinks, food, books, massage. You name it."

She smiles through her weariness and closes her eyes. "Thank you. That sounds lovely. I'm gonna change and crawl into bed. If the food is still downstairs, I would really like a plate. And some ginger ale too, please. I'm starving. I was nauseated and nervous leading up to tonight, so I haven't had much to eat today."

We get up from the floor, and I pull her into me for a hug. She then turns and heads for the bathroom. Just as I'm about to tell her everything is going to be fine, the bathroom door shuts, so I don't say it. I need to give her some space.

I peer into the dining room, surprised to see everything is still there. No one took their dishes with them. The table is set beautifully, with no indication a family brawl broke out minutes earlier. From the kitchen, I spot Claire straddling Ryan, getting hot and heavy on the family room couch. Claire doesn't have a shirt on, but thankfully she hasn't removed her bra yet. I loudly clear my throat.

Claire swings herself around in my direction. "Oh, shit!" She snatches her shirt from the floor and climbs off Ryan. He sits up and adjusts himself, because he is undeniably pitching a tent.

"Bro, I figured you'd be up there a while," Ryan says, embarrassed. "Sorry, dude." Once Claire is presentable, she leads Ryan through the kitchen, grabbing their belongings and heading toward the door.

"Come on, Ryan. Let's take this back to my place." He smacks her ass and she squeals just as the door shuts. All I can do is roll my eyes. I mean, I know my family can be a little much at times because there are so many of us, but what the hell happened tonight?

There's a quiet knock at the door.

Irritation instantly floods me.

"Okay, Ryan, what'd you forget this time? I don't have any cond—Mom! Hi." My annoyed expression transforms to astonishment as I see my mother standing meekly in front of me.

"Can I come in?"

I hang my head in resignation and usher her inside. A waft of snowflakes follows her.

I fix Billie's dinner and pop it in the microwave. "I was just about to take Billie some food."

"Let me," my mom interrupts, wrapping me in a hug, just like she used to when I was little. My mom always knows what I need exactly when I need it.

"I'm really sorry about tonight," my mother apologizes. "I should have stopped Elodie. She hasn't been the same since Christine died either. It's no excuse, but the surprise probably sparked her meltdown."

Elodie and Christine were best friends, so close they were the maid and matron of honor in each other's weddings. In fact, Elodie is the one who introduced me to Christine when we were kids. I know Elodie has taken Christine's passing extremely hard, but it doesn't excuse her inappropriate blow-up tonight. It's unconscionable. We were inseparable growing up, considering we were born only fourteen months apart. After Christine died, our relationship became tumultuous, and that's putting it mildly.

"Billie seems like a wonderful woman. I'm glad you've found happiness again. You look like the Scott I remember. I've missed him." My mom releases me and cups her hands on my cheeks, her eyes glistening. "Is she expecting? Are you giving me a grand-baby?" My eyes well up. I grin as wide as my face will let me.

"August 18 she's due. We're thrilled. And I didn't ask her to marry me because she's pregnant. I had already planned on it." I sniffle and wipe my eyes with my shirtsleeve.

"That doesn't even matter, honey. What matters is that you and Billie are happy and that the baby continues to thrive." The microwave beeps, alerting us that the food is heated. "I'll take this up to Billie and talk to her. I'll be back down shortly to help clean up." She pats my shoulder, then carries the tray away. I pour myself a large glass of wine before tackling dinner's other mess.

CHAPTER FORTY-FOUR

BILLIE

I hear a light tap on the door just as I climb into bed and turn on the TV. It can't be Scott, because why would he knock?

"Come in," I call warily. Scott's mother enters with a can of ginger ale and a plate of hot food, which makes my mouth water. I feel nauseated as she approaches me, not because of the food but because of what might come out of her mouth. She hands me the tray and sets the ginger ale on the nightstand.

"Thank you," I say, accepting the tray onto my lap.

"I need to apologize for this evening," she begins. Her voice is calm and quiet, just as if she were going to soothe a child. "That behavior is not typical of our family, and unacceptable at that. I should have spoken up and put a stop to it, but I froze, and I'm sorry." She places her hand on top of mine in remorse. I offer her a forgiving nod.

"I really do love your son, Pearl." I love the name Pearl. It's on my list of middle names if the baby is a girl. So timeless. I place my other hand over hers and lightly squeeze.

"I know you do, and he loves you. I saw that tonight. I knew it when all he could talk about at Thanksgiving was you. At Christmas, all about you. I recognize my son again, and I have you to thank for that. Grief can do awful things to people, as I'm sure you're experiencing now, going through it with your father. I'm so sorry for your loss." Pearl says in a motherly tone.

I break eye contact to prevent tears from forming. "Thank you. It's been tough navigating these last few months. My mom is living in France with her boyfriend. Other than my dad's companion, Rick, my friend Claire, my cousin Abbey, and Scott, I really don't have anyone else here."

"Well, you have me," Pearl reassures me. "I cannot wait to spoil this precious little one, plan a baby shower, and spend more time with you." She rises from my bedside and smoothes her skirt. "Eat and rest, sweetheart. We'll talk again soon."

"I look forward to it," I reply. I sit back against the headboard, rub my belly, and sigh in relief.

CHAPTER FORTY-FIVE

BILLIE

Twenty Weeks Pregnant

Would you like to know the gender?" the ultrasound technician asks as she approaches the baby's genitals for examination. I can know right now if Scott and I are having a boy or a girl.

"*Yes! No!*" Scott and I say in unison.

"You don't want to know?" Scott looks at me, stunned that I voted *no*. In all actuality, I don't want to know. If it's a girl, I'm worried Scott will go on a downward spiral and it'll dampen the rest of our pregnancy experience. At least when the baby is born, we will be so overjoyed that it hopefully won't matter to him.

"I just think a surprise would be fun, don't you?" I ask innocently. I'm lying. I want to know, *badly*, but only if it's a boy. Unfortunately, that's not how gender ultrasounds work.

"No," Scott contradicts. "I like to be prepared. We can finish the nursery and choose a name. You know, all the fun stuff."

Scott attempts to persuade me, but I'm not budging. I don't think I could handle the news if the baby is a girl either. What if I'm just like my mom? What if I can't handle motherhood? I mean, if we have a girl, I'll be ecstatic but terrified. But I never want my child feeling the way I do about my mom—not that I hate her, because I don't. It's just that the emotional neglect has profoundly affected my relationships. I do want a baby girl in my parenting journey. But given the circumstances, I'm afraid that having a girl will cause a whole new intense wave of grief, for me and the practically dead relationship with my mother, as well as Scott with the loss of Maggie. I don't have the emotional stamina at the moment. I need to figure out something to say to get him on board.

"I'll just do these other measurements while you two decide," the tech adds.

Think, Billie. Think!

I take Scott's hand and kiss it. "Babe, I guess I had it in my head that when the baby gets here, you would announce to the whole room what the baby is and everyone will be overjoyed. It'll be such a beautiful moment. I don't mind neutral colors in a nursery. I'm not particularly a fan of pink anyway. Pretty please?" I roll my bottom lip down, pout, and bat my eyelashes. I can see he's starting to crumble.

Come on, Scott, cave. Please.

"It would be pretty amazing to tell everyone after he—*or she* —is here. Are you sure this is what you want?" Scott isn't fully convinced yet. I bend my index finger, indicating that I want him to come close to me.

I whisper in his ear, "If you let me win this one, I'll let you do anything you want to me later." Scott startles. His reaction then morphs into one of mischief and lust.

"Anything?" he mouths.

"Anything," I mouth back, and then I wink at him.

"Deal." He holds out his hand and we shake on it.

"We do not want to know the sex of the baby," I announce. I look at Scott tenderly, but inside I'm so relieved. It may be selfish of me, but I want this experience to be with Scott and me. I don't want it riddled with anxiety and comparisons. Moreover, Scott has been through a pregnancy before and I haven't. Even though the circumstances were out of our control, I'm a little jealous that his first experience with fatherhood wasn't with me. Maybe admitting that sounds terrible, but it's how I feel. I want Scott to feel excited and relaxed so that I can feel excited and relaxed. I want him to enjoy this pregnancy with me.

"Good choice!" the tech agrees. "I'm almost finished. You'll be able to empty your bladder while I get this over to the doctor."

"Thank God! Because I'm about to burst!" I haven't peed myself in years, but this may be the time.

Fortunately, I am able to survive the rest of the ultrasound and get myself back together before the doctor comes in to speak with us. Dr. Moseley doesn't even shut the door fully before she starts talking. I like her. She's bubbly, witty, and a no-bullshit type of person. I'm not bubbly. I consider myself a bit witty, and I don't take shit from anyone—well, when I'm not pregnant and hormonal. She has been my only gynecologist. I won't see anyone else.

With fiery red hair and baby-blue eyes, Dr. Moseley is the type of woman others would kill to resemble. She has freckles that speckle the bridge of her nose and scatter over her cheeks. Her tall, slender figure looks stunning in her complementary blue scrubs. She's not much older than me, maybe five years or so. As a matter of fact, I was one of her first patients.

"Everything looks great! Baby is growing perfectly. I'll take your blood pressure and measure your belly. Then you're outta here." She opens a drawer and pulls out the blood pressure cuff and soft tape measure. "Do you have any questions?"

"No, I don't think I do. I feel great right now, other than being tired all the time. I love this little bump. I finally look pregnant, and it is not questionable as to whether I'm pregnant or just gaining weight." The three of us snicker. "Actually, I do have a question now that I'm thinking about it. I've been experiencing these little bubbles occasionally. I'm not sure how else to describe it. I don't have any pain or gas with it, though."

"Does it feel like a flutter?" Dr. Moseley asks.

"You could say that," I agree.

"That's your baby. Those tiny little flutters are coming from your baby wiggling around in there."

"Really?" I become teary-eyed. My baby is moving, and I can feel it. How awesome!

"Can I feel it too?" Scott perks up. I see his eyes glaze over, then glimmer ever so slightly.

"Probably not yet, but within the next few weeks you should. Soon you'll be feeling all kinds of headbutts, kicks, and punches," Dr. Moseley assures me. Scott gazes at me lovingly, so overjoyed, and gives me a kiss.

I think this is what emotional stability and happiness feels like. It's fucking beautiful.

CHAPTER FORTY-SIX

SCOTT

Billie Is Twenty-six Weeks Pregnant

Today is the day I say goodbye to my first house. In true Pittsburgh fashion, I am running late, white-knuckled, attempting to merge onto the Fort Pitt Bridge toward the outbound tunnel. I have what appears to be a hundred feet to cross four lanes. It's brutal.

"Siri, call Billie." She answers on the first ring. "Hey, babe! I'll be there soon. Pittsburgh traffic. Can you hold the fort until I get there?" I'm maneuvering between lanes, and some idiot almost causes an accident. "Turn signals, people! Jeez!" I holler.

"Are you all right?" Billie asks, concerned.

"Yes, I'm fine as long as this *jagoff* doesn't cause a ten-car pileup."

"Be careful and take your time. I'm at the house now, making sure we haven't left anything behind."

"Got it. Seeya in ten."

I take one final sweep through the house, remembering all the memories I made here with Christine, as well as the ones I've created with Billie. There has been so much love in this house, a bittersweet end to this chapter. I realize the time has come. What Billie and I are building will create wonderful memories in our new home together.

"Remember when you tore your shirt off and flashed me while I was trying to make breakfast?" I nod toward that area of the kitchen.

"Wait a second, you made me spill scalding hot coffee all down the front of me!" Billie scoffs.

"Purely an accident! I got an up-close and personal view of your boobs, though." I waggle my eyebrows.

Billie closes her eyes, smiles, and nods slowly. She heads toward the entryway and recalls the night we got it on for the first time. "And there is the floor where I fell on top of you and you kissed me for the first time, and then it was all over after that." She shivers. "When you said, 'Something is already going on between us,' I about lost my mind. That was so hot." She starts fanning her face.

We laugh and reminisce until we are ready to say our final goodbye. "Do you want to go back to the nursery or your bedroom at all?" Billie asks gently.

"No, I'm good. Today is a little sad, but it's a happy day."

Billie rubs my back, then gasps. "Give me your hand. Quickly!" Billie takes her hand and places it on the bottom left side of her belly. "Press right here and just wait." We get quiet and still. I haven't felt the baby move yet. It seems every time the baby is active, the little bean stops moving as soon as I touch Billie.

We wait a few moments. Nothing. "This baby is stubborn already," I sigh.

"Just wait! You're being impatient," Billie demands, hushing me. I wait again and soon feel the faintest nudge on my thumb. It is gentle and brief. My eyes grow wide. Billie places her hands over mine. I feel a few more light pokes. I am entranced. This is my baby *finally* saying *hello* to me. In just a few short months, our baby will be here. A part of me feels terrified that I'm going to screw it up, but mostly, I am overjoyed.

"Hello, little one. Daddy and I love you," Billie says to the baby, patting her belly.

God, she is breathtaking.

"This couldn't have gone any better. I'm able to leave with a cherished last memory here," I say, kissing Billie softly on the lips. "Come on, sweetie, let's go close on this house so a new family can make beautiful memories here too."

When we cross the threshold, I look inside one last time to see the absence of things but a space filled with love. This time, instead of blowing a kiss, I wave goodbye. Selling this house is cathartic. I will always hold my time and memories here dearly, but the life Billie and I are building together fulfills me. I know it. I feel it deep within me, and I am no longer afraid of love. I exhale in a moment of requiescence and close the door one last time.

CHAPTER FORTY-SEVEN

BILLIE

Twenty-nine Weeks Pregnant

I've been debating on what to do with Dad's house. I stop over there several times a week after I visit my dad's grave to check on everything. Nothing changes, of course, but it helps with the grief, I suppose. There are so many memories here.

So. Much. Stuff.

It could take a year to go through the storage boxes and decide what to keep, and with the baby coming, I'm not going to have time to dedicate to it. Plus, I'm not sure I'm ready to go through it all.

Lately, on Thursdays after Scott gets home from work, we visit my dad, Christine, and Maggie at the cemetery. He stops with me at my childhood home, and then we go out for dinner. Today, we clean their headstones and place fresh flowers around each base.

When we arrive at my dad's house, I can't bring myself to get out of the car. I sit in the passenger's seat, surveying the porch, the windows, the landscape. The house, speckled with black, red, and brown bricks, looks as vibrant as it did when I was a kid. With the exception of some painting, new windows, a new black roof, and matching shutters, almost everything is original. I remember playing "five corners" with my neighbor friends as a child on that porch. One of us would swing and count to ten with our eyes closed while the rest of us scattered to a corner. The fifth "corner" is right in the center of the porch, a brick pillar attached to brown concrete railings, which have since been painted black.

My mom used to make the best sun tea and freshly squeezed lemonade, paired with fresh fruit and veggies, for all of us to snack on when we were hungry and overheated. Occasionally, she'd bake chocolate chip cookies or grill hamburgers and hot dogs for lunch. I miss those days. They weren't riddled with pain or stress yet. At the time, my rose-colored glasses shielded life's reality. The summers were particularly fun, especially because I had a tight-knit group of friends. We played nearly every day each summer until junior high. Sadly, busy schedules took over and we drifted away. I don't know where most of them are these days.

"Everything okay, Billie?" Scott asks, breaking my reverie.

"Every time I come here, I think today's the day I'll feel good enough to say goodbye and put this house up for sale, but I cannot bring myself to do it. You sold your house, but I feel like a hypocrite because deep down I don't want to sell this one." I blow out all my air and inhale deeply. I get a whiff of the subtle sweetness from the hydrangea bushes.

It smells like home.

"Here, let me help you out of the car and we can talk about it." Scott holds out his hand and I accept. We take our seats on the wooden porch swing and rock lazily back and forth.

"What are your thoughts on making this place an Airbnb?" Scott asks as he puts his arm around my shoulder. The thought never crossed my mind to do something like this with the house. As I sit with the idea for a minute, everything becomes clear.

"You'd be okay with that?" I ask with a quiver in my voice. This man never ceases to amaze me. He may not be perfect, but he's absolutely perfect for me.

"I think it's a great idea. This is a well-built house in a cutesy neighborhood. It would be a convenient place for visitors to stay that's close to the city but away from its congestion. We can come here anytime. We can store or move what you want to the attic. Give it some thought." Scott gives me a kiss on my head. I notice him breathe in my orchid-scented shampoo.

"I don't have to. I think it's perfect. It's absolutely perfect." I snuggle into him, and we enjoy the scenery until the sun sets and the sky turns pink.

CHAPTER FORTY-EIGHT

BILLIE

Thirty-two Weeks Pregnant

T his is ridiculous! I look silly in this outfit." I shake my head in reluctance as I eye myself in the large full-length mirror inside the walk-in closet. Scott slithers behind me, snaking his arms through mine, his hands landing on my baby bump.

"You look so great! It'll be the best costume there!" Scott reassures me, but this is partly his fault. Claire decided she wanted to have a costume birthday party this year. I do enjoy costumes and getting dressed up, but at eight months pregnant, I am not feeling the vibe. My '80s-style shoulder-length light-brown wig with teased bangs is cemented with Aqua Net, which I didn't even know was still available. I have a tight black off-the-shoulder shirt with a giant handmade purple bow pinned to the top left side of my shoulder. I opted for black maternity leggings and an oversized purple knit sweater. To top it off, my belly has a fabric globe adhered to it. If you know, you know.

Scott wiggles his hips to show off his fitted black jeans, black t-shirt, and black leather jacket, which he borrowed from his brother. He slicked and sprayed his hair back to finish the look. We give ourselves a once-over in the mirror, standing side by side. "We got this in the bag, baby," Scott says confidently.

I should be surprised Claire is having a costume contest, but I'm not. She told me she wants to go all out. Something about living it up and it being her year. I'm sure she will be dressed in something elaborate, winning her own contest.

We pull into Claire's housing development and park at the far end of the road. We can hear music blaring as soon as we open our car doors. Unsurprisingly, Claire's robin's-egg blue front door stands out from all the rest in the condo building. The cookie-cutter housing development is located in a nice suburban area of town. Many of the condos are occupied by single or divorced millennials.

I open the front door and hear a delighted screech.

"Shut. The. Fuck. Up! Bills! You're here!" Claire charges toward me. Her eyes are a tad glassy, so I'm sure she's indulged in a cocktail or five already. And, just as I suspected, she is dressed over-the-top as Medusa, complete with an intricate updo that mimics snakes, with her body bronzed and shimmering from head to toe. Her costume consists of a golden bustier, also covered in glitter, with a long sheer golden skirt that overlays gold satin underwear.

Claire opens her arms and embraces me awkwardly, since my belly is in the way. "Girl, I swear you grew overnight. Look at this baby!" She starts rubbing and patting my bump, then bends down to talk to it. "Hey, this is your Auntie Claire. I can't wait to meet you, Baby!"

Claire has been fussing over me and this baby since the second I announced I was pregnant, which is slightly odd, considering she said she didn't want kids. "Come on, I have sparkling white grape juice just for you!" Claire snatches my hand and excitedly leads me toward the makeshift bar in the kitchen, which is crammed with partygoers.

Meanwhile, I glance around the condo, getting a vibe from the party. Almost immediately I spot Ryan playing beer pong in the corner of the living room with Sherlock Holmes and Watson. He's clearly dressed as Perseus, sporting gray full-body paint, a chest of body armor, a Roman gladiator skirt and—how he obtained this I will never know—an intricate cap of Hades.

"You do realize Perseus kills Medusa, cutting her head off, right?" I quip. Claire hands me a champagne flute of sparkling juice, and I take a sip. Hot damn! It's delicious. I take a second drink, this time downing half the contents.

"Slow down there, killer. I need you to make it 'til at least 10 p.m.," Claire teases. "And yes, I know. I plan on letting him destroy me in the bedroom later. Just look at how hot he is in that costume! I can't wait to smear our body paint all over each other." Claire looks dreamily at Ryan. He glances our way, giving us a slight nod and winking at Claire, who responds by biting her lip and tipping her chin.

"Spill, sis. I need the deets. Now. Are you guys together yet?" I give her an expectant look, waiting for her response.

"Nothing to spill. Like I've said before, we're just fucking." Claire shrugs her shoulders and pours herself another drink.

"Oh, no, you don't! You're not getting off that easily!" I argue.

"No one in the history of my sex life has ever gotten me off easily...except for him," she smiles, nodding toward Ryan. She takes a stealthy gulp of her cocktail.

"Okay, so he's a good lay, but you have no other feelings for him? Not at all? Does he know this? Come on, Claire! I'm not leaving until you tell me ev-er-y-thing," I enunciate.

"We are what we are, and that's all I can and will say. We're not together, if that's what you're asking." Claire throws back the rest of her cocktail, then swirls her index finger around the top of the glass, staring into its empty contents.

"Claire," I respond, unrelenting, "why aren't you being honest with me?" I'm rather annoyed that I've spilled my guts out to her, and she's being surface-level about her boyfr—well, whatever Ryan is. Claire shoots me a snarky look.

"I am being honest...I'm just being...vague," Claire continues, revealing her reticence. Before I can probe her for more tea, her sister, Joy, enters the conversation. Now, Joy is the definition of a paradox. Her hair is long and thick, dyed black as night, styled in two low braids that hang just below her chest. Her face is purposely pale from makeup, and she has thick black eyeliner winged perfectly on each side. Naturally, she is wearing black lipstick, and her stiletto fingernails are painted matte black. Joy is dressed as Wednesday Addams, of course, but even if this weren't a costume party, I could see her wearing this as an everyday look.

"Ew, why is the energy off over here?" Joy sneers.

Claire has mentioned only bits and pieces about her sister, but she made it a point to tell me that Joy has *abilities*. Like... communicating-with-dead-people type of abilities. I know that when she was little, Joy had a near-death experience. Ever since, she has been able to communicate with those on the other side. I had previously told Claire I wanted to keep myself away from any type of negative energy. She assured me that her sister's abilities are used for good. Joy interacts with only positive energies.

"She's not an evil witch or anything. She does not dabble with questionable devices. She dresses in black because she 'always carries a sadness with her,'" Claire said, using air quotes. "And honestly, Joy tries to block out whatever she sees and hears, but she really does have a gift. She provides a lot of healing for so many people. My parents thought she was schizophrenic, but she had countless evaluations, and she doesn't have it. Hey, maybe someday she'll connect you with your dad."

She'll connect you with your dad.

Those words hang on me. Communicating with the dead isn't something I've ever been open to before, but who knows what the future holds? To be able to communicate with my dad again, even for just a minute, would mean everything to me.

"Get over yourself," Claire teases, as she hands Joy some type of spiked concoction she mixed together.

"Hi, I'm Joy, this wacko's sister." Joy hitches her thumb and plucks the drink from Claire.

"Belinda Carlisle. Nice to meet you." I hold out my hand to shake hers. Joy cracks a smile as she returns the handshake.

"Yes, I see that. You must be the famous Billie that Claire has been raving about for months on end." My eyes briefly meet Claire's and see her cheeks flush with embarrassment.

"I go by Billie, yes, but my actual name is Belinda Carlisle," I admit.

"Your name is Belinda Carlisle?" the sisters say in unison. Their eyes and mouths pop open. I shake my head in disbelief. "Claire, you knew my name is Belinda. I told you this forever ago." I distinctly remember telling her about my full name when I was visiting Dad at the hospice center.

"Nope, it wasn't me," Claire says, shaking her head vigorously. "I didn't know this at all. That's badass!" She holds out her glass to clank it with mine.

"My dad always called me Billie, so that's what I prefer to go by," I reply, *verklempt.*

"No, don't you start the waterworks here, missy. It's my damn birthday!" Claire pulls me toward her living room to dance. I'm getting motion sickness from all the pulling and yanking. Plus the place is full of people, most of whom I have never met. Besides Claire, Joy, Ryan, and Scott, I have no idea who's here celebrating. Everyone is wearing a costume, so I wouldn't be able to name names even if I tried.

I'm slowly and gently waddling my hips while Claire gyrates the air. I can feel my swollen feet screaming at me to sit down, but I'm enjoying myself. I'm not feeling great either, tired and mildly lightheaded, but who feels invigorated at eight months pregnant?

The playlist is millennial Heaven, hits of the '80s, '90s, and early 2000s. Everything from Don Henley to Lil Wayne. As we dance, I can't help but notice how longingly Ryan stares at Claire. I've seen that look before on Scott's face when I became completely unhinged and subsequently pregnant at his office. Ryan's totally in love with her, and she is fighting it. I wish I knew why.

I'm making a mental note right now to find out more about Claire's previous relationships. I want to get to know her better, but she is guarded like Buckingham Palace. Why swear off relationships forever? That seems extreme. Plus, she has a smoking-hot young Bennington right in front of her, worshipping the ground she walks on! Surely, she sees him as more than just a fuck buddy.

As I attempt to move to the song's upbeat tempo, I swear I see Scott salivating from the corner of the room. He's chatting with a man dressed as the Joker, who is animating what appears to be a suspenseful story. Scott winks at me as he presses his beer bottle to his lips. I curl my index finger at him, seducing him out to the makeshift dance floor. He pats the Joker on the shoulder and makes a beeline for me. When he looks at me, it's like no one else is in the room.

How lucky am I? How insanely lucky I am to have this wonderful man marching straight toward me, wrapping his arms around me, moving his hips with mine, kissing me like no one can see us, loving me as no one ever has. I feel whole.

When we get home from the party, I practically crawl up the stairs to de-glam myself. This mama is whupped. I had a ton of fun but, at this stage of pregnancy, it's hard to feel comfortable unless I'm in leggings and a sweatshirt, with zero makeup on my face. First, I take off my wig and brush out my hair. After that, I do my skincare routine, removing all my makeup, washing my face, and then moisturizing. I change into an oversized t-shirt and kick off my black maternity leggings. I am pulling up my sweats when everything in my belly becomes extremely tight, and my stomach feels like it's churning. It's so intense I can't stand up.

"Scott, come here!" I cry out loudly and painfully. I'm doubled over, holding my belly. It's so tight I'm struggling to breathe. "Hurry!" I scream.

Something's not right. I'm not sure if the baby is coming now or what's happening, but I'm really scared because it's way too early to be having this baby. I'm trying my best to breathe slowly through it, using the techniques from the birthing classes we took.

Scott bolts into the bathroom within seconds. "Oh, God, Billie! What's happening?"

I shake my head and manage to utter, "I don't know."

"Okay. Let's get you over to the bed." He supports me entirely as we move carefully to the edge of the bed.

After a solid minute, my back and belly loosen up, and every-thing feels completely normal again. "Okay...Okay. I think I'm okay. It went away." I rub my belly gently, trying to relax myself.

Scott has a look of sheer terror on his face. "Are you sure? Maybe we should go get you checked out just for peace of mind." He swallows hard, his breathing becoming deeper and louder. Another wave of intense squeezing and churning strikes me.

"Ow, babe. It's happening again." Scott flies off the bed to grab his phone. He's got Labor and Delivery on speed-dial.

"Hello? Yes, this is Dr. Scott Bennington. My wife says her belly is really tight, and she's having trouble breathing."

There's a moment of silence. Scott is pacing and scratching his head. "Uhhh, she's like—"

"Thirty-two weeks," I blurt out as I try breathing through the tightness again.

"She's thirty-two weeks."

Silence.

"Okay."

Silence.

"Yes."

Silence.

"No."

Silence.

"We'll be right there." Scott ends the call, rushes over to me, and kneels down. He takes his hand and runs it through my hair. The tightness has gone away, yet I'm relying on him for support. I'm scared. Like, really, really scared. Both of us look into each other's eyes with uncertainty and fear. He brings our hands together and kisses my hands. And then, he begins to pray.

"God, please be here with us as we find out what's going on. Keep us calm and help us to stay strong through whatever is happening. Please keep Billie and our baby safe. Please, I beg of you." Scott stands up and helps me up. Once I get to my feet, I almost faint. I'm woozy and suddenly incredibly nauseated. My heart is racing, and I feel cold sweats coming on. My legs give out, and Scott catches me.

"That's it. I'm calling an ambulance." He dials 911 and within ten minutes the EMTs arrive. I haven't moved from the bed. The tightening has been occurring frequently. I get so dizzy that I puke into the bedroom wastebasket.

Time whizzes by as we make it to the hospital and into a room. There are needles and fluids and blood pressure cuffs and monitors. I must have passed out at some point because no one except Scott is in the room with me when I come to again. I sense Scott clasping my hand in his. I detect kicks and nudges in my belly, so I think the baby is okay. But I feel drained of every ounce of energy.

"Hey," I croak, barely audible.

"Honey, oh, Billie." Scott leans over from his chair, cups my face with his hands, and kisses me repeatedly. I'm so weak I don't kiss him back. "How are you feeling?"

"Tired. Even blinking my eyes hurts. Is the baby..."

"Our baby is fine. Everything is all right. We're just waiting on your labs. You vomited again and passed out while the nurses were getting you all hooked up, but your temperature and heart rate have stabilized. Blood pressure is normal."

The nasty taste of vomit hits me when he says that.

Yuck.

"We probably won't know anything until the morning. What can I get you?"

"I really need to pee and brush my teeth. I'd love some ginger ale and saltines, if you don't mind." I manage a crooked smile. His face releases his stressed look as he smiles back at me.

"By the way," I add, "I heard you call me your wife."

"I can't help it. I just love you so much and love how calling you *my wife* sounds." Scott's eyes light up, and my entire body flushes with warmth.

"I can't wait to officially call you my husband."

CHAPTER FORTY-NINE

SCOTT

"Well, your lab results are in," Dr. Moseley says as she visits us first thing this morning. She seems relaxed, so I feel confident she's delivering good news. "First, the baby is flourishing. The contractions you experienced was some preterm labor. The reason why it felt so intense is because it looks like the baby has turned and is currently breech. Not to worry, though. The baby has plenty of time to flip," she assures us.

"We had you hooked up to the monitor last night, and things looked great. I would like to check you to ensure your cervix is still closed. Since the contractions subsided with the medication we administered, you can rest assured this baby is not coming today. Next, you're extremely dehydrated, so we've given you fluids to rehydrate you. You'll need to start carrying water with you at all times. Or juice. Ginger ale. Something. Whatever you can drink to stay hydrated."

Dr. Moseley flips to the next page of the report. "Finally, you, my dear, are anemic. That explains the heart pounding, nausea, weakness, and dizziness. We'll schedule weekly iron infusions until this baby gets here and possibly a few after delivery. Sugar levels are normal, which is great. No gestational diabetes. No preeclampsia. Blood pressure is slightly elevated, but no cause for concern. Everything was normal on the ultrasound, so you'll have a baby here in about eight weeks. Questions?"

I can feel my body calming itself, releasing a massive amount of stress. The room suddenly feels so much lighter.

"What happens if I start having contractions again?" Billie asks.

"Some contractions throughout the day are normal, and you will likely experience Braxton-Hicks contractions until you go into active labor. They are just practice ones, helping your body gear up for the real deal. There's no need to worry about them, and they shouldn't feel painful. You'll feel that tightening, but it's nothing to be concerned about. It's typical, especially for this stage in pregnancy. The baby will probably flip again too."

"Phew, okay. This is good news." Billie sighs in relief.

"You're doing a really great job, Billie," Dr. Moseley reassures. "Unless your water breaks, or you start having contractions so bad you can't talk through them, or they're five minutes apart lasting at least one minute, there's a good chance your body is just preparing for labor. However, call me or just come in anytime you feel concerned. You know your body and what's best."

"Got it," she replies.

"I have a question," I begin. "How early could the baby come and survive?" I bite my bottom lip, apprehensive of the answer.

"The baby would most likely be okay now, with help from the NICU. The baby's lungs won't be developed enough to breathe independently. However, the survival rate of premature babies born past twenty-eight weeks gestation is now more than ninety percent."

"That's great to hear, Dr. Moseley. Thank you." I look over at Billie and soak in her beauty.

"I'll let you two be for now. Billie, I'd like to keep you here one more night until we get your dehydration and iron levels under control. I'll be back later to check in, but if you need anything in the meantime, don't hesitate to ask," Dr. Moseley stresses.

"Will do, doc," Billie says.

After Dr. Moseley leaves, I help Billie get cleaned up and ready for the day, then it's back into bed to rest. She's still very weak. It reminds me of when I cared for Christine toward the end of her cancer. This time, I know everything will turn out in our favor.

It has to.

CHAPTER FIFTY

BILLIE

Thirty-five Weeks Pregnant

I've spent the last few weeks taking it easy. I've been having Braxton-Hicks contractions like Dr. Moseley said I would, but no more preterm labor. I'm also fairly sure this baby is head down again. Now I just need to make it to full term. Today is my bridal shower, and I'm really excited. It's going to be a small gathering, with just Scott's family, Miranda, Claire, Abbey, and Rick, but I prefer it that way. I don't need a bunch of people I don't know buying gifts and fussing over me. Talk about awkward and uncomfortable!

Scott's mom generously offered to host the shower in her backyard. Fortunately, the weather is warm and sunny. Not too hot or humid for July—a perfect day for an outdoor party. She hired a decorator and a caterer, which is completely over the top and unnecessary, but she insisted, so I obliged.

The backyard looks gorgeous. Large oak picnic tables line the center of the yard, shaded by a grand white canopy. Each table is covered with either a blue or pink gingham fabric tablecloth, with fresh blueberries and watermelon as centerpieces. Down the center of each table lies a garland of daisies, black-eyed Susans, marigolds, violets, and hibiscus.

The menu consists of a strawberry balsamic salad, bacon-wrapped scallops, a variety of tea sandwiches, shredded pork sliders, and fruit salad, with a selection of bite-sized cheesecakes for dessert. Pearl is a gem, quite literally. As I take in the scenery, I see her and Elodie finishing the decorations for the gift table.

Truth be told, I haven't spoken with Elodie since the house-warming shit show. I feel a little anxious about seeing her, but Scott has assured me he has spoken with her, and she will be kind to me moving forward.

Abbey is the first guest to arrive. It's been months since I've seen her and, even then, we've had lunch or dinner only a few times since she's moved back to Pittsburgh.

"I thought you moved back here," I joke sarcastically. Abbey sets her gift bags on the concrete patio and gives me a side hug since my baby bump is boomin' these days.

"Ugh, I know. I'm sorry. I'm a terrible cousin. This job is sucking the life out of me, I swear. The entire network has been an epic disaster since Archibald Barney fell from grace."

Good ol' Archibald Barney. He is, well, *was* the CEO of Barney Health Network, Bellevue's conglomerate monster. Barney Hospital was originally Bellevue Hospital until he took over ten years ago and renamed it after none other than himself. An egotistical prick, that's what he is. I'm not sure how he did it. He built a huge empire, purchasing surrounding hospitals, private practices, and even the city's museum and library. Then the idiot had the bright idea to embezzle money from the hospitals and launder money from the private practices. As if he wasn't raking in enough dough!

Greedy bastard.

Greed is one of the seven deadly sins and, consequently, Barney's hamartia.

His wife was the one who discovered what was happening and turned his slimeball ass in to the authorities, believe it or not. It is probably one of the biggest scandals the city has ever seen. Barney is in prison now for, like, decades and his wife divorced him. However, the mess he left behind has caused the Barney Health Network empire to nearly implode. As Chief Medical Officer, Abbey is helping to salvage the company. She has serious brains and is a force to be reckoned with.

The baby shower goes without a hitch. Everyone is obscenely generous. Rick gifts us our crib, bassinet, baby swing, and a battery-operated car the baby can drive when he or she is old enough.

Scott's mother made us a stunning knitted green blanket, just as she's made in various colors for all her grandkids. I can't hold it together when I open it. My grammie used to crochet Barbie doll clothes for me when I was little. I keep them in a storage bin with other special mementos that I can't bear to part with. I miss my grammie so much. Everyone else tears up right along with me. It's a beautiful moment.

Scott surprises me with solitaire diamond studs and a yellow newborn outfit, a nod to my dad I'm sure, perfect for bringing home our little one whether it be a boy or a girl. Words can't describe how supported and loved I feel today. I could get used to being part of a family again. I welcome it.

The evening is quiet as I start putting baby items where I want them—the light items, of course. No heavy lifting for this mama. Scott is still at his mother's house helping with cleanup, but he should be home anytime.

As I'm searching for a pair of scissors, I open my desk drawer to find an envelope with a name and address on it.

Upon further inspection, it reads:

Christine & Maggie Bennington

123 Heavenly Way

Paradise Island

My heart drops to my stomach because this has to be the letter Scott wrote to Christine at the start of his therapy sessions with Shelly. He said I could read it, but I thought I would be intruding. But now that this envelope is sitting here staring at me, I can't help myself.

I slice through the top of the envelope with a letter opener, pulling out the several handwritten pages in Scott's messy but legible handwriting, bracing myself for impact.

Dear Christine,

It's hard to believe you and Maggie have been gone for a couple of years now. Some days it seems like you just left, and others it feels like it's been decades. I miss you so very much, Maggie too. Sometimes I wonder what life would be like now with us, where we'd be, how big Maggie would have grown, if we'd have any more children. I know you two had to leave, and I'm sorry I couldn't come with you. I'm sure Paradise Island is exactly how it sounds.

I have a dog named Bruno. He is a wonderful dog. When he was a puppy, I had him trained to be a therapy dog. I take him to the hospice center several days a week to visit the residents. I always make it a point to stop at the gazebo too while I'm there. Rain or shine. It's not any different than when we sat out there all those times. When I look out into the landscape, I think of you.

Lately, I've been struggling. Actually, I've been grappling with your departure since the moment you left. I know there was no way to avoid your leaving, but the last two years I've been trudging through each day, hoping it was all a bad dream.

Christine, I need to tell you something. Recently something beautiful has happened. I met someone. Her name is Billie.

I know before you left we spoke about the future, encouraging me to find someone else to share my life with. Never in my wildest dreams did I ever think I'd find her. I wasn't even looking. She showed up one night out of the blue, and I knew I wanted her from the moment I laid eyes on her.

Billie is ravishing, such a beautiful person inside and out. She is kind to me, patient with me, and in love with me. I am hopelessly in love with her too. In fact, she doesn't know this yet, but I plan on asking her to marry me. I am looking at houses for us. She knows exactly what she wants, and I am determined to give her everything she could ever dream of because she deserves it. I want to have children with her and grow old with her.

She and I will be the crotchety couple yelling at the hooligans riding bikes outside the retirement home. We will be the ones with grandkids who stay over on weekends and kids we vacation with every year. I see it all with Billie.

I don't know how to explain it, but I know I'm meant to be with her. She is everything I didn't know I needed and all I've been waiting for.

I am so blessed to have been loved by you and now loved by Billie. How fortunate I feel to have had you in my life, and I am grateful for the time we shared together. Not many men can say they've been lucky enough to experience true love twice. I look forward to building a life with Billie. She makes me the happiest man in the world.

Although I bid farewell for now, know that I will always remember you fondly. You and Maggie will forever be in my heart.

Love always,

Scott

Tears stream down my face. A teardrop splashes onto the bottom of the letter. What a beautiful man! What heartfelt words! How reverent he is of Christine and of me! Knowing that's how he felt about me even then touches me to my core. I can't help but read the letter several more times to absorb it all.

"Hey, what's wrong?" I hear from the doorway. Scott is leaning against the door frame, propping himself up with his forearm.

"Nothing, I just..." I hold up the letter and run to his arms. I cling to him and sniffle and hiccup through the overload of emotions. Scott doesn't hug me back right away. If I had to guess, it's because he's processing that I read his letter. His stiff stature eventually relaxes, and his arms engulf me. "You are such a good, good man, you know that? I love you so much, Scott."

Although he doesn't say anything back, I don't need him to. My love, appreciation, and adoration for him only grows stronger.

CHAPTER FIFTY-ONE

SCOTT

We're counting down the days until our baby arrives, and I have this nervous excitement I can't describe. We've nearly made it to the finish line. The only thing we have to get through is childbirth—and by *we*, I mean Billie. Then we can go home and live happily ever after.

We deserve the "happily ever after."

Before reaching my office, I pick up coffees and some bagels and soak in a few sunrays on this beautiful morning. There's something about the morning sunlight that boosts my whole mood for the day. I walk into reception with a smile on my face and a growling stomach.

"Gooooood morning, *Miran*—" I halt. Something is wrong. Miranda stands abruptly when she sees me walk in. Her face looks like she's seen a ghost.

"What's wrong? Are you okay?" I hope her family is all right. Anything she needs, she's got it.

"Scottie, I have some bad news," Miranda chokes out. I go to her, setting the bagels and coffees on her desk and putting my hand on her shoulder. "I'm afraid..." Miranda sniffles, "I'm afraid Layla didn't make it. She passed away this morning." She looks at me with the most painful eyes, and tears stream down her face. My mind becomes blank. The news does not register right away.

"What do you mean she died, Miranda?" I'm in denial. I just saw her at the beginning of the week. She was battling a respiratory infection, but we had everything under control. I put both my hands on Miranda's shoulders, gripping them firmly, nearly shaking her. "What do you mean she died?" I bark.

My emotions are choking me, strangling me, fighting to break through. I attempt to swallow them down but exhale instead, letting out an anguished sob. Miranda hugs me tightly, crying with me. When we finally get ourselves under control, I ask what happened.

"Her heart. The meds seemed to be fighting the infection, but she took a turn and her poor heart gave out. They tried to revive her, but she was gone. I'm so sorry, Scottie. I know how special she has been to you," she soothes.

My pain bubbles into anger.

"Why didn't anyone call me?" I bellow, ripping my phone from my pocket to make sure I hadn't missed any calls. Zero missed calls and no voicemails. Miranda remains calm and comforting, although I can hear in her tone that she is shaken too.

"It all happened so fast. Even if you had been called, you wouldn't have made it here in time. She went from stable to gone quite rapidly. There was nothing you could have done. I'm so sorry." Miranda gives me another hug, more tender this time, and I embrace her back, letting my guard down and vulnerability consume me for a moment. I attempt to regain my composure because it won't be long before patients start arriving for their scheduled appointments. In the meantime, I book it down to

Layla's hospital room to see if the family and Layla's precious little body are still there.

Now, I've lost patients before, but Layla is one of a kind. She has an inner joy that lights up a room. She is hopeful and positive. She has never been angry or bitter about her diagnosis and treatment. Maybe that's why she's always fascinated me. It's as if she came to terms with her possible fate during her first round of treatment, so there were no ill feelings toward potential outcomes. Perhaps that's why she's so remarkable. She remained peaceful and accepting, two things I struggle with. And maybe in a way I'm jealous of her ability to practice gratitude during a time of despair.

And, too, maybe when Layla went into remission, I thought of it as my redemption for failing Christine. That since she and Maggie are gone, that Layla would live. That Layla would be granted the long life Maggie never had and the success of the treatment that Christine didn't. But none of that matters now. I was wrong to think any of that this entire time.

When I get to the corridor, I notice Layla's parents, red-eyed and robotic, speaking with Dr. Turner, my colleague. Layla's mother, Sophie, spots me first, with puffy eyes and tears streaked down her face. Then her husband, Brandon, glances over with tightly pressed lips and gives me a subtle nod of hello.

I enter the hospital room to find Layla still lying there. I've seen dead bodies before, small children included, but this one is different. She doesn't look dead. She doesn't look sick. She looks angelic. Peaceful. Her little lips are still pink, her cheeks rosy. Pallor mortis hasn't set in, so she had to have passed less than thirty minutes ago.

There are no monitors or machines, only a bed reclined and little Layla, with a butterfly hat on her head, her eyes closed, and her hands resting on top of her chest.

"I'm sorry I failed you, Layla," I whisper. "Rest in peace, sweet child." A surge of heat courses through my body as I force myself to contain my emotions. Now is not the time or place to express anything other than sympathy to Layla's parents. I extend my condolences when they come back into the room, Brandon shaking my hand and Sophie hugging me with what energy she can muster. Before I return to my office, I give one long final look at Layla and her parents, remembering that it was Christine and me once with Maggie, under different circumstances. Grieving the loss of your child is unmatched agony.

The day goes painstakingly slowly, but I make it through the motions, pretending I haven't failed again, acting like there's hope for all my patients and providing good news the rest of the day.

When I get home, I march straight upstairs without so much as saying "hello" to Billie. I know she sees me come in because I hear a "hey" from the couch, but I cannot hold it in any longer. I shut myself in the bathroom and turn on the shower as cold as I can stand it.

I lose it.

I break down.

I let out every emotion I've been pacifying all day, and I'm leaving it all on the shower floor. The sobs erupt viciously and they stop for nothing.

CHAPTER FIFTY-TWO

BILLIE

I knock softly on the door when I hear weeping coming from the master bathroom. It's unusual for Scott not to greet me when he arrives home from work. Something is very wrong.

"Scott?" I say gently.

No response except more crying.

"Scott, honey?" I repeat. This time I open the door to see Scott hunched over and weeping uncontrollably in the shower. "Baby, what happened?"

"I can't, Billie. I can't do this anymore," he babbles. Panic activates because I have no idea what "this" is, and that terrifies me.

I carefully open the shower door and freezing cold water splashes me, causing me to retreat in surprise. I manage to shut off the water and grab a towel. Scott may not be fully aware I'm in his presence. His cries are that intense. I dry him off with the towel and wrap it around his shoulders, escorting him out of the shower.

"Shhh. It's okay. It's all right. I'm here for you. Talk to me. What's wrong?" I attempt to soothe him, but I'm not convinced it's working. He slides down to the floor, his breath hiccuping, and stares blankly at the wall. I carefully sit myself down beside him and maneuver the best way I can to comfort him.

"I lost a patient today," he mumbles with disbelief. "A little girl. She died and I couldn't save her. I didn't save her!" His voice cracks and he coughs out another cry. I wrap my arms tightly around him to warm his frozen body.

"I can't do it anymore, Billie. I don't want to do this job any longer." Alarm bells sound. It wasn't long ago I decided to stay home permanently and just do occasional consulting for Rick because Scott promised he'd take care of us. I'm trying not to show my fear because I know he's emotional right now. I don't want to add fuel to the dumpster fire that was his day.

"Let's get you dressed and warm, and then we can talk about it."

I just finish pouring the tea when Scott slips in behind me to rub my baby bump. The baby gives his hand a swift kick, and Scott silently chuckles. I relax into his embrace. We sway back and forth while our bodies bond.

"I'm sorry," he whispers as he kisses my temple. "I didn't mean to scare you. I've had everything bottled up for so long, and my patient's dying was the final straw that broke me." I place my hands over his, which are still snuggled on my belly, and lightly squeeze, acknowledging I've heard him.

"I've been giving a lot of thought lately to what I want to do, even before this happened. Don't worry, I will take care of us just as I promised before." I wait for him to continue because I'm not sure what to say yet.

"What are your thoughts on starting a foundation? Between your dad and Christine and my involvement with the hospice center, what if we started a foundation for those on hospice? I know a lot of people in the medical field. I can put out feelers for donors. We can apply for grants, and you know you're a whizz with writing and advertising. I can see about moving into full-time research at work while we get everything up and running." A note of excitement lifts his tone. "Think it over."

I perk up because I like his idea...a lot. I could stay mentally fresh in a professional sense while devoting my time to the baby. If we run the foundation, things would be pretty flexible. I'd get to see Scott more, and advocating for families with terminally ill family members would bring more joy and less sorrow. Between the two of us, we have experienced devastating deaths the last few years. We're both emotionally drained of grieving, of feeling hopeless with no end in sight.

We slip outside to the patio to enjoy the clear, starry sky. His cup of chamomile tea and my raspberry leaf tea steam like extinguished flames.

"I'm in. Let's do it," I say, moving my gaze from the sky to a pair of glistening green eyes.

"Are you sure you're ready to take this on? You want to do this with me, babe?" Scott's expression looks excited and hopeful. He reaches his arm out and grabs my hand, kissing the top of my fingers.

"Every day. I want it all with you."

CHAPTER FIFTY-THREE

SCOTT

Layla's viewing and funeral are gut-wrenching. As soon as I walk into the funeral home, I excuse myself to the men's room because I can't breathe. I can't go in there and start crying, so I take a few deep breaths, splash some water on my face, and get myself together.

There are so many people here. The line is out the door and down the street. Billie was adamant about coming with me, even though I told her she should be resting. She at least compromised and took a seat in the community lounge while I waited in line.

I extend my condolences to the family and move to the casket, where angelic little Layla lies in eternal slumber. She's wearing the cutest little black-blue-and-white butterfly dress, with a complementary butterfly headband. Layla's favorite color was blue. Sophie, her mother, told me that before Layla died, Layla insisted she be dressed like a butterfly if this time came because she would break from the cocoon of her human body and turn into a butterfly angel.

How wise to say, coming from such a small child. I'm not surprised, though. Layla was wise beyond her years. May she rest in peace.

After the funeral, we attend the luncheon held at the church hall. Miranda is there with her husband, and the four of us sit together while we eat.

"Miranda, I'm afraid I have some bad news," I say. Normally Miranda would give me a smartass answer, but today she doesn't. She looks at me warmly with brows furrowed with concern.

"I'm afraid you're going to have to retire soon," I continue. I know Miranda has been wanting to retire and that she's stayed on longer than she had planned because we have such a close working relationship. Since I'm moving into full-time research soon, which just got approved this morning, I won't need an administrative assistant.

Miranda stops chewing, the corners of her mouth turning into a frown. "What are you talking about, Scottie?"

"Well, I'm moving fully into research in the coming weeks, and I won't be needing an administrative assistant anymore. I know you've been joking about retiring over the last year, but I know you want to, and...it's time." Cedric, Miranda's husband, places his hand on Miranda's shoulder and smiles.

"I don't know what to say." She doesn't become emotional often, but in this moment, we understand that our time together in a professional setting is coming to a close. Miranda will always be a part of my life. She's family to me. I look forward to birthday parties and cookouts together with our families.

"Say, 'thank you, Scottie,'" I joke. Miranda clicks her tongue and rolls her eyes. "Oh, and one more thing." I pull out an envelope and pass it to her. She cautiously takes it from me and opens it up. I watch as she pulls out the check for $10,000. Miranda gasps in shock.

"Scottie, what is this?" Miranda breathes audibly.

"It's a thank-you for your dedication all these years. I figured it would be a nice gift to take on your cruise in a few weeks." I smirk because I enjoy seeing Miranda speechless.

"But this is a *personal check*. Not some kind of bonus for a job well done. I can't accept this," Miranda argues, handing me the check.

"Take the damn money and retire already, Miranda! Jeez! Or I'll be forced to fire you," I tease. Miranda meets my eyes, and a tear streaks down her face. It's the end of an era for us. I will miss working with her. We all have to move on at some point. She deserves to spend her remaining years enjoying her family.

"Thank you," she mouths to me. I nod my head and wink, an unspoken understanding between us.

When we finish mingling and saying our goodbyes, Billie and I are more than ready to go home to unwind. I see her visibly wince in pain as she walks through the parking lot. I carefully help Billie into our new baby-ready SUV. She's been a warrior through this last trimester. Only a few more weeks to go.

I round the other side of the vehicle and reach for my door handle. There sits a black butterfly with bright blue wings.

A *blue* butterfly, Layla's favorite color. I stick my finger out toward the handle, and the butterfly crawls onto my finger. It flaps its wings while I examine it for a moment, then flies on its merry way. I smile to myself because that had to be a sign from Layla, letting me know she's okay. I couldn't make this up if I tried. There's no explanation other than that those who have passed are always watching over us.

CHAPTER FIFTY-FOUR

BILLIE

Thirty-seven Weeks Pregnant

Scott has become a stage five clinger. Not that I mind more attention, but I feel huge and am not enjoying the constant hovering. I know protecting the baby and me is a top priority for him, but I wouldn't mind running to the grocery store alone. Since I'm in the last month of pregnancy, I get that he'd want to be with me every moment he can in case I go into labor.

Since I met Scott, I've never prodded him about church or religion, but I've continued to practice mine, going to Mass weekly, praying, and just trying to live a good, spiritual life. Pregnancy out of wedlock and "living in sin" with Scott hasn't stopped me from fostering my relationship with Jesus. This past year, I have been focusing on spirituality versus the constructs of religion.

However, I've seen the stares, heard the whispers behind my back. And while the gossiping bothers me a little, I remind myself that Jesus never turned away from anyone—*no one*—and acting Christian-like does not include shunning unwed mothers from the Church.

It's Sunday morning. I'm slipping into the coolest sundress I can find because this July heat has me swollen like a sausage link. The winner is a tea-length white cotton sundress, patterned in purple and orange flowers, paired with white slip-on sandals that fit my swollen feet. The summer heat is no joke. I'm braiding my hair when Scott enters the bedroom and gives me a kiss on the cheek.

"I think I'm going to come to Mass with you today," he says, selecting a purple polo from our closet.

"Babe, you really don't have to do that. I'll be fine. If anything happens, I'll call you right away."

"I know I don't have to, but I want to," he replies, wrapping his arms around me from behind and rubbing my baby bump. I love when he does that. "You're so pretty, you know that?"

"I feel like a giant Easter egg," I sigh.

"I love Easter eggs," he replies, kissing my neck.

"Now, you listen. You can't be getting me all worked up before church, so you just keep your paws down, boy." He gives me another lingering kiss before readying himself for the day.

I'm hyper aware of the influx of stares and whispers today. Maybe it's because everyone has finally seen me with a man and realize that I'm not knocked up by some random one-night stand. And even if I had been, they can still mind their business.

Scott takes notice and offers his reassuring affection—not in a weird sort of way, but he holds my hand and sits close to me.

After Mass, most people congregate outside for a while and chat, greeting the priest while the kids burn off some energy climbing on the playground and playing tag in the large grassy area. I usually don't stick around, but several people make it a point to greet me and meet Scott. The interactions seem genuine, but it's hard to feel welcome and included when you know half of them are gossiping behind your back.

At some point, Scott and I get separated. I'm talking to Agnes Bailer, the church organist, who knew my dad very well. Scott is chatting with Isadore Rice, who owns Rice Dealership. I'm guessing he's schmoozing for sponsorships for the foundation he's been working tirelessly to build for the last few weeks. Any spare second he has, he's researching, making phone calls, and whatever it is one does to start a foundation.

I happen to glance over and see none other than Betty Ann Barber approaching Scott and Isadore. She has removed her sweater to reveal a tight pastel-pink spaghetti-strapped sundress that accentuates her breasts, which are in full bloom. I can't help but roll my eyes and spy on her. Betty Ann has no reason to go over there and speak with them, so it's only a matter of time before I lose my shit outside of a Catholic church.

Dear sweet Agnes is still going on about some event she and my dad organized years ago. I nod along while staring directly at Betty Ann. She flirtatiously touches Isadore on the arm and laughs way too loud at something he says.

Watch yourself, Betty Ann.

The last thing I remember Agnes saying is "puppy parade" when the *biatch* does it. Betty Ann puts her arm on Scott's shoulder. I notice Scott stiffen and take a step back, kindly removing her hand. Her boobs are unmistakable, but neither men pay the voluptuous ladies any attention. My blood is boiling as I observe her use her fake southern drawl to converse with Scott and Isadore. But when she playfully touches Scott's chest, I go berserk.

I waddle my very pregnant self right over to them and slide in between her and Scott. "Betty Ann," I say politely through gritted teeth, "how lovely to see you." Her smile morphs from flirtatious to disdainful. She eyes me up and down, sucking her teeth stained with pink lipstick and rolling her eyes as she looks away.

"Well, I think it's time Billie and I take off for the day. Nice to meet you both. Isadore, I look forward to our lunch next week," Scott says, wrapping his arm around my waist and gently squeezing my hip in reassurance.

"It was nice to meet you too, Dr. Bennington," Betty Ann says as she squeezes her breasts together to reveal more cleavage.

"Betty Ann, if I may," I say calmly but with a clear tone of sarcasm, "would you be a dear and put your tits away? No one wants to see your fake deflated sacks. Scott prefers these babies." I squeeze and push up my swollen breasts so she gets a good look at them, then shimmy. Scott's cheeks puff out and eyes pop to hide shock and laughter. I pivot squarely and walk away, taking Scott's hand to follow me. I hear Betty Ann scoff, clutching the string of white pearls around her neck.

How symbolic.

I hear Isadore guffaw and, when I look back at Betty Ann, she's staring at me with daggers in her eyes. Then she whips herself around in the opposite direction and stomps off to wherever it is she's going next.

"If you're going to do that with your boobs, Billie, you need to be prepared for me to jump you. You're so hot when you're fiery mad," Scott says lustfully.

My grimace turns into a smirk, and we laugh ourselves the whole way to the car. I'm not going to lie, telling off Betty Ann Barber feels invigorating. I don't think anyone has ever had the guts to put her in her place before, except me. I'm tired of her hypocritical bullshit. This reinforced backbone I have since being pregnant is as solid as steel.

CHAPTER FIFTY-FIVE

BILLIE

August 1st

C an you believe it's officially baby month?"

I can't stop smiling as I assess the nursery. Mint walls with white trim provide a calm, relaxing environment, furnished with a gray crib and changing table. The accent wall contains a painted mural of baby forest animals, compliments of Scott's sister Scarlet. A white glider sits in the corner, waiting for a baby to be rocked to sleep. We received enough diapers and wipes at the shower to last us the first month or two at least. The hospital bag is packed, the yellow coming-home outfit washed up and neatly folded on top of everything else in the suitcase.

I think I'm ready to meet this little boy or girl in a few weeks. I rub my belly to soothe the kicks and headbutts from a baby who is very active today. He or she will undoubtedly be an acrobat.

I will miss the baby kicks.

Scott and I are sitting on the floor, folding the last of the newborn baby clothes. Most of them are neutral, just to get us started.

"No, it feels really surreal. I feel good, about as ready as I can be. I'm here for you all the way. It's going to be great," Scott says. He seems relaxed and excited today, which helps me feel more at ease.

He stands up and starts stacking diapers, wipes, and other baby necessities onto the changing table.

I truly want to believe he's feeling okay. Recently, though, I've heard the sound of panic attacks coming from the bathroom in the middle of the night. I want to go comfort him, but the last time he had one midday, he said not to concern myself with them because he doesn't want to stress out me or the baby. He has emphasized time and time again that he has everything under control and is working through it. I'm not the least bit convinced, but I respect his wishes.

He continues to attend therapy and grief counseling weekly. I'm wondering if maybe he should see Shelly twice a week for now, at least until the baby comes.

Nevertheless, my nervousness about labor and delivery is increasing by the minute. I have no idea when or how it's going to happen, and there's only so much preparing I can do for the pain. I've had Braxton-Hicks contractions since the preterm labor incident at thirty-two weeks, but those contractions aren't really painful. Dr. Moseley knows to have the epidural on standby when it's *go time.*

"You're right," I say, holding up a tiny onesie patterned with tiny brown teddy bears. I lay it over my baby bump. "Well, little babe. We're ready for you whenever you're ready." I rub my belly again and feel another kick.

I fold the last few items just as Scott finishes stocking the changing table. I attempt to stand up, but my baby bump is simply too big.

"Babe," I frown, "can you help me up, please?"

"Of course. Here, grab my hands." He leans down and firmly holds my hands as I rock backward just slightly to get enough momentum to stand up. When I get to my feet, I feel something wet. I think I peed myself.

"Oh, my gosh! Scott, I just peed myself!" I laugh.

"Baby pushing down on that bladder pretty hard today, huh?"

"I think so. There's a lot of pressure down there too. I feel like I have to pee every five minutes, I swear. You stay here and put that pile of baby clothes away while I attempt to change my clothes."

I take two steps and feel a little gush. It's not quite like a water balloon popping, but it definitely isn't pee. I lean over and hold up the bottom of my belly to see if releasing some of the pressure of my bladder will help. More fluid comes out.

"Scott?" I say nervously.

"What? What's wrong?" He rushes over to me.

"I think my water just broke."

CHAPTER FIFTY-SIX

SCOTT

It's happening.

It's now.

It's too early.

We're supposed to have seventeen more days.

Cue internal panic. I knew the triggers were going to hit hard. This labor and delivery is about making sure Billie and the baby are safe. That I support her in any way she needs me. That I don't freak out. But I didn't expect it to happen *right now*. First babies usually surpass their due dates, or so I thought.

"Okay, let's go. I'll grab our bags. We can leave right now. It's going to be fine. Are you in pain?" I am officially in dad mode.

"No, no pain. Wait, I don't want to go yet," Billie protests.

"Why? Dr. Moseley said if your water breaks, we have to go to the hospital to reduce the risk of infection." I've listened to every single word out of that doctor's mouth. I've been to all of the prenatal appointments, and I've read everything I can get my hands on.

"She also said if my water breaks and contractions don't start right away to take our time and not get all worked up. Now, I really want to get a shower to relax me. You double-check the bags. Call the hospital to give them a heads-up that we're coming. Tell Dr. Moseley to make sure that epidural is on standby. Call Claire to come get Bruno. When I'm finished, we will go to the hospital regardless. Deal?"

Billie is breathtaking. She's about to deliver our child, and she's talking *me* off the ledge.

"You're the boss." I pull her in and wrap my arms around her, holding her tightly. I feel her breathing change against me.

"Are you having a contraction?" I ask, fully alert.

"No, you're squeezing me too hard," she strains to speak. I quickly release her.

"Ah! Billie, I'm so sorry." She looks up at me and smiles. "It's all right," she sighs. "I guess we're having a baby today. Let's do this."

CHAPTER FIFTY-SEVEN

BILLIE

I didn't have "going into labor seventeen days early" on my bingo card. Technically, I'm not in labor yet, but this baby is coming today whether we're ready or not. If I don't start contracting within six hours, Dr. Moseley wants to administer Pitocin to jump-start labor. I've heard all the stories about how hard labor is right out of the gate with inducing, and I'm already scared of how bad the pain is going to be.

Change of plans. Instead of heading to the bathroom to shower, I change my underwear, put on a super pad and some fresh leggings, and descend the stairs.

Gush. Gush. Trickle.

Scott notices me round the corner of the staircase while he's talking to Claire.

"Hey, where are you going?" he asks, alarmed. "Do we need to leave? Are you having contractions?"

"No, not yet. I'm going to walk the curb first to try to get labor started before I take that shower." I open the door and waddle out.

"Please be careful. I'll be right out," he calls after me.

"I will be fine, I promise. I'll be thirty feet away."

I pull up my '80s playlist on my phone and press play. The first song "Heaven Is a Place on Earth" by—of course—Belinda Carlisle pumps through the speaker. I'm flushed and don't want to put earbuds in, so I just turn the volume up and start walking. I get to the house next door and feel a tightness across my stomach. It's not painful and I can still walk just fine. I get to the next house and it happens again. Still, not painful. I turn around and go the other way.

Nothing. No tightness. No contractions. No pain. Just more fluid trickling.

Scott comes bursting out of the front door onto the porch, with the phone to his chest.

"Anything?" he calls.

"Nope! All good," I call back with a thumbs-up.

"I'm talking to Shelly. If anything happens, you call me. I'll be done in fifteen minutes unless you need me."

"Go. I'm fine, I promise."

I curb walk back and forth until my swollen pancake feet can't take it anymore. Still no contractions. This is disappointing. I know labor can take a while, especially with the first baby, but the intrusive thoughts of Pitocin are psyching me out. I need to get myself under control. If I stress, the baby will notice and become distressed.

Calm. I need to remain calm.

I inhale deeply and blow out all my breath, focusing and grounding myself in the moment. I place one hand on my belly and one on my chest. I inhale and exhale slowly a few more times until I feel clear and peaceful. As I walk back into the house, Scott is ending his call.

"Anything?" He walks over to me.

"No," I shrug, clearly looking defeated. "I'm going to try that shower to see if it helps."

"Okay, but not too hot. Dr Moseley said—"

"Babe?" I put up my hand to stop him from talking. "I know. Everything is going to be fine. I'll call for you if I need anything."

Scott softens his expression and cracks a mischievous smile. "You know, sex can cause contractions. Maybe that'll put you into labor. Would you like my assistance with that?" He rubs my shoulders slowly and firmly. The massage releases the tension I've been holding in my shoulders.

"At this point, I'd be willing to try anything, but my water broke. I can't have you poking around in there. I'll let you know if anything happens. I'll be right upstairs."

I start the shower and ensure the temperature is lukewarm. I'm starting to feel more flushed, so I turn it to a cooler temperature. I give my hair a thorough wash. I put in the fancy conditioner and let it sit for a few minutes. I shave my armpits. I'm not even going to attempt my legs or vag because I can't bend down or see anything beyond my belly. I wash what I can of myself and call for Scott. He dashes into the bathroom in record time.

"Is it happening? Are you having a contraction?"

"I need you to wash my back and my legs," I say, pouting.

"You got it." He stands behind me and gently moves the soapy loofah up and down my legs. He washes my back and rinses me off, then steps into the shower, fully clothed and everything.

"What are you doing?" I ask, surprised by the unexpected gesture, but I welcome him in.

"I just want to relax you. I won't try anything. Put your hands up against the shower wall and let the water run down your back. I'll massage your neck, shoulders, and back."

He's the best. Whatever Shelly told Scott is working because for the first time since my water broke, I don't feel petrified. The cascading water paired with the massaging is kind of turning me on.

How? No clue at a time like this.

I feel heavy pressure down below, but it eases when I feel a surge of pain right under my breasts. Everything from my belly to my back tightens.

Okay, this is new.

The squeezing intensifies for a few seconds before easing up, then nothing.

We stay in the shower for a while because I don't want to move yet. The steady noise and water from the shower put me into a trance.

Pressure and tightness waves in again, with deeper pain this time. I take some deep breaths because the squeezing is making it hard to breathe. It's still bearable, but I feel pretty confident this is it. Scott notices my change in body language.

"Are you all right?" he asks quietly.

"Contraction." It's all I can muster saying until the wave starts to subside. Scott shuts off the water, grabs a towel, and starts drying me off. "Thank you. Can you please grab my phone and start timing them?"

"Anything you need. I'm right here." After a quick swap into dry clothes and delicately drying me off, Scott helps me get dressed and gathers all the stuff we need for the hospital. He stops to hold me through the next couple contractions.

"How long was that one?" I take a cleansing breath as the contraction finishes.

"About thirty seconds long, and the last one was about eight minutes ago."

"Go get an actual shower. We still have time. We don't have to leave until they're five minutes apart, lasting a minute."

"I am not leaving you, Billie."

"It'll take you five minutes. You'll probably be done before my next contraction." I argue.

"Fine, but—"

"Yes, honey, I will call for you if anything happens," I snap. Scott hurries to the bathroom. I wanted to dry and straighten my hair, but why? I'm going to be sweating anyway. I decide to go for the double French braids look. As soon as I secure the first braid, a strong contraction waves in so powerfully I can't call for Scott. I prop myself on the edge of the bed, trying to breathe through it.

That was not eight minutes!

The pain of the contraction paralyzes me. I'm determined to secure this last braid, though, before we leave for the hospital. I've still got time. *I think.*

"I was in and out in four minutes. How are you doing?" He's practically breathless, dashing around the room like a chicken with its head cut off.

Another contraction hits. *Hard.* I don't have to say anything. Scott panics due to my pained expression and heavy breathing. The contraction subsides, but it was longer this time.

Five minutes, my ass! It's time to go!

I quickly finish my braid. Claire hasn't made it over here yet.

What is taking her so long?

He must know what I'm thinking because he randomly blurts out, "Claire is on her way, but we do not have to wait. Bruno will be fine. Are you ready to go have this baby?"

I nod my head when another contraction hits. I grip onto him, crying out in pain, and he holds me through it. Once I can talk again, I choke out, "I think we need to hurry."

Scott carefully leads me to the car. His body is shaking. His face remains strong. I know he's scared, but he's doing well holding himself together. Another contraction surges before I'm in the passenger seat.

"I'm scared. I thought labor was supposed to build intensity gradually. It's happening so fast. Too fast. How long between contractions?"

"Uhhh," he answers, fumbling for the phone. "The last one was less than three minutes ago, a minute long."

"Shit. Shit. Okay. Stay cool, but you need to drive as quickly and safely as you can."

"I'll get us there, baby, I promise. Focus on your breathing and hold my hand when you need it."

God, I love this man.

We get five minutes down the road when the contractions change intensity. I'm starting to moan through them because it's the only thing I can muster.

"Billie? What's happening?" Scott asks nervously.

"Hurry. Please!" I scream when the next contraction hits me. Scott hits his flashers and speeds up.

I better not have this baby in the car.

CHAPTER FIFTY-EIGHT

SCOTT

I breathe with Billie through her contractions because it's the only thing keeping me sane right now. We're less than a mile away from the hospital, and Billie is groaning and grunting. I don't know exactly what that means, but I sure as hell don't want to deliver this baby in the car. It's been less than two hours since her water broke. Labor is moving rapidly and fiercely. I have been this terrified only one other time. That was when Maggie was born. So far, the experience of Billie's labor is dangerously close to Christine's. My PTSD is surfacing, but I'm stuffing it down as best as I can.

I screech up to the emergency room entrance and burst through the doors. "Wife. Baby coming. Car. Help," I heave, pointing toward the entrance. The receptionist calls Labor and Delivery and instructs an orderly to get a wheelchair and bring in the patient.

I hear Billie shriek. I bolt out the entrance and open the car door. She's breathing heavily and her forehead is dewy with sweat.

"We need her up there now!" I shout.

After her contraction ends, the orderly helps me get Billie into the wheelchair. When we get to the correct floor, I see nurses racing toward the Labor and Delivery entrance to let us in. They can probably hear Billie screaming. I'm semi-calm on the outside, but I am freaking out inside.

What if something's wrong? God, please don't let anything be wrong.

Several hazy minutes pass by as the staff gets Billie on a bed and monitors set up.

"Billie," a nurse says in a stable voice, "how far apart are your contractions, honey?" Billie is breathing heavily, sweat dripping down her face. If there's one thing I've remembered so far, it's timing these contractions. I glance at my phone.

"They're right on top of each other, about a minute apart," I answer for her.

"All right. I need you to relax your legs so I can determine how dilated you are. I'm going to stick my fingers in you. You will feel pressure and it might hurt some."

The nurse pulls down Billie's leggings and underwear.

"Oh, shit," the nurse whispers under her breath.

"What's wrong?!" I panic.

This cannot be happening again! I can't lose them! Don't take them from me. No. No. NO!

A blast of dizziness threatens my consciousness.

It has to be okay. Everything will be okay. I need to be strong right now. Billie needs me.

The nurse calls out, "She's crowning. I need a doctor in here right now or I'm catching this baby myself."

Billie manages to cry out, "I need to push. NOW!" I see her face turning red. She squeezes my hand as she bears down. Any second now I'm going to be a father.

"You're doing so great, Billie. I love you so much."

She lets out a guttural scream and begins to push again when Dr. Moseley rushes in with a blue gown and gloves on.

"Sounds like we're having a baby in here," she says chipperly.

"Oh, thank God you're here," Billie cries.

"The head is out. She's going to have this baby in another push or two," the nurse says as she trades places with the doctor.

"On your next contraction, I need you to breathe in deeply, put your chin to your chest and push like you're trying to poop. You're almost there," Dr. Moseley instructs.

Billie nods her head. She looks exhausted.

"You got this, baby," I whisper.

Billie inhales deeply and pushes.

"Shoulder is out, Billie. Give me one more big push, and we will have a baby." The doctor is wiggling and maneuvering down there, but if I look, I may pass out. I'm barely holding on.

Billie grunts through a primal scream. There's a moment of silence before I hear the most beautiful sound I have ever heard.

Our baby's cry.

Immediately, I'm overwhelmed with emotion. "You did it! You did it, honey!" I weep happily.

The doctor places the baby directly onto Billie's chest. Billie shakes uncontrollably.

"She's shivering, Dr. Moseley," I point out.

"That's normal," she reassures me. "Her vitals are stable. Her body is just in shock."

"Hi, Baby. Hello there, sweet one. I'm your mommy," Billie soothes as the baby cries. She has been fantastic through this whole ordeal. Tears flood as I kiss her on the forehead. We stare at our child, mesmerized.

"I'm so proud of you," I murmur.

"Did you see the baby's sex?" Dr. Moseley asks.

We both shake our heads.

Billie turns the baby over and...

A boy. I have a son.

"It's a boy!" I announce.

Billie begins crying and looks up to kiss me. I kiss her with everything I have because I love her with my entire body and soul. All the nurses congratulate us. We both sigh in relief.

He's here. And everyone is safe and healthy. Thank you, God.

CHAPTER FIFTY-NINE

BILLIE

I can't stop ogling over my precious, perfect little boy. I am shocked at how fast labor and delivery went, from zero to baby in a matter of a couple hours. I was fully prepared for a twelve-hour or longer labor, with an epidural somewhere in there. But not this hurricane. Yet something instinctual took over. I felt so empowered.

Scott did exceptionally well too. I became terrified after the contractions picked up momentum. But once we got in the car, I let my body do what it needed to do. Instead of working *against* the pain, I worked *with it*. It still hurt like hell though.

I hold my son against my chest to experience the skin-to-skin bond. My body feels warm and peaceful, even though it's trembling uncontrollably. Scott is sniffling and wiping tears from his eyes. I reassure him that everyone is okay. Once I'm ready, Scott cuts the umbilical cord, and the nurses begin cleaning up the baby.

Dr. Moseley is currently stitching me up because I tore a little, but at least I'm numb down there now. "See, that wasn't so bad, was it, Billie? Didn't even need that epidural," She chatters. I can't tell if she's being sarcastic or not.

"Ha. Yeah, piece of cake!" I exclaim.

"You can consider yourself lucky with how fast and smoothly that went. Precipitous labor isn't typical, more like a sprint versus a marathon. You delivered beautifully. Just a few stitches. You'll heal up in no time." I know she does this all the time, but Dr. Moseley is going about her day as usual, like I didn't expel a baby the size of a watermelon out of a keyhole—*unmedicated*—a few minutes ago. I'm skeptical to think anything looks "beautiful" down there.

"Eight pounds, one ounce, and twenty inches long," a nurse announces.

"Wow, that sounds big," I huff.

He felt big too.

"For just over thirty-seven weeks gestation, that's a hefty baby. If you had gone to your due date, you could have been pushing a ten-pounder." Dr. Moseley doesn't say that in jest. She is serious.

"Yikes! I guess you're right then. I will consider myself lucky."

And I am. I am the luckiest girl in the whole world.

A perfectly healthy eight-pound, one-ounce baby on August 1, both inversions of the number 18. That's not a coincidence. My dad is here watching over us, no doubt about it.

Once we're all settled, I am finally able to rest.

Scott cradles the baby and sways back and forth, enamored by his tiny coos and grunts, looking him over from head to toe. At this moment, everything is right with the world.

"You know," Scott begins, "we need to choose a name for this little guy."

"That's right. We never really decided." I put my finger in the baby's palm. He latches onto my finger instantly.

"I was thinking we could name him Theodore after your dad. We could call him *Theo*. What do you think?" Scott looks at me with a hopeful expression.

I choke up a little before answering. "I love that. He looks like a *Theo*," I agree.

"What about a middle name?" he asks.

I pause. There's only one that comes to mind so that the baby's name honors each of the people we cherish so deeply.

"Considering he's a boy, how about *Christopher?* In honor of Christine." Tears well up in Scott's eyes, and that's when I know it's the perfect name for the baby.

"Thank you, Billie. You have no idea how much that means to me."

Even though we've been through so much pain, this is a poignant moment of healing for both of us.

We have fallen out of grief.

"Theodore Christopher Bennington," Scott gushes, "welcome to the world, my son."

EPILOGUE

SCOTT

One Year Later

F ive minutes!" calls the wedding coordinator.

Today, August 18, I am honored to marry Billie and become her husband. It was Theo's due date, and 18 is the number sign from Billie's father. The number pops up multiple times every single day. It's unexplainable. I know Teddy is watching over us and showering us with love.

This past year has been wonderful. Billie is a natural mother, so loving, so patient. I feel well. I am in a place of healing, rather than trapped in a pit of grief I can't climb out of. I still have bad days sometimes, but Billie has been graciously understanding and supportive, just as I am when she has bad days grieving her father. We have a joyous life together, and I am grateful to have been given a second chance to love and have a family.

I get into place at the altar. Then the bridesmaids process down the aisle. I'm chewing my lip, holding back the waterworks, but I know the tears are coming.

Here comes little Theo, pulled in a wagon by his older cousins Meredith and Maren. Everyone "ohs" and "ahs" over them.

The music changes and the back doors to the church shut. When they open, the most beautiful soul is standing there.

My Billie. My wife.

She is escorted by Rick, who has continued to treat her like his daughter. When our eyes meet, tears begin streaming down my face. She has pure love in her eyes for me. I have said it before and will say it forever. Billie is breathtaking.

Her white dress has a modest sheer v-neck bodice and long sleeves, overlaid with a floral lace appliqué. The curve-hugging bodice and silhouette accentuate everything I love about her. Her floor-length veil meets the train of her dress and highlights her luxurious wavy chocolate-brown hair, which reaches her hips. She's carrying a bouquet of yellow roses, naturally.

Billie doesn't cry as she walks down the aisle. Instead, she smiles from ear to ear. She is confident and ready. So am I.

The day is like one out of a movie—the kind where everything goes smoothly and looks perfect. Everyone is having a fantastic time. August 18 will always be a special day, the one Billie and I chose to celebrate our commitment to a lifelong journey together.

If I didn't have faith, my life circumstances would seem contrived. I've never been a particularly religious man, but I have to believe there's something more for us after this life. I need to believe that Christine and Maggie are restored into perfect beings, living in Heaven, watching over me. It's impossible for me not to think that Billie's dad is clearly showing us signs he's still here with us. The repetitive numbers and yellow roses are just two of the many little things she and I both notice that reinforce the notion that he's guiding us.

As the last two years have passed, I've reflected on life much deeper than ever before, and here's what I've discerned:

I once told Billie about the waves of grief. And the more I think about it, the more I believe that everything is a wave: our heartbeats, labor contractions, the movement of the ocean, the sunrise through sunset, sound waves, light waves, heat waves, the life cycle. The list is endless.

There are times in our lives when everything contracts and relaxes, just like the peaks and dips of a wave. The peaks being the happiest moments of our lives. The dips being our struggles. The waves can be big or small, tumultuous or subtle, but one thing I know for sure is that when times are low, they will always rise again.

That's what grief has been like for me: many types of waves. What once felt like a tsunami is now small rolls onto white sands where I watch from afar. My life is good, better than I could have ever hoped for. If I had to crash through these waves in order to get to the stability I have today, well, I understand that now.

I guess what I'm trying to say is that the pain of loss will always be there. Eventually, it won't be all-consuming. There's no timeline to heal or right or wrong way to endure the waves. But someday, somehow, life will become bearable again. And if I hadn't opened myself up, I never would have met my wife and had my son.

Life is funny, you know. Not in a "ha-ha" sort of way, but peculiarly. Everything had to happen just as it did for my life to be this way. And I'm content now, happy with my job, my family, and our lives together. I'm not sure if everything happens for a reason. In my case, the reason was to create a life with Billie and Theo, two more loves of my life.

So when the flood tide crashes onto land again, I will protect my family, just as Billie will undoubtedly nurture us. We will get through the hard times. We will not drown in grief.

...I did it. I finally made it out of the water.

BILLIE

Mrs. Scott Bennington. The name just sings, doesn't it? I married the man of my dreams today and couldn't be happier. The ceremony was perfect. Gorgeous. Everything I ever wanted and more. I wish my dad could be here today, but I know he's watching over us. I wanted to honor him in some way. To incorporate something old, something new, something borrowed, and something blue, I purchased a new pair of white heels. I then had a seamstress cover the shoes in one of my father's old button-down blue shirts that I permanently "borrowed" from him. This way, he could still "walk" me down the aisle today.

Rick is the perfect stand-in. Theo simply adores him, calling him *Pupup*. Rick spoils Theo every chance he can get. My mom is here with her now-husband, Pierre. Of course, Claire is my maid of honor, with Ryan as the best man. I feel deeply loved and supported.

Currently, my relationship with my mom is better and more stable, as I've grown to accept her as she is and embrace what she's able to give me as a mother. She's been around a lot more now that Theo is here, doting on him and spending quality time with us. It's been nice to move into a solid place in our relationship.

We've just finished all the formalities at the reception—the entry, the dance, the cake-cutting—and now we get to drink, relax, dance, and have a great time. I watch my husband (that sounds *so good* to say) thank our guests for coming, giving handshakes and hugs. He's just the best.

When he spots me staring flirtatiously at him, he finishes his conversation and makes a beeline for me.

"Mrs. Bennington, looking ravishing as always," Scott says, kissing me tenderly on the cheek.

"Wanna blow this popsicle stand for a minute?" I whisper in his ear, winking as I step away from him.

"Now?" he mouths with devilish excitement. Before I nod my head, he whisks me away to the groom's dressing room. Once we're away from our guests, even before we reach the room, he begins wildly kissing me and undoing my dress. I remove his bow tie and unbutton his shirt as he opens the door.

The ear-piercing shriek makes me cringe. I hear a male voice call out, "What the fuck, man?!" I turn to see Claire and Ryan going at it on the couch. Claire plants herself on Ryan's chest in an attempt to shield their nakedness.

Scott pulls the door shut, and we giggle like teenagers. "Try locking the door next time, asshole!" he hollers to Ryan. Before we go to the bride's dressing room, I can't help but knock on the groom's door again.

"Hey, you two," I say unrelentingly.

I hear the crash of something being knocked over and an agitated "Ouch! What do you need, Billie? Can this wait?" from Claire.

"Are you two together or what? Or are you still just fucking?" They've been beating around the bush long enough. It's time I finally get the truth.

"Yes!"

"No!"

I hear their voices in unison.

"Wait, what?" a muffled voice asks. I walk away, rolling my eyes and shaking my head.

ACKNOWLEDGEMENTS

This novel would not have been possible without the following people. First and foremost, thank you, God, for the blessings you've given me and for carrying me through life's trials.

My husband, Jason, deserves the highest acknowledgement for his support through this entire process. From my late nights writing to weekends at various coffee shops, you always gave me the time and space to work when I needed and wanted to. For that, I am grateful. Thank you also for being my front-cover model for Scott and braving your first manicure. You were the perfect choice for him! I appreciate your honesty with the storyline, for challenging me, for picking out little details that paralleled our love story that I wrote subconsciously. We helped each other fall out of grief. I often think about all the things that had to perfectly align in order for us to be together. Even though it took five years of friendship before our life circumstances aligned for more, I would choose it all again to end up with you. I have loved you since the moment I laid eyes on you and will continue to love you beyond my last breath. Thank you for giving me this beautiful life.

Rachelle, my dear cousin, beta reader, and unofficial book promoter, thank you! Without your support, both emotionally and financially, this book would not have happened. Your zest for not just the story, but also for me as a person, pushed me through the challenging times. Thank you for funding the bigger expenses so that this story could become a reality.

Carol, my copy editor extraordinaire, thank you for your wealth of wisdom and knowledge during the post-production of the book. I appreciate your time and expertise. It's unmatched!

Bry, my beta reader and developmental editor, thank you for fleshing out my ideas and giving me integral feedback on content and continuity. I appreciate you not only professionally, but as a good friend. I admire you and your strength. You have a beautiful soul.

Anthony, thank you for broaching homosexuality, relationships, and language with me so that I could portray this story delicately. You are like my Claire, the best friend a girl could ever have. From our notes about *Days of Our Lives* (that darn Stefano DiMera!) passed through our religion book to ziplining in your backyard to sneaking cigs in the hot tub to blasting Tina Turner from the poolhouse to our yearly visits where we emotionally dump for hours, I cherish you deeply. You make me a better person. And as Glor would say, "Oh, Nicole!"

Dr. Dennis Dobrzynski, thank you for sharing your expertise as an oncologist so that I could craft an accurate depiction of cancer and its effects physically, mentally, and emotionally. I value and appreciate your insight regarding your profession and those affected by cancer.

Jennie, my front-cover model, thank you for being brave and willing to be Billie. I'm so pleased with how everything turned out. You have been fantastic to work with. May life continue to bless you every day.

Serena, thank you for shooting the front over, marketing photos, and my headshots. You captured my vision for the cover perfectly and made me feel beautiful. The pictures are stunning. Your talent and eye for photography is truly special.

To my beta readers: Jason, Rachelle, Kass, Bry, Krystal, Michelle, Tara, Lisa, and Mike, you are all rockstars! I appreciate your honesty, feedback, insight, and time in critiquing the story. Your thoughts have been invaluable and have made this book better than I could have ever expected.

To my readers: By the end of this book, I hope you take away comfort, peace, and healing in whatever and whomever you're grieving. When the pain seems unbearable, please keep going. Stay. You will make it through.

I hope you love Billie and Scott just as much as I do! Stay tuned to follow Claire, Joy, and Abbey through their unique "falling" journeys.

Follow me on TikTok, Instagram, and Facebook.
Nicole Thompson | Author
@nicolethompsonauthor

A NOTE ON THE NUMBER 18

Although this novel is fictitious and not based on real events or people, one thing I did incorporate that is true to my life is the frequent encounters with the number 18. This number has a long history, including the day I was born. My birthday is 2.18, which is Teddy's room number. My heaven-side brother, whom my mother miscarried many years ago, was due on 8.1, the inversion of 18, and the reason why the character Theo is born on that day. This year (2025) I have known my husband for 18 years, the year I decided to finally spill my guts on paper, not holding *anything* back, and achieving my bucket list item of publishing a novel.

This number has followed me the whole way through writing and publishing this story. When I needed encouragement to keep going, 18 would pop up almost instantly: bus numbers, receipts, house numbers, time, the number of social media likes or comments on a post, to name only a few.

While the story is not intended to be religiously influential, I do believe in God and the afterlife. Given the undeniable signs I've experienced from loved ones who have passed, I know that they're sending little messages from Heaven.

ABOUT THE AUTHOR

Nicole Thompson discovered her love for writing in middle school when she wrote a story about marine life. It was then she made a commitment to publish a novel some day. A devoted wife to Jason and mother of four girls, one son, and two fur pups, Nicole lives outside of Pittsburgh, Pennsylvania, where she enjoys reading, trash TV, all things music, and playing bingo. (What a millennial!)

Nicole has more than a decade of experience in professional writing and instructional content development. She hopes to inspire her children to follow their dreams, whatever they may be.